THE GIRL ON THE RUN

A.J. RIVERS

The Girl on the Run
Copyright © 2025 by A.J. Rivers

PROLOGUE

S HE KNEW WHAT SHE WAS SUPPOSED TO DO.
She had the skills. If it ever happened, she had the knowledge at the back of her mind. She'd heard it a thousand times. She'd watched the videos. Memorized the tips.

She knew what she was supposed to do.

Until she didn't.

When his arms clamped around her, she didn't have the chance to think. There wasn't time to dig through her mind and find the knowledge of what she was supposed to do. She didn't have a chance to fight back before she felt the ground fall away beneath her feet. Her spine bent backward, folding over his stomach as he arched to lift her. She managed to cry out, but he muffled the sound with his hand. Even thrashing against him, she was no match for the strength of his arms and the determination of the plan he so clearly already had in his mind.

He knew what was coming. He already had the next breath in his lungs, the next moment in his mind. He could see ahead while the seconds fell around her like grains of sand in an hourglass, submerging her beneath them so she couldn't breathe.

Her heart felt like stone, and her breath strained against her lungs. The screams she couldn't force out of her mouth swelled inside her chest. She wanted to close her eyes the way she did when she rode a roller coaster. If she couldn't see the turns and drops ahead, it wasn't as terrifying. But she knew that wasn't true. They still came. There was nothing she could do to stop them. This time she wasn't strapped into a seat. She wasn't going to be brought safely back to a platform to walk on shaky legs with breathless laughter away from it all.

She had to know what was coming. She had to try to stop it.

With her eyes forced open, she saw the edge of the open trunk and the dark-gray carpet inside. There was something in the back corner, but she didn't have the chance to see what it was. She tried to struggle against him so he couldn't get her inside, but he easily overpowered her. She didn't remember that going limp, forcing deadweight into his arms, would likely cause him to drop her. She didn't remember to kick backward or bury her elbow into his stomach.

She could barely process the speed of everything happening before her arm scraped against the carpet. She managed to flip over, but before she could even think of how to climb out of the trunk and get past him, he pressed something to her side and a shock of pain radiated through her.

She couldn't move. She couldn't do anything to resist when he grabbed her wrists and bound them together. He didn't cover her eyes. His were the last thing she saw before a final flash of light from the setting sun, and then her ears rang with the slam of the lid.

Darkness.

The sting of the burn on her arm, the shiver of the currents that rushed through her, and the almost tangible darkness immersed her senses. It wasn't until the car lurched forward, bouncing over something hard enough to make her lift off the trunk bottom and into the closed lid that she felt like she came back into herself.

There was no way to know how long he would drive. She had no idea where he was planning on bringing her, though she had no doubt he did have a plan. This wasn't entirely spontaneous. He didn't just decide when his eyes fell on her to toss her into the trunk and drive off. He wasn't sitting behind the wheel panicking because of what he had done or wondering what he was supposed to do next. He had known when his eyes opened that morning. He had known when he carried the Taser and the bindings with him to the car and when he put the key in the ignition. It might have all fallen into place when he saw her, but he'd already planned exactly how he wanted this to play out.

She just had to change it.

The car kept moving, every bump and jiggle of the road amplified by her lying in the trunk. She moved around as much as she could, trying to orient herself and create some leverage that would help her escape. A hard turn and another rough bump made her tumble, and dizziness rolled through her already-addled mind. She lay still for a few seconds, staring into the darkness. She no longer really knew which direction she was facing.

The air inside the trunk felt thick and heavy, getting harder to breathe with each inhale sucking away the oxygen and each exhale pumping more carbon dioxide into the small space. She didn't know if that was actually true. It was just what she felt.

It seemed like hours had passed since he forced her into the trunk, and they were still driving. For a short time, she had tried to pay attention to the movement of the car, hoping somehow she could keep track of the swerves and turns, or how long they were moving in one way or another. Maybe then she could tell where they were going or have an idea of where they were when they stopped. But she quickly realized it wasn't so easy to keep it in her mind. The fear clouded her thoughts. Being jostled around made it harder to tell which way they were going. She kept track for a time, but then it all fell away, and she put all her concentration on getting her wrists out of their bindings so she could try to escape.

It didn't matter where she was. All that mattered was getting out of the trunk alive.

Whispering encouragement to herself that became instructions that became demands that became prayers, she struggled with the bindings on her wrists.

The sides of her fingernails scraped across her skin until the thin layers tore and bled. She kept digging, thinking of every painful millimeter as less of a hold the bindings had on her hands. Finally, with the blood dripping down her palms and the tips of her fingers, the bindings fell away. With the release of her hands came the release of her thoughts. Suddenly, she remembered.

Pressing her hands to the sides of the trunk, she felt for the back seat. She knew many newer cars were designed so that the back seats could be opened directly into the trunk, allowing for more storage space. If this was one of those cars, she would be able to push through and crawl out. As she was pressing her fingertips around the seat to find the release lever, it occurred to her that even if she was able to move the cushions out of place, crawling out this way would put her directly behind him. He would see her immediately. She couldn't go that way.

Instead, she moved around so she could feel what would be the back of the car. She found the taillights and tore away the wires, then kicked at one until it broke through. A tunnel of light came through, just enough illumination to show her there were stars.

She waited for more light, for the wash of headlights from other cars, but it didn't come. There was no one else around. She couldn't let that discourage her. She had to get out. Shoving her hand through the opening, she reached into the cool air beyond. She felt around but realized there was no way she would be able to reach the handle for the trunk from that angle. She pulled her hand back inside and ran it along the inside edge, finally finding the safety latch she should have searched for to start with. Popping the trunk open, she pushed the lid up and tossed herself out.

She hadn't given herself time to think about what she was doing. She hadn't considered the impact on the pavement or the way the gravel bits on the hard surface would rip at her skin. She felt bones crack and hair come away from her scalp. Crying out with both pain and relief, she rolled across the worn pavement until she came to a wrenching stop in a heap several yards away. By the time she stopped, so had the car. She heard the tires squeal as she tried to pull herself up from the road.

Her heart desperately pleading for anyone to come along and help her, she forced herself to her feet. She saw him get out of the car and wrench open the back door. He reached inside and took something out. In the glow of the moon, she could only see the outline, but it was easy to recognize the tire iron clenched in his palm as he came toward her.

She cried out as she pushed herself through the pain to run as fast as her injuries would allow her. There was strength inside her. She knew it was there. She just had to dig for it, to reach beyond what she thought was possible and demand her body do what she wanted it to do.

Now that she was out of the trunk, she could see that he had driven her out to the middle of nowhere. It was far outside the edges of town, well beyond the businesses and homes that would typically have people in them at this time. All around her was shrubby desert and the lonely stretch of road.

She ran off the road and looked for anything that would tell her which direction she should go. She could go back the way they came, but they'd driven for so long she had no idea how close the nearest outpost of civilization would be. The same went for going in the same direction they were traveling. It could be miles more until there was anything.

A sudden rumble in the distance and a wash of lights on the road made her heart jump. Someone was coming. She turned, ready to jump out into the road so they would see her and stop to pick her up. The headlights blazed down the road. She heard him mutter a profanity behind her and glanced back to see him heading back to the car. She stumbled back to the edge of the road and raised her arms over her head, screaming as she waved. One arm wouldn't go up further than her shoulder, but she made herself as visible as she could as the lights came toward her.

They passed without slowing down.

Her hands dropped to her sides. Hope crashed in the red glow of their taillights.

She couldn't give up. He had gone back to the car and was bent into the open trunk like he was searching for something. Her mind went to the object she'd seen when he first threw her in, and she didn't want to know what it was. Even if he was only poised like that to create a scene for whoever was driving by, his hands were dangerously close to whatever was in the trunk. But he was also distracted. He wasn't looking at her. Wasn't moving toward her.

She ran.

Clouds shifting across the sky seemed to be in her favor. They moved over the moon and dimmed the glow. It made it harder for her to see, but that meant it would be harder for him to see her too. Several yards ahead of her she saw a thick patch of scrub. She limped toward it and climbed through the thick, sharp stems to crouch in the middle of the patch and hide. Trying to control her breath so it wouldn't be so loud in her ears, she strained for the sound of his footsteps. The rumble of the truck that had gone by was long gone, and there was only eerie silence around her.

Her hand shook as she reached into her pocket for her phone. He hadn't taken it from her when he shoved her into the trunk, and she could only hope it hadn't been destroyed when she jumped out of the trunk. She opened the screen and cupped her hand over it to dim the light. The screen was cracked, and small pieces of glass were missing, but it was still working. She nearly sobbed with relief, but it was short-lived. There was no signal.

She could still dial emergency services, but without a signal, there would be no way for dispatch to track her location.

She dialed and turned the volume down as low as she could so that it wouldn't carry in the air. As soon as she heard the dispatcher's voice, she whimpered.

"I need help. I've been abducted."

"What is your name?"

When the dispatcher heard her name, it wasn't from her. Instead, his singsong call sent a chill along her spine and made her hand clamp harder around her phone so she wouldn't drop it.

"Ma'am? Ma'am, are you there?" the dispatcher asked.

She couldn't force her voice through her throat. He was close. She could hear his steps on the ground and her name drifting through the night chill. She didn't know if he was trying to coax her out or if it was just a taunt meant to paralyze her. She could hear the dispatcher talking to her, but she could only manage a whisper pleading for help. Her phone beeped, telling her the battery was rapidly draining, and it made her heart clench. It beeped again and went silent.

She had a choice. She could stay where she was, crouched in the shrub hoping somehow he would walk past her or she could outrun him. She didn't know where she was. She didn't know where she would go. All she could do was hope that she would be able to stay out of his grasp.

If she could just stay away from him until the sun came up.

As soon as the thought flickered through her mind, she knew how ridiculous it was. There was something reassuring about the thought of the sun. There was comfort in light. A sense of safety in the thought of the pink and purple burning away the darkness. And yet, she knew there was no sense in that. There was nothing inherent about the sun coming up that would make her safer or end her torment. If she did manage to evade him until dawn, all it would mean was that she would be more visible. It would only mean more hours of pain and fear.

She didn't need to wait for the morning.

She needed to look for help.

There had to be someone, somewhere. This road existed for a reason. She would never know why that driver didn't stop for her, but they were driving down the road. They had to be going somewhere. There was something beyond this desolate stretch. She just had to find someone willing to see her and care.

He called her name again. This time it sounded farther away, like he had turned in the opposite direction. This was her chance. Her phone dropped from her hand as she scrambled out of the brush and ran.

But there would be no help. No sunrise.

She didn't hear him coming up behind her. The sound of her ragged breathing covered his footsteps. She didn't see the tire iron lift over her head. The clouds over the moon she thought would save her hid the shadow.

One blow brought her to her knees.

The next dropped her to the ground.

The third sent blood across the dirt.

She wasn't moving anymore when he took the knife from the sheath on his belt, but he wasn't taking any chances. After the first plunge of the blade, it was purely for enjoyment.

He didn't keep count of the times he stabbed her. There was no target, no quota. He went until he felt finished, then got back to his feet. He looked behind him toward the road. It wasn't as far away as she probably thought it was. He knew she was going to be found eventually. If he really cared that she would go missing forever, he could have arranged for that. As it was, he only cared that it took a little while. He didn't want her to be so obvious or for the trail that might lead to him to be so fresh when she was found. It was why he brought her out this far. He didn't think anyone would be out there. He didn't expect the truck to go by.

The driver didn't so much as pause, so he doubted they took notice of his license plate or any kind of description of the car. By the time she was found, if the driver even remembered that they came this way and saw a car, they wouldn't be able to describe it or make any link to her.

Just to make sure, he put the knife away and scooped her off the ground, flipping her over his shoulder to make it easier to carry her further away from the road. He walked until he couldn't see the road behind him when he glanced over his shoulder, then let her drop down into the dirt.

Without another look, he walked back to the car and reached into the trunk. Moving aside the crowbar at the back, he took out his duffel bag and got a fresh shirt. He replaced the one he was wearing, wrapping it in a towel before putting it back in his bag. Closing the trunk, he stepped back and eyed the broken taillight. It aggravated him that she would do that. Now he would need to drive a few towns over and have it fixed.

He got back into his car and headed down the dark stretch of road. A couple of miles ahead, a sign advertising a hotel made him turn. He'd stay there for a few nights for good measure. He could use the rest.

CHAPTER ONE

Emma

"FOUND THE MISSING GROUND STAKE," SAM ANNOUNCES, COMing into the house and wiping his forehead with a bandanna he stuffs back into his pocket.

"Good. Just leave it on the table. I'll bring it up and put it in the box later," I say.

"I will when I find all the pieces," he says.

I look up at him from the notes I have spread across the coffee table.

"I ran over it with the lawn mower."

I nod, going back to the photocopied note I've been studying. "Well, that's what we get for getting dazzled by the flashy world of oversized Christmas inflatables. We flew too close to the sun."

"But you have to admit, they were fun. Did you see the look on the neighbor kid's face when he saw the twenty-foot snowman?"

"Do you mean did I see the look on *your* face when you saw the twenty-foot snowman?" I ask.

"He is delightful," Sam says as he walks out of the room.

I couldn't see out of half of the windows in my house for the month of December. But he was pretty delightful.

"Does that mean you're planning on adding the reindeer this year?"

I hear my husband digging through the refrigerator for the glass bottle of sugarcane cola he stashes in the back corner sometime in February, where it waits to be his reward for the first time he has to mow the lawn come March. I'm not sure where this tradition originated, but it's been a hallmark of spring for as long as we've been married. It seems like the weather caught up with him earlier this year, and he's had to break out the cola before he usually would, but I'm glad for the sunlight and the warmer temperatures breaking through a particularly gloomy, cold late winter. Usually, I'm all for the colder weather letting me snuggle up in my favorite sweats and blankets, but after all I went through the last several months, I'm craving springtime.

"Absolutely not," Sam says emphatically, coming back into the room with his drink. "You think I'm going to willingly subject myself to that particular Xavier existential crisis?"

"It isn't an existential crisis," I tell him. "It's a philosophical conflict."

"Over science versus canon."

"Which is a very common ideological conflict," I point out.

"He's talking about mythical reindeer!"

"Yes, yes, he is. But that doesn't change that it's hard for him to grapple with the names of the reindeer changing and Donner being Rudolph's father…"

"Even though scientifically, all the reindeer are female because they are all presented as having antlers and only female reindeer still have antlers in late December. Yes, I know. I got the laminated reference card in my stocking. But here's the thing… When I pointed out that he is so concerned about the science saying they are all girls but seems just fine with them flying and asked his explanation for that, you know what he said?"

I can't help but grin. "What?"

"'Christmas magic,' Emma. The man said, 'Christmas magic.'"

"That makes sense."

"No, no, it doesn't. I checked out when he started saying something about the sleigh being powered by sugar snowflakes and candy cane elf breath."

"To be fair, I think he knew you'd checked out before then, and that's why he said that," I tell him.

"Whatever. My point is ... I'm not doing reindeer."

"So ... Santa?"

He takes a swig of his drink. "And probably that giant-ass tree with the big star on top."

He comes over to the sofa, and I reach up to take the bottle from his hand and steal a sip as he leans over to look at what I'm doing.

"You're still looking at that?"

I let out a heavy sigh and drop back against the couch, running my fingers back through my hair.

"Yep. And I'm going to keep looking at it until I can make it make sense." I scoot back to the edge of the seat and pick up the paper. "If they had just given me the original rather than this trash copy, I might be able to get somewhere."

"Why would an original make a difference? Doesn't the copy have the whole note?"

"The file notes say it does, but I just feel like there's something missing. If I could see the original, I could get a better feel for how it was written," I say.

"Don't handwriting analysts usually use copies of documents for comparisons?"

I lean back away from the table as Sam opts not to walk around the table and instead climbs over me to get to the spot on the couch beside me. I look over at him flatly, and he flashes me the boyish smile I fell in love with when I was seven years old and he rescued my ball from rolling across the street.

"Hi," he says.

"Hi." I look back at the paper. "Yeah, they do. I mean, sometimes they have the originals, but it's pretty rare for them to have multiple original pieces for comparison. That's not what I'm talking about though. I don't have any verified original sources of handwriting to make a real comparison. Just some things that are alleged to be from Sebastian. I'm not trying to get a better feel for the handwriting. It's the actual way it was written. The depth of the pen strokes. If there are any hesitation marks or places where whoever wrote it went back and forth over the letters multiple times. Things like that."

"So you're trying to determine if someone faked the note," he says.

"Or at the very least what kind of state of mind they might have been in or if they were overthinking what they were writing for some reason."

"What would that tell you? What do you think it might mean?"

I hesitate for a few beats, waiting for some brilliant response to come up. Nothing does.

"I don't know. But there's something here. I know there's something here. None of this is lining up with what his wife said about his disappearance."

"Has she changed her story?" Sam asks.

"Not at all. And I mean, *not at all*." I emphasize each word. "There has been no deviation from the first story she told the police when she first reported him missing. Down to the detail. If you look at the different times she's made statements, the interviews, even the social media posts she wasn't supposed to make but did anyway, she uses some of the same exact phrases at certain points in the story."

"You think she has some kind of script?"

"It could go one of two ways. She could have planned out exactly what she was going to say because it's a story she came up with and she had to memorize it to make sure she wasn't tripped up by anything." I let out another breath. "Or she doesn't have any variation on what she's saying because it's really what happened. She could be in so much shock and so unsure of what she's supposed to do next that all creativity has stopped and she just keeps going through the same motions because she doesn't want to use the energy to come up with a different way to say the same thing."

"Why does it sound like the thought of that disappoints you?" Sam asks. "Do you want this woman to have had something to do with her husband going missing?"

It's a pointed question I'd probably take offense with if it came from anybody but my husband. The ring on his finger and the many years he's dealt with my never-ending train of nonsense and mayhem grant him some extra wiggle room in that area.

"Obviously, I don't want her to have something to do with it," I say.

"No, not obviously. You've been hyper-focused on that note, and you're looking for a reason for her staying consistent with her statements to be some kind of red flag. I get that it can be weird for someone to stick so hard to what they've said and not have any variation, but like you said, it could just be that she only has those words for how to describe what happened. It just seems like you're trying to find a way to prove she did something to him."

"I don't want her to have done anything to him. I hope nothing has happened to him. I didn't become an FBI agent because I have a ghoulish fascination with all the creative ways people screw each other up," I say.

He nudges me with an elbow. "You sure about that?"

I choose to roll my eyes rather than indulge him. "The ideal way this would work out would be Sebastian would just walk back through the door, be absolutely fine, and it would be some big misunderstanding. The chances of that are nothing. He's been missing for almost three weeks, and there have been five notes either found in the house or sent through the mail to Lavinia. Something has happened. And it's not what it seems on the surface. That's what everyone wants to think. It's the logical path to follow. It's not right. I just know it's not."

"All right," Sam says, setting his now-empty bottle down on the table away from my notes. "Let's go over the whole story. Hit me with it again."

I sift through the papers on the table until I get to a photograph. I pull it out and set it on top of the papers. The face of a man not too far away in age from me smiles away from the camera, but the angle is sharp enough to show his whole face. The bottom edge of the photo is crowded with blurred flutes of champagne, showing the moment the glasses clinked together. The glass nearest to the screen, like it's in the other hand of the person taking the picture, is partially in focus. Some of the bubbles inside build a delicate, teetering tower from the stem toward the surface, sparkling in some unseen flash of blue light like a firework out of frame. The action shot of the elite.

"Sebastian McDonnell, thirty-five. Son of heiress Anita McDonnell and late old-money business tycoon Rile McDonnell. Known for being much more involved in the community than the rest of his family. Didn't jump straight into working for the company when he got out of college. Did the whole 'traveling the world to find himself' thing, including backpacking around a couple continents. He's spearheaded a bunch of philanthropic and volunteer efforts through the company and his connections.

"Married Lavinia five years ago. Rumor has it there was some controversy around them getting married because she didn't come from money and he met her while he was traveling. I haven't been able to find anything that actually supports that. Anita never spoke out against her, was at the wedding, had been photographed with her. But there were whispers."

"As there tend to be," Sam says.

"Yes, because people are the freaking worst."

"You know, it's when you say things like that that people start to question your motivations," he says.

"All right. Some people are the freaking worst," I amend.

"Better."

"Okay. So they get married. Rice and cake. Two-month honeymoon with a photo safari in South Africa and bathing elephants in Cambodia. Back home. Settle down. Sebastian takes on more responsibilities for the company while still trying to actually do something that will make a positive impact on the world. That's the buildup. Fast-forward to three weeks ago. Lavinia took a last-minute trip back to where she grew up because of a family emergency. This is where we get into what she has been telling the police and everybody else.

"According to her, the trip happened very suddenly and without a lot of planning. Sebastian wanted to go with her, but because of some obligations here, it would be difficult for him to work it out and she told him it was fine, that she would just go by herself and if he was able to join her before she came back, that would be great. They kept in touch for the first few days she was gone. Texts, phone calls, video calls. Checking in with each other pretty frequently, trying to catch up with her before bed despite the time difference. Everything was fine.

"Then he stopped responding. She went a full day without hearing from him. That was very unusual. Things had settled down with her family, so she was planning on coming back, but she still hadn't heard anything from Sebastian. She contacted Anita, who said she'd gotten a few messages from him. He hadn't been in the office, but that didn't really mean much because he frequently worked from home or was out doing meetings and things, so they didn't think much of it. But Lavinia still hadn't heard from him through the whole time she was traveling back. He wasn't at the airport to pick her up.

"When she got home, she found his cars in the garage and the back door of the house open. All the security cameras had either failed or were turned off the night before Sebastian stopped responding, so there was no footage of him leaving or anyone coming into the house. There were no security system alerts, and the security company said the system had been deactivated. Which means either Sebastian turned it off purposely or someone who knew the code did.

"She searched the house and found the notes. She specifically stated that there was nothing else out of place in the house and no other signs of anything happening. None of his personal belongings were missing, including his phone and his wallet, with the exception of one bank card. That card has not been used in the time he has been missing. She immediately called the police," I say.

"Which sounds like the right response considering the circumstances," Sam says.

"Absolutely. I've seen way too many situations where people think they need to try to figure things out on their own and that the police should be a last resort option once they exhaust everything else. It's good she didn't decide to go that route, especially considering it had been a couple of days since she heard from him by the time she got back home."

"What about the messages to his mother?" Sam asks.

"That's one of the odd things about this whole situation. She definitely got messages. She was able to show them to the police. And they did come from Sebastian's phone. But like I said, his phone was at the house when Lavinia got back. The messages were found on the phone, so it wasn't that someone used a spoofing app. They were definitely sent from his actual device. The question is whether he sent them or if someone else did. And if he sent them, why was he messaging his mother and not his wife?

"Anyway, over the last three weeks, there's been essentially nothing to show what might have happened to him other than the notes. Lavinia brought the ones she found in her mailbox to the police. But they don't really give any information. They are all in the same handwriting, which looks like Sebastian's, and they all say pretty much the same thing: 'Bottom of the lake. Top of the mountain. End of the trail. Beginning of the road.'"

"And nobody in his life has any idea what that could mean," Sam says.

"Right. The police talked to Lavinia, Anita, friends. Then when I came in, I talked to them again and tried digging into social media and contact with other people. No one knows what they mean. So now we have conflicting interpretations causing all sorts of problems. We have people who say it sounds like a suicide message or at the very least like he decided he wanted to totally separate himself from life and start over. And then we have people who say that's not Sebastian and it sounds like he went off on some sort of spirit quest but is planning to come back. And then we have people who say it sounds like someone took him and they are sending some sort of warning.

"His mother thinks he just got a wild hair and just ventured off to some random corner of the world to spontaneously do some humanitarian work. Which is like him. So she's convinced he just got wrapped up in that, jetted off, and will eventually come wandering back home having lost track of how long he was gone and filled with stories."

"Sure, that's like him, but to the point of leaving his phone and wallet behind? Just disappearing with a cryptic note?" Sam asks. "If he has a lot of responsibility in the company, it doesn't sound like he would be that flighty. He might want to jet off to help people, but couldn't get away from work to come with his wife for a family emergency? I just don't see it."

"Exactly my thought," I say. "And the fact that he didn't tell Lavinia where he was going and hasn't used any money just doesn't fit."

"So optimistic thinking from a worried mother, or disconnection from reality based on a warped view of the world?" Sam asks.

"Either. Both," I say. "His wife is on the other end of the spectrum. She says she absolutely knows in her heart he would not have killed himself. He didn't have any reason to, as far as she knows. But she says even if there was something going on in his life she didn't know about, he wouldn't take those measures. They'd talked extensively about mental health, and he knew she'd lost more than one person to suicide when she was young. She says he would have sought out help. Even if that meant going to the hospital by himself, he would have done it.

"She believes someone took him. He's very wealthy and has a lot of connections. The problem with that theory, though, is no one has gotten any kind of ransom demand or instructions. She is the only person who has gotten any kind of communication, and it is only those notes. Three weeks is a really long time for abductors to hold someone while thinking about what they want to do with them or trying to word a ransom note.

"She has no explanation of why someone would take Sebastian without making a ransom demand and has insisted over and over that she has had no contact with anyone beyond the notes. In all her interviews, she has said the same things. She doesn't know of any threats he received. She doesn't know of any direct enemies he has. She doesn't know where he is or what happened to him. But she is sure someone did this to him. There's no evidence of violence in the house, but the security cameras weren't active. He didn't have anything with him. She insists the handwriting on the notes is his. And that brings us here."

Sam shakes his head. "All right, now I think I see more where you were coming from. This is a doozy."

CHAPTER TWO

MY PHONE RINGS IN THE KITCHEN WHERE I LEFT IT PLUGGED IN earlier, and I get up to go answer it.

"Agent Griffin," I say as I pull it from the charger.

I walk over to the pantry and open it so I can search the shelves for inspiration for tonight's dinner. We were supposed to go over to Janet and Paul's house for game night, but the flu that missed Paul when it took down half of Sherwood late last winter finally caught up with him. Instead of laying out snacks and deciding if we were going to take Clue out of board game jail, he's apparently wrapped up in a giant blanket on the couch with copious amounts of tissues and chicken soup. I'll graciously forgo the need for tissues, but the chicken soup sounds good.

"Hi, Emma. This is Baron. Just checking in."

The words are pleasant enough, but Baron Johnson's tone gives away his frustration. He hasn't come right out and said it, but it's obvious he is quite done with these check-ins I've insisted on since he decided to leave the hotel right after the New Year.

"Everything okay?" I ask.

"Everything's fine. Nothing new."

"No contact with the Game Master at all?" I ask.

This is one of those conversational quirks I always cringe at when I see it in a movie or a book or it's directed at me. And yet, here I am, spoon-feeding a grown man how to update me on his situation. A situation he is very well informed of and calls me about three times a week. Excessive? Possibly. Going to continue into the foreseeable future until I get this twisted son of a bitch behind bars where he belongs? Absolutely.

Clearly, Baron wouldn't tell me everything was fine if he had actually been in contact with the Game Master. He doesn't need me reminding him about the sadistic serial killer who has called him out as one of his targets. It's not like he's going to say everything is good and then when I mention the Game Master he's going to be like, *You know what? That's right. He did show up at my house last night with a game of Twister where all the spots are blue and red and the spinner only has yellow.*

But I still have the compulsion to pry. I have the need to specify and hear confirmation—and for it to be every couple of days. It doesn't escape me that this situation could turn on a dime.

Baron was staying at a hotel in Sherwood for a few weeks so he could be monitored and I would know for certain he wasn't in danger. But there was nothing legal keeping him there. He was not in witness protection. He wasn't being detained. He was staying there under my recommendation after the Game Master's attempts to lure him to his own potentially dangerous challenge and the threats that came when he didn't do what he was told. As the year drew to a close, he lost patience. He didn't want to be in Sherwood any longer, and there was nothing I could do to stop him from leaving.

Technically, there's nothing I can do to force him to do these check-ins either, but he's been going along with it. Hearing from him regularly gives me reassurance that he is still safe. I know if he doesn't call at his appointed time, I should start to be concerned. There are police and other agents poised and ready to do welfare checks if it becomes necessary. I hope it never will be.

"No, I have not heard from him," Baron humors me.

"Good."

"How about Mike?" he asks. "Anything new?"

I am under no obligation to reveal any details of my investigation or keep him updated on the search for Mike Morris, and if I did have new details, it's unlikely I would divulge them to him. I think Baron knows that, but he's still going to ask. He is understandably worried about his friend.

"Nothing to report," I tell him. "We're still investigating."

"Do you think..." he stops. "Never mind."

He doesn't want to say any of the potential endings to that question:

... *he's still alive?*

... *he's still in those woods?*

... *the Game Master has him?*

"We're still investigating," I say again.

I end the call and set my phone on the counter to keep going through the kitchen, making my grocery list. Sam is dozing off on the couch when I walk back into the living room.

"Babe," I say, jostling him awake. "You should go take a shower. I'm heading to the grocery store."

"Who was on the phone?"

"Just Baron," I tell him. "Checking in, asking about Mike Morris."

"You're going to find him," Sam says.

He knows how frustrated the search for Mike is making me. I never could have imagined this case would stretch on like it has. From the beginning, when the mysterious death of Terrence Brooks first brought the existence of the Game Master to light, I knew it would be complicated. This wasn't going to be a fast investigation or a clear-cut explanation. But I didn't expect it to be as tangled and sprawling as it is being.

Since Mike was instructed to go to the National Park months ago, I've uncovered many more players in the twisted game.

The first person contacted police as soon as he was selected and was put into a secure location. And though it's frustrating, I'm grateful that Baron has continued to work with me.

The next was Coleman Harris, who was found where we thought Mike would have been. I'm not exactly certain whether or not Coleman was a player himself, but I do believe he was murdered by one of the players. Possibly Mike.

Richard Fine is recovering from his injuries after his ordeal with the Game Master, and his attacker, Solomon, is still behind bars but not volunteering any information that could help us.

It wasn't long after that that we found another victim, floating naked in a bitterly cold lake. It added a sharper edge to the search for Mike Morris.

Sean Coolidge had gone missing from a hunting cabin, and it took several days to find him. Even then, it was a series of events falling into place perfectly that made it possible to locate him. The lake was so far from the hunting cabin where he was supposed to be, and the winter weather made the water treacherously cold. It was barely even considered when the initial search was planned. If it wasn't for a local with a drone posting footage from the area that happened to catch the attention of one of the officers assisting with the search, we might not have gotten to it for days longer.

The officer noticed a partially submerged canoe at the edge of the water, looking like it had drifted up to the shore. It was enough to pique his interest. Another look at the video revealed footprints in the wet dirt at the edge of the water. Even still, if we hadn't gotten there just when we had, we might not have found Sean's body. It hadn't been visible in the footage, and evidence on it suggested it had been trapped under the surface, tangled in submerged plants and logs.

We don't know how it dislodged or why it was floating exactly where it was. It doesn't really matter. All that matters is that we were able to find his body and recover it. But it also brought to mind a stark reminder of Mike Morris.

I arrived with the park rangers at the ledge where Mike was supposed to be, only to find blood splattered on the rocks and no other sign of him. DNA comparisons to materials collected at his house connected the blood to him, and shreds of fabric that could have been clothes were found near the ledge. But the trail ended there. And the body that was found was that of Coleman Harris—not Mike.

With no trace of Mike for weeks, I switched directions in my investigation and started monitoring his financial accounts and properties, wondering if there was a possibility he had decided to try to escape on his own, the hot breath of the Game Master on the back of his neck. I thought he could have gone to the ledge, encountered whatever horror was waiting for him there, and run for it. But there's been no activity on any of his accounts, and despite his name being flagged on all airlines, there's been no indication of him traveling.

Discovering the body of Sean in the lake, so long after Coleman's, was a harsh reminder of what is possible. If we'd searched the area around that lake the day before, we might have missed his body completely because it was still submerged, and we might not have seen evidence that it was there. Without any clear reason to think he was in there, it's unlikely we would have gone to the extent of having divers go into the dark, cold water. And if we'd waited and gone later, it's very possible his body would have gone back beneath the surface. We could have left the area convinced he wasn't there.

I put everything into my investigations. I pour every ounce of myself into digging as deep as I need to go, considering things from every angle

I can, looking at every detail in ways that other people don't, so I can find the answers. I always want to believe that will bring me to where I need to be. Seeing Sean's frozen, discolored corpse on the surface of the water, however, his face turned up to the sky as if his crystallized eyes were watching the gray clouds move overhead, reminded me it isn't all in my hands.

Sam peels himself off the couch and gives me a kiss on his way toward the stairs. I grab my keys and bag and head for the car. I pause by the door to tilt my face up toward the sky and feel the sunlight on my cheeks and across the bridge of my nose. It glows orange and red against the back of my eyelids and warms my lips. I let my shoulders drop with my exhale and get behind the wheel. I know I'll end up immersed back in my cases tonight while Sam and the rest of the neighborhood sleep. But for now I want to make chicken soup and spend the evening catching up on quality bad TV time with my husband.

CHAPTER THREE

Nadia Holmes

I T FELT LIKE SHE SHOULD HAVE GOTTEN THERE BY NOW.

Nadia had known when she stuffed every inch of her car with luggage, bags, and boxes that morning and hit the road that it was going to be a long journey. She and Amelia had been calling it their "quest" for weeks as they prepared for it. Calling it that rather than "a long-ass road trip into the outskirts of nowhere" made it a lot more palatable. And Nadia was determined to do whatever she could to make this whole experience easier for her daughter.

She glanced in the rearview mirror and watched the little girl with her head rested on the pink-and-purple unicorn neck pillow she'd picked out at the first rest stop they hit on the drive. She was asleep and oblivious to anything happening. At least there was that. At least she wasn't getting antsy or seeing her mother getting increasingly anxious as the lonely road continued to stretch ahead, the milky headlights illuminating nothingness.

Thick clouds splashed massive drops onto the windshield and obscured the moonlight. It made the area seem even more desolate. There were old streetlights scattered every now and then along the sides of the road, but they didn't offer much in the way of reassurance.

This is good, she had to keep telling herself. *It's our new start.*

She and Amelia were leaving the stress and hardships of the last three years behind them and getting the fresh chapter she'd been working so hard for.

Soon this would be behind them too. Despite feeling like they had somehow veered far off the route, the GPS still said they were going the right way. Soon it would all be all right. They would arrive at Jeff and Lisa's house. She'd take a shower and go to bed, and in the morning, everything would look brighter.

Nadia was doing everything she could to hold on to optimism. Her body was sore from the long hours on the road. She stretched her neck from side to side, sitting up straighter in the seat to try to release the pressure on her hips and relax her back. She kept trying to push them away, but difficult emotions were right at the edge of her mind. She didn't want to show them. Amelia could wake up at any moment, and she didn't want the nine-year-old to see the tears in her eyes. She'd been smiling through them for this long. She only let them fall when she was behind closed doors.

If she just kept pushing through, she wouldn't have to hold them any longer. When Jeff and Lisa offered to let Nadia and Amelia stay with them while they got on their feet, she jumped on it. There was no way she could turn that offer down.

A new town. New friends. New opportunities. Amelia was worried about going to a different school, but Nadia knew it was going to be good for both of them. They wouldn't have to think about any of the pain of the divorce and how much they had lost.

The rain started falling faster and harder, reducing visibility on the road, and with the stress of being unable to see, the rhythmic pitter-patter added to her exhaustion. The GPS said less than an hour to go.

"One more hour," she whispered. She wiggled her body closer to the steering wheel and stared through the streaks of water at the old, weathered road. "Just one more."

The words had barely gotten past her lips when the car lurched slightly. Nadia pulled back and looked at the dashboard. The car lurched again, a strange noise coming from under the hood. She patted the dashboard.

"Come on, old girl. You and me. We can do this."

The entire car shivered, and a warning light popped up on the control panel. The orange glow looked more glaring in the gloom of the stormy night.

"All right. Well, I guess you can make different choices for yourself," Nadia said. A sigh made her chest sink. "Shit."

She glanced at the screen of her phone attached to the holder on the windshield to check the GPS again and noticed that something had shown up in the distance. Little symbols on the map showed a gas station and a motel ahead. Not knowing what was going on with the car, and with the weather getting worse, made her feel unsure about another forty minutes of driving. She decided that if they were open, she was going to stop.

Lights appeared ahead, and Nadia willed the car to keep going to get there. She didn't know what was going to happen with the car tomorrow. There might be no mechanic anywhere nearby where she could have it towed to if it completely gave up the ghost by the time she got there. But at this point, that was a problem for future Nadia to deal with. Right now all she cared about was getting out of the increasingly bad weather and making sure Amelia was safe for the night. She'd figure everything else out from there.

The car was shuddering and making some unsettling sounds when she finally saw the entrance to the parking lot. It occurred to her in a fleeting moment of panic that they might not be open. It was late, and they were out in an open expanse close to nowhere. It was entirely possible that the little spot had closed up shop hours ago. She could only hope that if that were the case, the motel would still be taking new guests. She might not be able to grab the snacks she was hoping for from the gas station, but she could fall face-first onto a bed. And that was top of the priority list right now.

As she pulled into the parking lot and up to a spot right in front of the door to the convenience store, she let out a breath of relief that all the lights were on. There was a young woman inside behind the register. She was looking down, doing something on the counter. Nadia didn't see any customers inside or any cars in the lot, but at least the store was open.

Amelia let out a little groan when Nadia turned off the engine.

"Mama? Are we there?"

"Hey, honey," Nadia said softly, turning around to look into the back seat. "We're not all the way to Mr. Jeff and Ms. Lisa's house. We're going to stop here for the night."

"Stop where?" Amelia asked.

"We're at a motel," Nadia told her. "It's getting stormy outside, and it's really late. I thought we'd get some snacks and have a slumber party at the motel, then go to their house tomorrow."

Amelia's eyes lit up. "Yay! A slumber party!"

Her innocent excitement made Nadia's chest feel lighter. Even with the tears stinging in the corners of her eyes, her little daughter could make brightness shine through.

"Come on, let's go inside," Nadia said.

Amelia snuggled down into her seat, tugging her blanket up from where it had fallen around her knees.

"I'm warm and comfortable. Can't I just stay in the car?" she asked.

After hearing one of the popular girls at her old school talk about her mother leaving her in the car at the grocery store, Amelia had been trying to convince Nadia to do the same. It was not working.

"No," Nadia said, shaking her head. "It's too late at night, and we don't know this area."

It wouldn't matter what time it was or if they were in their own neighborhood. The answer would still be no. Nadia wasn't going to walk away from a car with her nine-year-old sitting inside.

"But… there's no one around," Amelia said.

"Come on, you don't want me choosing all the slumber party snacks myself, do you?"

Amelia kicked off the blanket. "No, you won't get the right gummy bears."

Nadia would most certainly get the right gummy bears, but it was enough to stop Amelia from trying to stay in the car, so she'd take the insinuation.

She locked the door behind them, and they walked through the cold rain to the welcoming glow of the glass doors. The girl behind the register looked up as they walked in. Nadia saw she was playing a game of solitaire on the counter. The deck of cards looked well-worn. She must be used to not getting a lot of foot traffic through here at night.

The woman, who appeared to be around Nadia's age or possibly just a few years younger, offered a genuine, vibrant smile.

"Hi there," she said.

"Hi," Nadia said.

Amelia took off running for the display of chips and cookies at the far side of the store, and the woman grinned.

"I like a girl who knows what she wants," she said.

"That's definitely her."

"Well, look around. Take your time. We're open all night, so there's no rush. Let me know if you need any help."

She shuffled her cards, and Nadia made her way over to the snacks. Amelia's arms were already overloaded, but Nadia picked out a few things for herself and went over to the drink machine for a massive lemon-lime soda. She'd been trying to cut fizzy drinks out of her diet since the turn of the year, but tonight called for sugar and bubbles.

"Let me take those," she said.

Amelia handed over her selections, and Nadia brought them to the counter as her daughter went to peruse the candy display. A pile of junk food hardly constituted dinner, but it was not like there was a restaurant they could walk to. And even if there was something around here willing to deliver, she highly doubted they would still be open at this time. Besides, a slumber party did sound like fun.

She and Amelia would be living with Jeff and Lisa for at least the foreseeable future. They'd been close friends for years, and Nadia was beyond grateful for their generosity and hospitality, but it would be a change. She and Amelia wouldn't have as much time just the two of them.

"Looks like you've had a long day," the cashier said.

Nadia lifted an eyebrow, and the other woman's face dropped. "I didn't mean..."

Nadia chuckled and swept her hand back over her wet hair. "No worries. It has been a very long day, and I'm sure I look every bit of it." She glanced over her shoulder at Amelia, then back to the woman. "Do you happen to know of a mechanic around here? My car seems to be having a little bit of a moment, and I'm not sure what's going on with it."

"I actually have a friend who has a shop up in Murphy. He has a tow truck and everything. He's not usually working this late. But he's come out for emergencies before. I could give him a call and see if he'll come out," she said.

"Oh no, you don't need to do that. It's really late, and it's raining. I was actually hoping to grab a room at the motel for the night. Like I said, it's been a really long day, and I need some sleep. Would he be available tomorrow?" she asked.

"I'm sure he will be."

She leaned back and looked under the counter, searching around for a few seconds before coming back up with a piece of paper. She grabbed a pen from a sticker-covered cup next to the cash register and jotted something down.

"Here. This is his name and information. I'm Maren, by the way."

Nadia took the paper from her and glanced at the information before smiling at her. "Thank you. I'm Nadia."

Amelia came over to the counter and dropped a mound of candy beside the rest of the snacks. Nadia put her arm around her and leaned down to kiss the top of her head.

"And this is my daughter, Amelia."

"Hi," Amelia said.

"Hi," Maren smiled. "Nice to meet you. Is this everything?"

"Looks like it," Nadia said.

"Okay. Let me get you checked out here, and then we can go over to the motel and get you checked in there."

Nadia smiled at the quip. She was glad she found this place for a variety of reasons, but meeting Maren was definitely one of them. The pretty dark-haired woman was like a breath of fresh air after the long day, and if she weren't so tired, Nadia would've liked to spend more time talking with her.

They finished the transaction, and Nadia took the bags. She and Amelia followed Maren out of the convenience store and paused while she locked the door. She flipped over a sign, letting anyone who might come by the store that she was at the motel helping someone and that she'd be back.

"Want to grab anything out of the car?" Maren asked.

They'd packed duffel bags to get them through the first couple of days, so while Maren and Amelia waited under the overhang of the building, Nadia grabbed them from the back seat.

The rain was still falling, but not as hard as it had been. They ducked their heads as they hurried around the side of the building and across the back parking lot to the motel. Nadia noticed what she assumed was Maren's car parked nearly behind the building, explaining why she hadn't seen it when they'd first arrived.

Maren led them to a small, glassed-in office at the end of the long brick building. She used another key on the same ring that held the key to the convenience store to unlock the door, and they ducked inside. She let out a sigh of relief and shook out her arms as she walked across the gray-and-white tile floor to an old wooden desk at the far end of the small office.

"You've got a lot on your plate," Nadia said as Maren went behind the desk and wiggled a mouse to wake up the computer.

Maren let out a little puff of laughter that let on just how much of a hassle the dual responsibilities could be.

"One of the glamorous perks of working the overnight or morning shift. During the day and in the evening, we've got a guy who actually sits in here and handles people checking in. I guess it's nice to break things up a bit though. You two are the first people I've seen in three hours."

"But you've got your cards to keep you company," Nadia said.

Maren flashed a smile. "Those were my auntie's. She taught me all the card games when I was little, and when she died, all I wanted was her pearl earrings, the shawl she wore to church every week, and those cards. They see me through a lot of very long nights."

Nadia looked around. "How does a place like this stay open? Wait. That sounded really bad. I didn't mean it to be as offensive as it came out. I just mean that it doesn't seem like it could keep going with so few people using it."

Maren chuckled. "Not offending me. I don't own the place. The motel is actually almost full. Most of the people who stay here are truckers. They park their rigs behind the building where they won't get in the way of people coming to the store. There are two other road trippers here, but they parked around back too. I guess they saw the trucks and thought that's where they were supposed to go." She shrugged. "Doesn't make a difference to me. I might be their check-in clerk, but I draw the line at bellhop. All right, I'm guessing just the one night?"

"Yes," Nadia said.

"Towels and soap and everything are in the room. If you need more, just give me a ring. The number for the store is next to the phone. Can I see an ID?"

Nadia handed over her license, and in a few seconds, Maren was leading them to one of the light-blue doors lined up beside the office. They got nearly to the end of the building before she swiped the card through the reader and the magnetic lock clicked to let them in. Maren opened the door and flipped on a light, then stepped to the side to let Nadia and Amelia in. The air inside smelled of bleach and air-conditioning, and though sparse and basic, the room looked surprisingly comfortable.

"This looks great," she said.

Maren glanced around the room. "It's not too bad. I actually lived here for a few weeks one time."

"You did?" Nadia asked.

"Yep. I was in between places to live, and Mel, the owner, said I could take one of the units as part of my pay. It was a pretty convenient commute. It's nice to have more space in my place now, but I'll admit sometimes I do miss being able to just shuffle across the parking lot in my pajamas to get a bag of chips in the middle of the night."

Nadia laughed. "I don't blame you."

"Is there anything else you need?" Maren asked.

"No, we're good. Thank you for your help."

"If you think of anything, just give me a call. Number is right there." Maren pointed to a laminated note taped to the wooden nightstand next to the phone.

Nadia nodded and walked with the other woman to the still-open door. She watched her jog across the parking lot toward the convenience store before stepping back into the room and closing the door behind her. When she turned around, Amelia had already climbed onto one of the beds and was dumping the bags of snacks out in front of her.

Nadia laughed. "Why don't we get ready for bed before that?"

Amelia eyed the goodies but sighed in resignation and climbed off the bed. Nadia headed for the bathroom to start a shower for her daughter, thankful for the warm, dry room and Maren's kindness.

When Amelia came out of the bathroom, Nadia swapped in with her for a fast shower. The rain had stopped when she got out and changed into her favorite well-worn sweatsuit.

"I'm going to step right outside," she told Amelia. "Find something fun to watch."

She took her phone and stepped outside the motel room, closing the door behind her but staying on the sidewalk a step away. Lisa sounded groggy when she answered.

"I'm sorry I woke you up," Nadia said.

"No, no… I wasn't asleep," Lisa said. "I'm just watching a movie while waiting for you guys to get here."

"Well, that's why I'm calling. We're not going to make it tonight," Nadia said.

"What's wrong? What's going on?"

"Everything's fine. Don't worry," Nadia said, trying to reassure her clearly concerned friend. "The weather got bad, and the car started acting up, so I decided to stop for the night."

"What's wrong with your car?"

"I'm not sure. It was just making some weird sounds. I'm sure it will be fine. I'll have it towed and brought to a shop in the morning, and we'll figure it out. I probably should have replaced it by now."

"Where are you?"

"There's a little convenience store with a motel in the same parking lot about forty minutes before your house. Maybe a little less than that if the weather was better and I was driving faster. That's just what the GPS said."

"Before the exit?" Lisa asked.

"Yeah, there's nothing else before it for a long time. The woman working here mentioned a town called Murphy nearby," Nadia said.

"Oh yeah, I know that place. Mel's Corner Market."

"It's not on a corner," Nadia pointed out.

"Yeah, I know. That's not too far. You're right, probably not forty minutes if the weather is better. You're sure you're okay? I could come out there and get you," Lisa offered.

"No, you don't need to do that. It's late. Amelia and I are already all showered and in our pajamas. We're going to eat a bunch of junk food and watch TV until we fall asleep. I need to be here to call the tow truck in the morning. You go on to bed, and I'll let you know what's going on tomorrow."

"You're sure?" she asked again.

"I'm sure. Thank you though. I'm really looking forward to seeing you."

"You too. I'm happy you two are coming."

Movement ahead of her caught Nadia's attention, and she looked up as a car pulled into the parking lot of the convenience store.

"I am too. I'll call you in the morning when I know more."

Nadia hung up just as she saw Maren dart out across the parking lot toward the gas pump. A man climbed out of the driver's side of the car, and she leaped into his arms. He snuggled his face down into the curve of her neck and held her tight against him, her feet up off the pavement. It was obvious they were thrilled to see each other, and the sight was bittersweet. It warmed Nadia's heart to see the couple so happy, but it brought a sharp twinge of painful emotion like cold air rushing into a still-raw void in her own heart.

As she was turning around to go back into her room, she noticed a door two rooms down from her standing open several inches. It hadn't been that way when Maren was leading them to their room. She would have noticed. There were no lights on inside the room.

A strange feeling came over her, like somebody was watching from the dark gap. Nadia couldn't see anyone there, but the chill kept her in place for several seconds. Suddenly, the door closed, the sharp sound making her jump slightly. Trying to push away the discomfort, she went back into the room and plastered on a smile for Amelia.

"Did you find something?" she asked.

"Yeah, we can put on this channel that's playing the Minions!"

"That sounds perfect, sweetie."

Nadia crawled into the bed and grabbed one of the packs of chips, glancing over at the door to make sure the lock was firmly in place.

I'm safe, she told herself. *We are safe now.*

CHAPTER FOUR

A MELIA STAYED AWAKE FOR MUCH LONGER IN THEIR SLUMBER party than Nadia had expected. They ate most of their snacks, and she finally fell asleep snuggled up by her mother's side watching the second movie of the night. Knowing that her daughter would be taking up the entire bed and sleeping restlessly, Nadia considered slipping out and getting into the other bed. But the thought of the open door kept her right where she was, her arm snug around Amelia as she fell asleep.

Despite being up so late, Nadia woke up at her usual early time. She got out of bed and went to the window to check the weather. Pulling back the thick, dark-blue curtain, she looked out into the earliest pink rays of dawn. The rain was completely gone, and only a few clouds still streaked across the sky. It was one of those mornings that made you feel the soft warmth of spring just by looking outside.

After a few moments of watching the sun slowly creep into the sky, Nadia went to the dresser where the TV sat to start a pot of coffee. She immediately noticed there was no coffee. She checked the drawer and looked around the pot to try to find the little sachets she was accustomed to in hotels, but it looked like whoever cleaned the rooms forgot to refill the station. Behind her, Amelia started to wriggle in the bed, the first stage of waking up. Nadia got dressed and pulled out an outfit for Amelia, then stuffed her dirty clothes into a bright-yellow plastic bag hanging on the bare bar near the bathroom.

By the time she had put on some minimal makeup and pulled her hair up, Amelia was sitting up, rubbing her eyes.

"Hey, baby," Nadia said. "Did you sleep well?"

Nadia knew she spent most of the night rolling around and kicking, but that was normal for the little girl.

Amelia nodded. "Yeah. What time is it?"

Nadia knew her daughter well enough to know that was the start of her angling for some extra sleep. She was not the early riser that her mother was. While Nadia would usually let her grab a handful more minutes snuggled down in the blankets, this time she wanted to get a jump on the day.

"Early. But we've got to get going. How about we go over to the store and get some breakfast? Then we'll call and see about the car."

She was expecting Amelia to ask her to just leave her in the room while she went for breakfast, and she was ready to turn that suggestion down. But Amelia nodded and crawled out of bed to head for the bathroom. When they left the room a few minutes later, Nadia's eyes cut over toward the door that had been standing open last night. It was closed, and the curtains were pulled tight over the window. Amelia's hand took hers, and she smiled down at her daughter.

"What do you think they have for breakfast?" Amelia asked as they started toward the building.

"I don't know," Nadia said. "Maybe doughnuts. Or those little cereal cups and tiny bottles of milk."

Since this place was obviously frequented by truck drivers and long-distance travelers, she hoped there would be some more substantial options as well. Something warm, even if she had to zap it in a microwave, sounded much better than the breakfast version of the mound of sugar they had eaten last night. But her first priority was coffee. Pretty

THE GIRL ON THE RUN

much if she could get her hands on a hot cup of coffee, the rest was just details. Once she had that cup down, it was a different story.

They got into the shop, and Nadia made a beeline for the coffee machines while Amelia went to explore the food options available. Nadia was filling up a cup with freshly brewed medium roast when Maren appeared by her side.

"Good morning! You're up early. I wasn't expecting to see you for a while."

Nadia held up her cup. "I am shamefully attached to my morning caffeine, and there wasn't any in the room."

Maren's dark eyes narrowed. "There wasn't? I'm sorry. You should have called. I would have brought you some."

Nadia waved the suggestion away. "No, it would have been ridiculous for you to close up here just to bring me some coffee. This is perfect. I would have come over here for breakfast anyway."

"Well, I can definitely help you out with that. There's a diner in Murphy that makes the most amazing breakfast sandwiches, and every morning they deliver a bunch. They're over in that case."

Nadia followed where Maren pointed and found a heated display case with a variety of sandwiches wrapped in parchment paper. Each had a little sticker on the top, marking the type of sandwich. To the side were paper cups filled with little, round potato hashbrowns and what looked like sticks of French toast glittering with sugar and cinnamon. After looking over all the options, she couldn't choose between the bacon, egg, and cheese on a biscuit and sausage and cheese on a croissant, so she grabbed one of each along with two cups of hashbrowns. Amelia came up to her clutching a bottle of orange juice, and when she eyed the French toast, she grabbed a container.

Set with breakfast, they headed to the counter.

"Have you called Smith yet?" Maren asked.

"I didn't know if he'd be working this early," Nadia said.

"Definitely. That boy is usually up tinkering on something mechanical even when he still needs a spotlight just so he can see what he's doing. Go ahead and give him a call. Hopefully, he doesn't have much scheduled for this morning and will be able to get out here and take a look before long."

"That would be amazing."

The door to the store opened, and a girl with blonde curls bouncing around the shoulders of her vintage denim jacket rushed in. Maren gave her a look, and the girl cringed.

"I'm sorry… I know, I know, I'm late. I'm sorry."

"Again," Maren says. "You forgot to add 'again.'"

"I'm sorry I'm late *again*," the girl said. "Thank you for covering for me."

"What was I going to do? Just leave the store empty?" Maren asked. The blonde stopped and looked at her blankly for a second. "Yeah."

"I would not do that," Maren said. She looked at Nadia and nodded toward the blond woman. "This is Christy. She works the morning shift. It's supposed to be the *early* morning shift." Her eyes slid over to Christy, who sighed.

"I'm sorry."

"I'm Nadia."

"Nice to meet you."

Christy hurried around the counter, shucking her jacket as she went. She tucked it under the counter and pulled a name tag from a drawer beneath the register.

"I'm going to give Smith a call," Nadia said. "Thanks again. It was really nice to meet you."

"I'll be around for a bit longer," Maren said. "Let me know what he says."

"Will do."

Gathering their breakfast, Nadia and Amelia returned to their room. Amelia sat on the bed to eat, peeling the top off a little container of syrup that came with the French toast sticks. Nadia swiftly snatched it from the white comforter and set it on the corner of the nightstand, already seeing the sticky disaster impending. She found the slip of paper Maren had given her the night before and called the number on it. The man who answered told her he could be at the shop within half an hour. Relieved, Nadia thanked him and sat down to eat her breakfast.

When she finished the delicious biscuit and crisp, perfectly oily potatoes, they walked back over to the convenience store to wait for the mechanic to arrive. Maren came out of the store as they got to the sidewalk.

"You get him?"

"Yeah, he'll be here pretty soon," Nadia said. "Hopefully, it won't be anything too serious."

"Hopefully. I hope you aren't missing any important plans or anything," she said. "I never even asked you where you're heading."

"Dogwood Valley," Nadia told her.

"Beautiful area. Are you visiting family there?"

"No, we're going to stay with some old friends of mine. Actually, we're moving there. Well, not there. Not officially. We're just staying with them until I figure everything out. Get a job and our own place and everything," Nadia said.

She stopped herself from elaborating any further. She felt the compulsion to open up to Maren and tell her all about Brent and everything she'd been through over the last few years. But she'd just met this girl. The last thing Maren needed at the end of a long night of work shift stretched even longer by a late coworker was a cascade of divorcée drama.

"You're going to be living in Dogwood Valley?" Maren asked.

"Yeah, I mean, thereabouts. I'm hoping to settle there, but at the very least close by."

"I'll be right back."

Maren turned and headed back into the convenience store. Nadia watched her go inside, and when she turned back, she saw a tow truck pulling into the lot. It parked off to the side, out of the way of any cars coming in for gas or visiting the store.

The driver's side door opened, and a young man—who Nadia knew her mother would have called "gangly"—swung a long leg out onto the step outside the door, then hopped down. He adjusted his dark-blue cap as he strolled toward the shop.

"Mrs. Holmes?" he asked.

Hearing that still gave Nadia a slight twitch. She remembered when she'd loved nothing more than to hear people refer to her by her married name. Not anymore.

"Nadia," she said.

"Smith," he said, holding out his hand to shake hers. "How can I help?"

She described the problems she'd been having with the car and how it had been acting the night before. He asked her to pop the hood, and when she stepped back onto the sidewalk, Maren had come out again. She eyed Smith hunched over the engine.

"Morning, Smith," she said.

He waved over his shoulder at her. This felt like the kind of friendship that'd been cultivated over many years. Nadia wouldn't be surprised to find out they'd known each other since childhood.

"Listen," Maren said, turning toward Nadia. Her eyes were sparkling. "You said you were looking for a job, right?"

Nadia was slightly taken aback by the question.

She nodded. "Yeah. The decision to move out here was kind of spontaneous. We just really started planning in a few weeks ago, so I didn't have a chance to get one before now," she said.

"How about here?" Maren asked.

It was a simple question, and yet that confused Nadia. She waited for Maren to say something else, but she just kept staring at Nadia, waiting for a response.

"Here?" Nadia finally said.

Maren bobbed her head with a bright smile. "Yeah, here. We've been looking for somebody else. There was a guy who was working here for a while, but he left a couple months ago, and we've just been filling in for his shifts and stuff. It's the main reason we have to do both the store and the motel at night and in the morning. So there's a position sitting here just waiting to be filled."

"What about the owner?"

"Mel? He knows we need somebody else. I've worked here so long he said if I found somebody I thought would be a good fit, I could hire them and he'll deal with all the paperwork and stuff later." She bounced slightly, like she was eagerly anticipating Nadia's answer, and said, "So?"

Nadia couldn't believe this was happening. Finding a job was her most important priority after getting Amelia enrolled and settled into school. She didn't know much about the area and didn't know what would be available that she would qualify for. While she was willing to do just about anything, she worried it was still going to take a while to find something. Now here she was with someone offering her a job before she even got to Jeff and Lisa's house. Someone she had already clicked with. It seemed like—as much of a cliché as it was to say—it was too good to be true.

So much so that she almost said no.

There was a lingering feeling of worry in her getting the offer. It was like something incredible was being dangled in front of her just to taunt her. She was afraid of the stinging pain of it being snatched away. The reaction was involuntary, coming from a deep corner she had tried to block off.

Nadia swallowed the doubt. She'd come this far. She already took the risk of leaving everything and trying to start over. This was a stepping stone toward achieving that.

"Um… I'll do it," she said.

"Yes! That's fantastic," Maren gushed. "Christy is going to be so happy. And you're going to love her when you get to know her. I know it seemed… well, I was just annoyed with her. We've been friends since the second she started working here. I can't wait for you to get started. I'll call Mel when I get home and let him know. Can I have your contact info to give him?"

Maren took out her phone, and Nadia input her name, phone number, and email address in the contacts. Handing the phone back, she grinned at Maren.

"I don't know how to thank you."

"Well, I can't promise good hours or that you're not going to have to explain to far more people than you'd think that this is not a full-service station and they're going to have to pump the gas themselves. Or that you're not going to get way too familiar with all the different kinds of junk foods that exist while you're stocking," Maren said.

"Or that I won't have to run outside in the rain to check someone into the motel?" Nadia asked with a cheeky grin.

"Only if you're lucky," Maren said. "Real talk. It's not the most glamorous gig in the world. The hours can be long. You end up with some nasty people who are tired of being on the road and take it out on you. It can be really boring, or it can be crazy busy. People are going to ask you to answer questions you don't have the answers to, give them directions to places you've never heard of, and ask if you can fix their car, carry their luggage, or deliver things to them at the motel.

"But all in all, it's a good job. Mel is great, and for the obnoxious people you end up having to deal with, you get a lot more who are either genuinely nice or who just want to pay for their gas, buy their snacks, and be on their way. It's solid, and it's something to give you a head start on your new life here."

"I can handle all of that. Not a problem. I really do appreciate this more than I can't possibly tell you. All of it."

"I'm glad to have met you," Maren said. "Just think, maybe if that car hadn't started giving you trouble, you never would have stopped here."

"That's true. A definite blessing in disguise, I guess you could say," Nadia said with a chuckle.

"Speaking of that blessing in disguise," Smith said, emerging from under the hood of Nadia's car. "This isn't something I'm gonna be able to fix here. It won't be hard back at my shop, I just don't have the tools I need here. If you want, I can tow it over there and have it done for you in a couple hours. You two could hop into my truck with me and wait."

"I wanna ride in the tow truck!" Amelia said excitedly from where she had slowly drifted over to a stand next to the car, watching the mechanic work. "I've never done that!"

"Actually, you have," Nadia said.

"I have?"

"You were just a baby, and your father was driving us home from your Aunt Jackie's house. It was snowing, and we skidded off the road. It wasn't a big deal."

Nadia said that almost like she was still trying to calm down her angry ex, who'd definitely thought it was a big deal when it happened. Even though he was behind the wheel at the time, he somehow managed to make Nadia feel like the situation was her fault. The tow truck driver roadside assistance sent out to help them wasn't as young and friendly as Smith. She could still smell the motor oil on him and feel the very hot blast of the heater on her face from the tight, uncomfortable ride.

"That doesn't count," Amelia protested. "I don't have any memories of that. Don't you want me forming core memories?"

Nadia had to laugh. For better or worse, her daughter was certainly a product of her generation.

"I'm not so sure this is one of those things I'm going to be eager to scrapbook about, but I do appreciate the ride. That will make everything a lot easier."

"There's a waiting room at my shop, but it's not much. There are a couple of restaurants nearby if you'd rather go have something to eat while you wait for your car to be ready. Do you need to get anything from the motel room?"

"No, I already put everything in the car."

"Great. Then I'll load it up, and we'll get out of here."

He headed over to his truck, and Nadia tugged Amelia backward further onto the sidewalk so she wouldn't be in the way when he picked up the car.

Maren rested a hand on her arm. "I've got to get home, but I'll see you soon!"

She hurried down the sidewalk toward the other side of the building where Nadia had seen the car parked the night before. It took a few minutes for the car to get up onto the tow truck, then the two of them climbed into the cabin.

"I didn't mean to listen in or anything, but was Maren saying you're going to be working at Mel's?" Smith asked as they made their way toward Murphy.

"Yeah," Nadia said. "Well, I mean, I guess. I haven't even met Mel, and I haven't filled out an application or anything, but Maren seems pretty confident I can have the position."

"Then you've got it," Smith said. "Congratulations."

Nadia gave a short laugh. "Thanks."

"So it sounds like you're going to be living in the area," Smith said.

"Technically, Dogwood Valley," Nadia told him. "A bit of a hike. But not too bad."

"Nah, it's a nice drive too."

Considering the amount of time she spent on the long, desolate road, she was not sure how much she actually believed that assertion, but she smiled along anyway.

Amelia was sitting next to the window and was stretching up as high as she could to watch everything go by from her new vantage point. The ride was not as long as Nadia expected, and Smith chattered the whole way until they arrived at the blue-and-white-painted concrete shop.

"You can go ahead on in if you want," Smith said. "There's a couple of machines and a coffee maker. Help yourself. And if you don't want to hang around here, about a five-minute walk up the road is a little shopping center."

"Thank you."

Nadia and Amelia got out of the truck and headed inside. She made herself another cup of coffee and handed Amelia a few dollar bills to go to the vending machines. They settled into chairs set up on a rug taking up one corner of the lobby, and Nadia took out her phone. She did a quick check of her email and her social media before shooting off a text to Lisa to update her. When she was finished, she pulled up her collection of audiobooks.

"Want to read a story?" she offered, scrolling through the options she accumulated for Amelia.

"Yes!"

Amelia wriggled up close beside Nadia and opened a pack of cheese crackers. Nadia chose a book and clicked on it.

This was one of those differences between parenting these days and the way she had been raised that Nadia felt conflicted about. She remembered how it felt bringing her big, pink canvas tote bag during her visits to the library with her mother and leaving while lugging it full of books. She'd loved the way it felt to reach into the bag and pull out a book, to feel and smell the pages. A physical book was better for curling under a blanket on a rainy day or hiding under a blanket fort with a flashlight when she got older. Holding a tablet and turning pages by swiping on a screen didn't have the same effect.

And yet, she had to admit the appeal of having the equivalent of several of those canvas totes right there at her fingertips. At moments like this, she could read as many books to Amelia as she wanted and then instantly flip to something for herself when she was done. No papercuts or overdue fines to be seen.

The time went by quickly as they read a book in the fantasy series Amelia had become thoroughly wrapped up in recently. They were swept up in a battle between factions of cats when Smith appeared at the door between the waiting area and the garage.

"All done," he said. "It's running great now. I even took it for a spin around a few blocks."

"Thank you so much," Nadia said, getting up and leaving the book with Amelia so she could keep reading.

She took her debit card out of her bag, bracing herself for the impact of the unexpected expense. She reminded herself of the job offer and told herself again it was going to work out. This was a bump in the road, but it would be far worse if she didn't have the prospect of a paying position waiting for her.

Smith took a piece of paper out of the printer and laid it down on the counter in front of Nadia. It detailed the work he'd done on the car and broke down the cost of each element.

"This is the down payment for the total and the increments of the payment plan," he said.

She was stunned by his words. "Payment plan?" she asked.

"You have the option of paying the whole thing now if you want, but I offer payment plans for repairs to make it easier on folks. I know when things come out of the blue like this, it can be a challenge. Especially when you're already going through all the hassle and everything of moving. If it helps, think of it as a 'welcome to the area' gift." He gave a friendly wink.

Nadia smiled. "Thank you."

She paid, and they went outside to where the car was waiting. The sun had fully filled a clear blue sky, with no sign of the clouds and rain from last night. She was starting to feel the same way. Things were getting brighter. The clouds were behind them, and everything was going to be better now.

She sent a text to Lisa to let her know they were on their way. She expected her friend to be at work and was surprised when Lisa immediately called.

"Hey," Nadia said. "I've got you on speaker."

"Hi, Ms. Lisa," Amelia called from the back seat.

"Hi, Amelia," Lisa said. "How are the two of you doing? You say you're on your way? The car is all fixed?"

"Yep, the mechanic was great, and we are headed that way. Should be there in about twenty-five minutes, it looks like. What are you doing calling me? Aren't you at work?"

"I took the day off so I can be here when you get here."

"You didn't have to do that," Nadia said.

"I wanted to. This is really exciting! and I didn't want you to show up and just walk into an empty house anyway. Jeff got called away on a business trip this morning, so he's not going to be home for the next three days. I know you could use the hidden key. I have one for you, obviously, by the way, but that would be anticlimactic."

"After the packing and the drive and storm and the car…" Nadia said, sighing, "'anticlimactic' is welcome. But I am looking forward to seeing you."

"Good. I actually called because I wanted to see if you're hungry and what I could throw together for lunch for you. Or if you want to go out. Or what would work," Lisa said.

"I'm hungry," Amelia said from the back.

"I am too," Nadia said. "Breakfast seems like a really long time ago at this point. If it's good with you, I'd prefer to just stay at the house once we get there. I just want to relax for a bit."

"No problem. I'll dig around in the kitchen and see what I can come up with. I'll see you when you get here!"

It turned out that "digging around in the kitchen" equated to a spread across the kitchen island that looked like it could feed ten. They sat in a sunroom to eat, chatting and catching up.

"Do you want to see your spot?" Lisa asked when they were done.

She led them down a hallway off the kitchen and through a door onto a set of beige-carpeted steps. She flipped a light switch to turn on a ceiling light past the landing below. They turned a corner and went down a few more steps to reach a large, open area. It was furnished like a living room with an overstuffed, gray sectional and a large TV. To one side was a tall bookshelf stuffed with books and another smaller shelf with stacks of board games. A door standing open behind the seating area revealed a full bathroom.

Nadia knew it was a basement rec room, and she felt a tug of guilt for taking over the space that was obviously designed for the couple to enjoy together and probably with friends. But she was too grateful for the help to let herself think about it too much.

"The bedrooms are over here," Lisa said. "This one is pretty small." She opened a door and glanced over her shoulder toward Nadia. "To be honest, I don't think it technically counts as a bedroom. Something about not enough electrical outlets."

"It's perfect," Nadia assured her, stepping into the room. It was already outfitted with a twin bed and a small dresser. "It's exactly right for Amelia."

"Let me show you yours," Lisa said.

They headed to the next door, and Lisa showed them a larger room with a queen bed and two dressers. A pink-and-white quilt draped across the end of the bed brought an unexpected lump of emotion into her throat.

"I really can't tell you how much I appreciate this," Nadia said. "It means so much to me. To both of us."

"I'm glad we can do it for you," Lisa said. "And I want you to know, I was completely serious when I said I want you to stay here as long as you want to. There is absolutely no rush whatsoever to get out of here. I know you told me about the job, and that is fantastic if it's something you want to do, but I don't want you to feel pressured just because you think you are going to overstay your welcome."

"I know. But I am actually excited about the idea. I mean, it's not the most glamorous position ever and not exactly the career aspiration I used to have, but that's okay. Maybe that's a good thing. I'm starting this whole new chapter of my life. Everything is different. Why keep holding on to my idea of what I can or should do? I need to try new things and take the opportunities that come my way. I have turned away far too many chances in my life. There have been so many times when I had the opportunity to do something or when a path opened up that I wanted to follow and I just didn't do it.

"Obviously, sometimes there were perfectly good reasons for me not to be able to take on those opportunities, but if I'm going to be honest, it wasn't always. And there were absolutely times when I just said no because I was scared of the change. Or because I felt like it was what I was supposed to do to keep everything calm and functional. I don't have to do that anymore. And I'm not going to. I want to see what life has to hand me." She laughed. "Maybe that was a lot more drama than a job working at the counter at a gas station really warrants."

"I think it was just the right amount of drama," Lisa said with a grin. "I think you deserve as much drama as you want. Drama and pomp and circumstance and all the things. You've been through enough."

"Thank you."

Lisa looped an arm through Nadia's and turned to head out of the room.

"Let's get your things inside and get you settled a bit. Then I need to go to the grocery store. You hang out here and relax."

"Actually, I think I'd like to go," Nadia said. "I might as well see the store."

"Mama, can I stay here?" Amelia asked.

Nadia gave Lisa a long-suffering look.

"No."

It took a few trips for them to bring everything they packed inside. Nadia knew she was going to have to go back with a moving truck for the last of what was in storage, but that could wait for a little bit. There was nothing too important in there. For now they had what they needed and could start setting up their home.

That evening they ordered pizza and sat wrapped in blankets on the living room floor watching movies until Amelia fell asleep. Nadia woke her up gently and got her downstairs into her new bed. She tucked her in and kissed her on the forehead before carefully closing the door. Lisa was standing near the seating arrangement.

"I hope she doesn't think that junk food and movies until she nods off are the new bedtime routine," Nadia said.

"You'll get her back on track," Lisa said. "She's a good kid."

Nadia let out a breath, rubbing her arms against a sudden chill. "Yeah, she is."

"How is she handling all this?" Lisa asked.

"Honestly, I wish I had an answer for that. It makes me feel like a terrible mother for not being more in tune with her and knowing exactly how she's feeling. Just so I can be there for her in the way she needs me to be. I want to make this as easy for her as I possibly can. I know there's nothing I can do to make it not hard. This is a huge change. She's old enough to know that things are changing and everything is going to be different. But she's still too young to really grasp why it's happening.

"And there are times when she is so excited about it. She's talked about making new friends, finding new things to do. She seems to really understand how important this is for us and that it's going to make so much of a difference.

"But then some days it's rough. A few days before her last days of school, she completely melted down. She burst into tears and was sobbing over leaving her friends. She said she couldn't believe she would never play in her playground again. Everything was completely overwhelming. She started saying that I didn't care about her and that all of this was my fault," Nadia said.

"Do you think Brent said something to her?" Lisa asked.

"I don't know. I don't think so. He barely even saw her over the last year and a half. Two years, really."

Lisa reached out and took Nadia by both her upper arms.

"Listen to me. I can already see what you're thinking. I've known you long enough that I know. She is not right. Look at me. Are you listening right now? She is not right. She is a child. She is just a child whose life is changing, and she's not sure how to make sense of it all. Like you said, she's at a hard age. Old enough and not old enough at the same time. But you need to get it out of your head that you did anything wrong. Because you didn't. This is not you. You are not to blame for the bullshit he pulled, and you are not the one who imploded all three of your lives. That is all on him. And if he did say something to her to make her doubt that, someday she would understand.

"But here's the thing. What matters now is that you did what you needed to do. You won't catch me saying it was easy. I know you could have done a lot of other things. You could have put your head in the sand and kept going. Instead, you decided to take a massive leap and start over. It was exactly what you needed to do for you and for Amelia. Both of you deserve a life that is stable, comfortable, and happy. And you're going to have that."

Nadia pulled Lisa in for a hug. "I don't know what I would have done without you."

"You don't have to worry about that," Lisa said. "Are you going to bed? Or do you feel like some tea and TV with fewer bright colors and anthropomorphized animals?"

"Let's go," Nadia said.

They chuckled as they went back up the stairs. Lisa went into the kitchen to make the tea, and Nadia headed to the living room to find something for them to watch. She got distracted by the pictures sitting on the mantel and went over to look at them. Most were of Lisa and Jeff on their various adventures.

Ever since she'd met Lisa in high school, Nadia had always described her as the restless type. It was not meant to be an insult, just an observation. She always needed to be doing something, discovering something, trying something. She bored easily and moved on to something else. No matter what, she was planning five steps ahead of her. Lisa was always looking to the horizon.

It actually stunned Nadia when Jeff stuck in her life. Lisa had gone through boyfriends with the same kind of attitude as she did just about everything else in her life—always moving on to the next thing. But it wasn't like that with Jeff. Something was different about him. Somehow he cracked the code of Lisa, and she was enamored. They fed off each other's enthusiasm for life and adventure and were constantly embarking on something together.

That meant a mantel full of pictures of them in front of various icons around the world or in the middle of whitewater rafting or zip-lining. Life and love glowed out of them in every image.

Nadia moved down the mantel following them on their various journeys and then noticed a picture different from the rest. This one was of Lisa alongside two women Nadia didn't recognize. It looked like they were standing in a park. Their long coats and slightly huddled posture indicated that it was winter.

"Did you find something?"

Nadia jumped slightly and turned to see Lisa coming into the room with a tray.

"To watch? Did you find something to watch?"

"Oh," Nadia said. "No, I got caught up in looking at your pictures. Sorry."

Lisa put the tray down and came over, shaking her head. "No need to apologize. I like looking at them too. That's why they're out here. They remind me of happy times."

"Who are they?" Nadia asked, pointing at the picture.

Lisa reached over and picked up the slim gold frame. "Do you remember a few years ago when my friend who went missing from my college was found? Julia Meyer?"

"I remember you talking about that," Nadia said. "The FBI got involved and ended up finding her alive."

Lisa nodded. "Yep." She pointed to the woman on the far right. "That's her. And that"—she pointed to the blonde woman in the middle—"is the FBI agent who solved it. Emma Griffin. We met in college and kept in touch after she decided to go to the Academy. This is right around the one-year anniversary of Julia being rescued. We met up on campus. It was the first time I'd seen Julia since she disappeared."

She looked at the picture, and a bittersweet smile came to her lips.

"Like I said, happy times."

CHAPTER FIVE

Emma

"WHEN WAS THE LAST TIME THEY TALKED TO HER?"

"Valentine's Day," Detective Melton says.

"Valentine's Day?" I repeat, shocked it was so long ago. "It's been a month since they've spoken with their mother, and they are just now getting around to noticing?"

"Apparently, it's not that uncommon in this family. Or at least with Denise. The daughter-in-law I talked to said she's known for being very independent. She travels a lot and is frequently out of touch with them for extended periods of time, and it's not unusual. When she comes back, they always get together to hear about what she did and catch up and everything," he says. "It doesn't sound like there's any kind of animosity or estrangement involved. Just a single, retired woman who goes about her life on her own terms."

"All right," I say, trying to get this situation straight in my head. "Then what's the problem? She's going off on her own all the time. Why are they worried about her now? Did she not tell them she was going somewhere?"

"They did expect Denise to be taking a trip right around that time, which is another reason why they weren't alarmed at not hearing from her for a few weeks. But she missed a couple of family birthdays, which evidently is something she never does. They tried to get in touch with her but haven't been able to. She didn't give them a firm itinerary of what she was doing, but they did know the hotel where she was supposed to be staying. When they contacted the hotel, they found out she checked out very abruptly, and that's what made them contact us. Emma, she fits the demographic. She's in the right age range. Financially comfortable. Well-known in the community and involved in a lot of things. Everything lines up," Melton tells me.

"Terrence Brooks wasn't in that age range or financially comfortable," I point out. "He wasn't scraping by or anything, but he definitely didn't suit the euphemism."

"But he's the only outlier. And we know what happened to him and why. All of the other players are a type. Maybe it's not as narrow and specific as Bundy's dark-haired girls, but they all do check off a list of specifications."

"And even Bundy had his deviation," I mutter. "Did you do a welfare check?"

"I sent officers to the house, but there was no answer. There's no justifiable cause for breaking into her house. No sign of any forced entry or anything. She's not responding to people, but you know as well as I do that doesn't give us the right to just smash her door down, even though that's what her children wanted us to do. She's a grown adult. She can do whatever she wants, including going somewhere without telling anybody and not checking in. She isn't obligated to call people on their birthday or come home when they think she should or respond to messages."

"I'm well aware of that," I say. "But you are the one telling me she fits in with the demographic of the Game Master players."

"Because she does. Unfortunately, that doesn't give me any actual extra wiggle room."

"All right. How about her kids then? You said you talked to her daughter-in-law? Where's she? Where's the son I'm assuming she's married to?"

"All three of her children live out of state. At least the daughter-in-law and son were making plans to come in tomorrow," the detective says.

"Do they have keys to the house? Or know where she keeps an extra?" I ask.

"They have keys."

"Good. All right. Give me their contact info. I'll let them know I'll meet them at the house, and we can have a look around."

"Thank you," he says.

"Let's just hope you're wrong. I don't want to mar your reputation or anything, but I would much rather her just having decided she wanted to opt out of expectations and sitting on a beach somewhere than to think she was selected," I say.

"She was traveling to a ski lodge," he says.

I pinch the bridge of my nose and close my eyes, my other hand tightening around the phone.

"All right. Sitting in a chalet sipping hot cocoa. Cozying up to a ski instructor. Inner tubing down the Black Diamond, for all I care. Something that makes her happy is infinitely preferable to the thought that the Game Master chose her."

Melton gives me the contact information for Vivica Stein, and I call her as soon as I hang up with the detective. There's an undertone of concern in her voice, but there's also the kind of steadiness that says she's good in emergencies. I assume this is why she was the one elected by the family to get in touch with the police rather than Denise Stein's son.

"FBI?" she asks, sounding slightly more alarmed after I introduce myself. "Why is the FBI involved?"

"It's not that the FBI is involved," I tell her. "Right now, I'm just looking into the situation. Detective Melton thought there were similarities between the situation with your mother-in-law and a case I am currently working on. He thought it would be a good idea to pass the information along to me and let me look into it. As of right now, nothing else has happened, and I don't know anything that you don't."

"Okay," she says with a breath.

"The detective told me you and your husband are coming into town."

"Yeah, we're boarding the train in about an hour," Vivica says. "We won't get there until tomorrow morning."

"Did you book a hotel?"

"Yes," she says. "Since we don't know what's going on, we figured we should be ready to be in town for a couple of days."

"Good. Go there directly from the train station. Don't go to Denise's house until I am there with you. What time do you get in?"

THE GIRL ON THE RUN

"Eight," she says.

"Would you be able to meet me at the house at nine?"

"Sure."

"All right. I'll see you then."

I set my phone on the coffee table spread with my notes and climb off the couch to head to the kitchen. Sam is working the late shift tonight, leaving me home alone. Other than a very brief video call with Bellamy and Bebe earlier, I've been fully immersed in work and barely noticed the time passing.

I grab a container of leftover Chinese food out of the refrigerator and get a fork from the drawer. I don't bother to heat it up or even dump it out of the little cardboard box. It's just me here. No one is going to care that I'm eating cold shrimp fried rice directly out of a takeout container.

The spring night has gotten chilly, and I reach into the wooden chest in the living room for a crochet duster Xavier made me for Christmas. He said he chose the color so it would feel cozy, like snuggling down into a bowl of warm oatmeal. I have to admit, that assessment is pretty accurate.

I sit cross-legged on the couch with my takeout and flip through the channels to find something to watch while I eat. At least that way I won't just work through and not even notice I'm eating. I settle on a rerun episode of a favorite true mystery show that's nearly as old as I am. There's something comforting about the grainy footage and wardrobes awash in earth tones and occasional jarring neon shades.

The show gets me to the bottom of the takeout container and through the remaining couple of inches in a pint of mint chocolate chip that's been stashed in the back of the freezer. But as soon as I add my spoon to the dishwasher and toss in a detergent pod, my mind is taken over by work again.

Thoughts of the potentially missing woman, Denise Stein, have been sitting at the edges of my brain throughout dinner. I've kept them at bay with the charming cadence of the host's voice and the nostalgia of the old cases, many long-solved. Now they rush in, filling all the little gaps and crevices around my other cases. It's like flooding a storage unit of stacked filing cabinets. It's all still there, but the new information is forcing its way in and taking up any little space it can find.

Just like I told Detective Melton, I don't want this to be part of the Game Master case.

The conclusion that Sebastian McConnell has nothing to do with the case is a massive relief despite the open questions still lingering there.

The loss of another player cut deep.

I don't want that to happen again.

As I do with any potentially missing person I am investigating, I take out my computer and run a search for Denise Stein. I have her address and the name of her son and daughter-in-law, so I'm able to sift through all the results and narrow them to the right woman. The results show me why Detective Melton thought it would be a good idea for me to look into her apparent disappearance.

He was absolutely right about her fitting in with the demographic of the people the Game Master has chosen as his unfortunate players. The search results are littered with images of Denise at a variety of galas and charity events. Articles from several years ago, before her retirement, praise her sharp business mind, intensity, and focus. These years of obvious hard work landed her in a tax bracket where she'd be in good company with other players.

I move on from the articles and blogs she's featured in to her personal social media pages. Here is where I'll get a chance to see more of who she actually is. She isn't overly active on any of the pages, but it looks like she posted fairly regularly. It's mostly just pictures with little to no caption. She clearly isn't the type to wax poetic about her views on life or blog incessantly about each detail of her day. Instead, I scroll through shots from her various travels or of a well-tended garden. Some offer a few words to give context. Others seem to just be there for the sake of sharing and remembering.

Getting back toward the holiday season, I find pictures of her with people I'm assuming are her children. It's all the usual holiday family pictures. Sitting around the table eating. Lighting the menorah. Walking through a light display. They all look happy and comfortable.

As I try to get a glimpse into Denise's life, I can't help but think of what I've uncovered about the Game Master. The players were chosen for their secrets. The cruel person behind the gimmick knows something about each of them. It's this secret that fuels him to choose them and put them through his games. Does Denise Stein have a secret? Is it enough to fall victim to the Game Master?

The next morning I pull up to the address Melton gave me a few minutes before nine. I don't see another car in front of the house or in the driveway, so I assume Denise's son and daughter-in-law haven't arrived yet. I park in front of the house and get out. I check my phone to make sure they haven't called me, then wait a few seconds to see if they drive up. When they don't, I start up the driveway.

Everything looks quiet and normal. Nothing seems obviously out of place. I'm not surprised at not seeing her car in the driveway, but I make a mental note to ask her son if he has access to the garage. I look around the front of the house, taking a cursory glance at the door and windows. They are the most obvious areas the officers would have looked at when they came for the welfare check. If there was a problem with them, they would have immediately noted it.

Instead, I focus on what might not have occurred to them to check. I walk carefully around the porch, looking down for signs of anything that might have been spilled or broken. Something like a dropped cup of coffee is easily missed if you're not looking for it, but it can be a strong indicator of something wrong. I don't see anything on the porch and move down the steps again to check the walkway and the yard. Something glitters in the sun at the edge of the grass, catching my attention. I lean down and pick up an earring.

The dangling earring looks like a long gold vine with leaves and clear stones. The back is standard for such a heavy piece, consisting of a long, curved hook rather than a straight post and a secure back. The tight curve of the top of the hook makes it difficult for the piece to fall from a person's ear without some force. Not impossible though. Especially if Denise wore them often, it's possible it could have maneuvered its way out of her ear. It could have caught in her hair and come out when she swept her hair away from her neck. There is a chance it's completely innocent and means nothing.

And there's a chance it means everything.

I hear a car behind me and stand, turning to see a nondescript sedan pull up the driveway and park. A man and woman in their early to mid-forties climb out. The man pushes his sunglasses onto the top of his head as he comes toward me.

"Detective Griffin?"

"Agent," I correct him.

"I told you, babe. She's from the FBI," the woman says, shaking her head slightly as she hurries to catch up. She puts her hand out toward me. "Vivica. We spoke on the phone."

I nod. "Right."

"And this is my husband, Rhys."

"Good to meet you," I say, shaking his hand. "Your mother is Denise?"

"Yes." He sounds anxious. His eyes keep flickering up to the house, and I notice him shifting his weight back and forth on his feet.

Vivica's gaze drops to the earring in my hand. "What's that?" she asks.

"I found it in the grass," I tell her, holding the piece of jewelry up so they can see it better. "I'm assuming it belongs to Denise."

"It does," Rhys says. "My brother gave them to her for her birthday last year."

"If it's okay with you, I'm going to keep a hold of this for right now."

"That's fine," he says. "I just... I don't understand what could have happened to her."

"We need to take this one step at a time," I tell him. "First, can you get into the garage?"

"Sure."

"I want to see if her car is there. Detective Melton didn't say anything about it when he was giving me the details of the situation."

We go to the detached garage, and he uses one of the keys on a ring he pulls from his pocket to open a side access door. It only takes a quick glimpse inside to see there are no vehicles.

"Do you happen to know the details about your mother's car off the top of your head? Make, model, license plate?"

There's no reason to think he would know something as obscure as the VIN, but if we can start with the basics, we can go from there.

"Yes."

"Good. That's a place to start. We'll put out the information and have local officers keeping an eye out for it as well as contacting the airport to see if it's there. Let's go inside and take a look around."

We leave the garage and start for the front door, but Rhys hesitates at the bottom of the steps. He looks up at the house nervously.

"Babe?" Vivica asks from the top step, looking down toward him.

"Are you all right?" I ask. "Do you want me to go inside first?"

He hesitates, but he finally nods.

"I can go," Vivica says.

"Actually, it's better if you stay with him. Give me the key, and I'll take a quick look around. I'll be right back."

He hands over the keyring with the door key held upright. I take it and let myself inside. The door opens without hesitation. Nothing seems off when I step inside. The climate control system is obviously working, and there is no concerning smell. Those are the first things I try to be aware of when stepping into a situation like this. The old cliché of people turning the air conditioner to a frigid temperature after committing murder is there for a reason. I've seen the tactic more than once and have heard of it many more times. The cold temperature can work to mask the time of death and throw off the initial investigation. The opposite can be true as well. I've seen perpetrators turn the heat up as high as it will go in an attempt to hasten decomposition.

A space that feels excessively cold or hot is an immediate red flag. After that, absent obvious visual clues, smells can be a strong indicator. Food that was abandoned, pets not cared for, or the most chilling, the unmistakable scent of death.

None of that is here.

I still walk through the house with my hand on my gun. I check each room and then return to the porch. Rhys looks at me with wide, worrying eyes.

"I didn't notice anything immediately concerning," I tell him, a sensitive way of assuring him I did not find his mother's body inside her house.

His body visibly relaxes as a heavy breath rushes out of him. "Thank God."

"I walked through the house and looked in all the rooms. I didn't do any in-depth searching. Like I said, I didn't notice anything immediately concerning, but I'd still like you to take a look around. You obviously know your mother and her house much better than I do. You might notice something that didn't stand out to me."

"I can do that," he says with a few nervous bobs of his head.

I go back into the house and hold the storm door open for them. Rhys takes a step into the entryway and looks around. Something flickers across his face.

"What is it?" I ask.

"No candle smell," he says.

"Candle smell?"

"Mom loves candles. She burns them all the time. It's part of her morning routine. As soon as she's up, while she's drinking her coffee, she goes around the house lighting candles. I've told her a thousand times it isn't safe for her to have them burning when she isn't in the room. She never listens. She says it's fine because she doesn't have any pets that are going to knock them over and she always uses the ones in the big glass jars," he says. "She used to complain because the different smells were all in different colors, and she didn't like the way they looked in the house. Then she found a company that makes different scents in all white. She really likes that. Says they go with everything."

He's starting to ramble. It's a normal reaction. Very often people babble when they are in difficult or uncomfortable situations that they don't understand or don't want to face. It fills their brain and slows everything down, but it's also just a side effect of trying to wrap their minds around what's happening. As they search for meaning or understanding, thoughts and tenuous connections start to tumble out.

"So the house usually smells like candles," I say, bringing him back into focus.

"Yeah. You can smell them as soon as you walk into the house. And they're on all the time. She only blows them out if she's leaving the house or going to bed. They're really strong, so the smell lingers. I've come over after she's been gone for a day or two and could still smell them."

"So the fact that you can't smell them now means it's highly unlikely she's been in this house any time in the last several days," I say.

Rhys draws in a breath. "Yeah."

"Can you give me that information about your mom's car?" I take the notepad out of my bag and write down what he tells me. "All right, give me just a second," I say when he's done.

I step back out onto the porch and call Detective Melton, quickly filling him in on what's happening. Then I ask him to put out the information about Denise's car and read out to him my notes about what Rhys told me.

"I'll contact the DMV and get the VIN," the detective says. "If somebody took her car and swapped plates, we can still make the identification."

"Good. Honestly, I would check with the airport first. If she went to the hotel she had booked and then left suddenly, we need to figure out if she made it back here and drove off somewhere or if she stayed back where she was vacationing. We should contact the airlines and airports to find out if she boarded another flight or if she even checked in at all. That's going to be a massive undertaking, so it's better if we can narrow it first," I say.

"I'll get on it."

"I'm still at the house. I am going to go through it more thoroughly with her son to see if he notices anything else that's unusual. Let me know if you find anything," I say.

"Will do," Melton says.

CHAPTER SIX

GO BACK INTO THE HOUSE AND FIND RHYS AND VIVICA STANDING at the entryway to a living room off the front foyer.

"Did you see something?" I ask.

"I'm not sure," he says. "It's just… I know this probably sounds ridiculous and like I am overthinking everything. But Mom is really particular about the way her house is kept. She has someone come and clean it a couple times a week, but even they have specific instructions for how everything is supposed to look. I've never seen her leave something sitting out on a table like that."

He gestures into the living room, and I see what looks like a few small pieces of paper scattered in the middle of the polished oval coffee table between two ivory floral couches. They didn't register when I was looking over the room earlier. They don't seem like much, but they're obviously enough to make her son take notice.

"Do you know what they are?" I ask.

"No, I haven't gone any further than this."

I walk past him into the room and up to the table. I see that they aren't just pieces of paper. They appear to be large stickers, like the ones I sometimes find tucked into the packages I order from small businesses. Before touching them, I take out my phone and snap a picture to show exactly where they were. Slipping my phone back into my pocket, I pick up one of the stickers.

"What is it?" Vivica asks.

"I'm not sure."

She comes into the room, and I hand the sticker to her.

"Does this mean anything to you?"

She shakes her head and gives it over to Rhys when he steps up beside her.

Each of the stickers shows what look like random slashes of red ink across a white background. It's not smears or brush strokes, but lines that don't appear to have any rhyme or reason. They are all different. No matter which way I turn them, to look at them from different angles, none of them have the same pattern. I flip them over to confirm they are stickers and to check for a company watermark or contact email that might be printed on the paper backing that protects the adhesive. There's nothing, which might mean these weren't actually ordered from a company but rather created by someone in their own home.

"Stickers?" Rhys asks.

"I guess you don't know what they are either," I say.

"No, I don't know why she would have stickers. Especially ones like this."

"I feel like I already know the answer to this, but I'm going to ask anyway. Is your mother a crafter?" I ask.

"Not one bit," Rhys says. "About as crafty as I've ever seen her get was when she used to color with us kids when we were little. One time she made a popcorn and cranberry garland for the Christmas tree because I'd seen one in a book and thought it would be special. That's the extent of it."

"So chances are low that she made these herself."

"I'd say almost nonexistent."

"I'm going to hold on to these as well," I tell him.

"Sure."

"Let's keep going."

We work our way through the house, and Rhys searches each room. He's obviously very familiar with the details of the house and what should and shouldn't be here. He checks for the candles he talked about and glances into the trash can and dishwasher. I remember what he said about someone coming to clean for her regularly, and I realize he's probably checking to see if they've been here. Everything looks in order on the first and second floors. When we get to the third floor and Denise's bedroom, Rhys immediately goes to the closet.

He opens the double doors to reveal a closet bigger than my bedroom when I was a teenager. The walls are lined with bars of hanging clothes and racks of shoes. Center islands offer cushioned seating around wooden platforms holding jewelry displays.

"There are things missing," he says almost instantly.

"You can tell?" I ask.

"Absolutely. There are a few things Mom always takes with her when she travels. She's really predictable that way. None of her really good jewelry, but some of the simpler pieces. A blue-and-purple caftan. Two pairs of khaki Bermuda shorts. Her green sweater. None of those are here."

"You said she always takes those with her when she travels," I say.

"Always. She packs other things depending on when and where she's going, but those are her staples that go everywhere," he confirms.

I glance up at the shelf above Rhys's head. Two large suitcases and a smaller matching carry-on bag are lined up neatly. I point at them.

"Isn't that her luggage?" I ask.

He looks confused when he sees the bags here. "Yeah. How is that here? Her car isn't. Her clothes aren't. She hasn't been."

"Is it possible those particular articles of clothing could be somewhere else?" I ask. "At the cleaners?"

"No. Well, I mean... I guess. But it..."

It doesn't make sense. He doesn't have to finish the thought.

"Do you notice anything else missing or out of place?" I ask.

He looks around the closet and then searches the bedroom. "No."

"Let's finish up the other rooms."

When we finish going through the house, we have no more answers than when we started. There's still no sign of Denise being in the house other than her luggage in the closet. Even that, though, doesn't conclusively prove that she returned from her travels and then left again. It's entirely possible she bought new luggage. Without some clear proof of what she had with her when she left, we can't really say it went with her and was then returned. It would be strange for her to buy a new set of luggage when she has this very nice set neatly stored in the closet, but it's not out of the realm of possibility.

The strange little details stand out to me. The fact that her car is not in the garage. The earring I found in the grass. The stickers in the living room. They don't seem like too much on the surface, but combined with what I've heard about Denise and what was happening in her life when she went missing, they seem extremely odd.

"Have you tried calling your mother since calling the police?" I ask when we return to the front porch.

"Yes," Rhys says. "A few times. It goes straight to voicemail. I've left so many, it's full now."

This means her phone is either purposely turned off or the battery is dead. Even still, it could be possible to track the phone's location.

"We could try to find the phone's location if she has the location-sharing feature activated. Even with the battery dead or the phone off, if the location tracking is on, it's possible to ping it. As long as the phone hasn't been moved since it was turned off, it could tell us where she is."

It's a lot of factors. But it's a step. As much as we'd all like to think investigations are a linear path of uncovering what happened step by step, this is really rarely the case. Most of the time it's more a matter of chipping away at it, eliminating individual possibilities until all that's left is the answer.

"We don't have the family-sharing set up," he says.

"All right. Then we'll have to get permission through the provider. It could take a few days, but hopefully not. Sometimes they expedite it for emergency situations like this. Just continue trying to get in touch with her. Call, text, send her messages on social media. Anything you can do to try to reach out to her. The detective is checking with the airports and trying to piece together a timeline of where she was and when. That can help them track her movements and better understand what might have happened," I say.

"What else should we do?"

"Keep doing everything you can to track down where she might have gone or what she might have done. Reach out to all of her friends and any associates or contacts you know. If you have access to her financial records, check them to see if she made any purchases or paid for another hotel."

"I don't have that information," he says. "Mom is very private about her finances."

"Then that's something else the detectives will have to do in their investigation. Right now, all you can do is think about every person she might have had any contact with and any location that she might have wanted to visit and follow up on those. The investigators can handle the more extensive steps," I say.

"The investigators?" Vivica asks. "Does that mean you aren't going to be moving forward with this case?"

"Like I said, I was contacted about this because it seemed possible it could be linked to another case. Right now, I don't see anything that really leads me to believe that's what's going on. Which means this is a missing person's case that needs to be handled by local investigators, not the FBI."

"Then why did you want to keep the earring and the stickers?" Vivica asks. "If you aren't going to be investigating the case, why do you want potential evidence?"

"I wanted a chance to look over it again and turn it over to Detective Melton," I say. "If it would make you more comfortable to do that yourself…"

"No," Rhys says. "Do what you need to do." He sounds slightly let down, like he's disappointed that I'm not going to be more involved in his mother's potential disappearance than I am.

I can understand how he's feeling. He's worried about her and wants as much help as he can get. But right now, this doesn't need my attention. Melton and the rest of the local team are more than capable of handling a missing person. If something changes, he knows where to find me.

I reassure Rhys again, reminding him of what Detective Melton and the officers are already doing in their efforts to locate Denise.

"How long are you going to be in town?" I ask.

"Two nights," he says. "At least that's the plan for right now. I guess it could change."

"All right. Detective Melton will keep you updated on what's going on with his team. Be sure to let him know if you find out anything from the people you contact or if you think of anything else."

"Thank you," he says. "I appreciate you coming."

Taking another glance at the house, I head down the driveway to my car. The warmth of the last few days seems to have just been a tease, and a chill has settled back in. I tug my sweater tighter around me before getting in the car and revving up the heated seat. I call Sam as I pull out of the parking lot.

"Just letting you know I'm on my way back home," I tell him. "How is your day going?"

"Good. We have some new ideas for the family fun day at the park this year, so I've been juggling calls and meetings about that along with everything else. A quiet day all in all though. How about you? Did you find anything?"

"Not really. This woman is definitely not at home, and no one knows where she is. Her car isn't at home. There wasn't anything too concerning at the house though. Everything was secure. The doors were locked. No blood or anything broken. Her son did say it was obvious she hadn't been there within the last several days, and I found a couple odd things," I say.

"But nothing that made you think she's part of your case," he says.

"No," I say. "Anyway, I know you're busy, so I will let you go. I just wanted to update you. Did you have anything specific that you wanted for dinner tonight?"

"Not that I can get right off the top of my head. Are we still going over to Janet and Paul's since he's feeling better?" Sam asks.

"As far as I know. I haven't heard anything different from her."

"Sounds good. I'll see you when I get home. I love you."

"I love you," I say.

CHAPTER SEVEN

D ETECTIVE MELTON CALLS ME WITHIN AN HOUR OF ME GETTING home.

"The parking lots at the airport were searched. Denise's car isn't in any of them. We're getting the security footage from them right now to see if we can find exactly when the car left. She didn't pay for parking ahead of time, so there's no electronic record of when she entered or left. All of the lots and decks have cameras at the entrance and exits though. Since we know when she got on the plane, we can track down where she parked by going through the footage from a few hours before that. Then it's just a matter of picking up after she left the hotel and watching until we see it move again."

"How about the location of the phone?" I ask.

"Still waiting," he says. "Hopefully, the provider will be cooperative rather than forcing us to get a warrant," he says optimistically, though he knows as well as I do that the chances of that are slim.

Phone companies, like anyone dealing with personal information, don't like handing over details about their customers without clear permission, unless they are legally compelled to. It's the fine balance between protecting the privacy of the paying customer and making sure they are safe. I'm not quite sure about how I feel regarding this type of situation. I think protecting life and safety should take absolute precedence over any kind of privacy in a missing persons case.

If a person is missing, time is critical. Every single second matters. The harsh reality is that in the majority of situations, by the time family or friends notice that a person is not where they are supposed to be, many of those precious seconds have already passed. It could be hours, days, or even weeks, and that puts investigators immediately behind. A tool that can pin their location can close that gap. Identifying the location of a person's device can help track them down or at the very least point out where they have been. This can literally mean the difference between life and death.

I don't think it's worth avoiding the chance that somebody has gone off on their own accord and simply doesn't want to be found. In a situation like this, investigators can use the location to get in touch with the missing person. If they don't want to be found by their family or friends, they can tell the police that and go about their business. But if they do need help, getting their location as quickly as possible is vital.

But that isn't how it always works out. Sometimes phone companies are more flexible than others. If an investigator explains the urgency of the situation, they may be willing to turn over the information. A lot of the time, however, they insist on a warrant, which requires more time and effort that could be spent on the search itself.

"Well, I found a couple of things at the house that I wanted to pass along to you. I don't know what they mean, but her son seemed to think they had significance. I'll be back in the area tomorrow, so I can come by the station and bring them to you if that works," I say.

"Sure. I'm sorry to have bothered you with this," he says.

"Not at all. She's still missing. This is still serious. And I appreciate that you are keeping your eye out for connections," I say.

That night after coming back from Janet and Paul's house, I take a shower and slip back into my oatmeal duster. Sam is absorbed in a replay of a spring training game in the living room, so I take all my notes with me into my office. Spreading everything out on the floor, I return to trying to put together the puzzle of Sebastian McDonnell's disappearance.

I line up stills taken from doorbell camera footage from the neighbors' houses near Sebastian and Lavinia's house. None of the footage showed enough to give us any clear idea of what happened, but these stills have some details in them that might mean something. I look more closely at one of them. Sebastian's house is at a diagonal angle, sharply to the right of the camera. It's only really noticeable if you know what you're looking for—or at least what you want to be looking for.

At the very edge of the lawn, what looks like a shadow cutting across an illuminated rectangle on the top of the driveway can be seen, like the garage door is open and someone is either standing just inside the door or walking into the garage. It's not close or clear enough to see any details about the person, if that is what it is. But it does offer a time stamp of at least some movement near the house.

Another still is from around the time the security system would have been deactivated. This particular detail is especially interesting to me. It isn't just that the system was disarmed; that could've been done as simply as by inputting a code. Instead, the entire system—including the cameras covering the house and surrounding grounds—had been fully disengaged well before the time Sebastian seemed to have vanished.

This would have required extensive planning and preparation on the part of someone aiming to abduct the wealthy man. They would have to be familiar with the house and the security system and have the wherewithal to approach the house in such a way that wouldn't trigger the cameras to record their actions. There's no footage from any of the cameras, inside or out, that shows anyone coming up to the house, walking through it, or tampering with the system. By all measure, it simply went dark. Either that person is the luckiest damn criminal who has ever walked, timing the abduction to the day after the entire security system just decided to fail for no reason—or this was targeted, intricate sabotage.

The still shot from the time just before the cameras stopped is from another house on the opposite side from the first. It shows a light glowing in the window of a room at the back of the upper floor as well as the lower floor. The front porch light is on, and a decorative lamppost at the end of the driveway is also illuminated. Another still shot from just a few moments later shows the upstairs light and the front porch light now off. In another from just a few moments after that, the front porch light is on again.

I go through all the notes, everything that's been collected throughout the investigation. I still need to speak with Lavinia and Annette myself, but for now I have their statement from when they spoke with the first detective who started the case.

Curious, I pull my computer down onto the floor with me and bring up Lavinia's social media page. She's been instructed not to discuss the details of the situation in any way. Since we don't know what's going on or who is behind any of it, it could be not only dangerous but also detrimental to the case for details to be revealed publicly. Just asking for something like this, however, is by no means a guarantee that it's actually going to be respected. I've gone through far too many cases where people did not heed the warnings and spilled everything out to the infinite void of the internet or skipped the middleman and just went straight to the media.

I haven't heard anything about the case on the news, and no one has contacted me to say they've seen anything, but I still want to check. Her page comes up, and I scroll through the very sparse feed of recent posts. Fairly vague, but pointed enough for those who know what's going on. It isn't realistic to expect she hasn't told anybody about Sebastian being missing. This has been released to the public, but the details surrounding his disappearance and any theories investigators might have are being kept confidential.

This leaves her carefully skirting the situation. Her posts make it obvious that she misses him, but she's careful not to talk about the notes left in the house or coming through the mail. She doesn't make any sort of plea for his return or for information. The most recent post is the simplest. No words, just an image of a piece of paper with a heart on it, torn in half.

It seems that it would be easy for anybody looking at these posts, particularly that picture, to misinterpret what's going on. Without the full information, it does look like they just broke up or are going through a difficult time. Knowing not just the full story surrounding his disappearance, but also the theories being bandied around, the picture teeters between meaning. If I choose to be optimistic, it is gut-wrenching. I can't imagine what it would be like to not know where Sam is. I can't even think about how I would deal with what she's going through if she truly doesn't know what happened to him.

But I am still struggling with the fuzzy suspicion at the edges of my thoughts. That makes the picture seem performative, like she is silently pleading for compassion and attention while also trying to not look suspicious. But as it usually works, efforts to deflect a suspicion only magnify it. And if that suspicion is rooted in anything, the picture of the torn heart isn't gut-wrenching; it's infuriating.

But until I know anything else, I have to keep my thoughts anchored in my responsibility toward Lavinia. I have to believe she is truly depending on me to find out what happened to her husband.

I'm about to move away from the page when my eyes are drawn back to the red of the heart against the white background. I focus on just half of the torn image. The perception of the heart drops away, and I'm only looking at the abstract red shape. Drawing my focus out again, I allow my eyes to settle on both halves, recreating the image of the heart in my mind.

I push the computer aside and rush into the living room. Sam is at the very edge of the couch cushion watching the last moments of the game intently. Even though it's just spring training, he is deeply committed to the outcome for his favorite team. We've talked about going on a baseball pilgrimage next summer. He wants to follow the team around and end up at their historic home field. He catches sight of me out of the corner of his eye as I stride past him.

"What's up?" he asks.

I find my bag sitting on the floor next to the front door and scoop it up.

"Remember when I told you there were a couple of odd things about Denise Stein's house when I went through it with her son and daughter-in-law?" I ask.

"Yeah," he says.

His eyes flicker back to the screen, but he looks back at me.

"One of them was some stickers that were on the table in her living room. Rhys Stein said that wasn't like his mother. She is extremely particular about the way her house is kept and apparently wouldn't just leave things like that out on a table. He also couldn't think of any reason why she would have stickers," I tell him.

"That does seem a little weird. What kind of stickers?"

I find the envelope where I put the stickers along with the earring to keep them safe. Leaving the earring, I take out the stickers and bring them over to the coffee table.

"That's the thing. I had no idea. When we first looked at them, they just looked like some red lines on a white background. It didn't mean anything. Rhys and Vivica said they didn't mean anything to them either. But then I was just looking at Lavinia McDonnell's social media, and she posted a picture…"

"Wait… Lavinia… Sebastian McDonnell's wife? This has something to do with that?"

"No, it's the picture she posted. It was a piece of white paper with a red heart drawn on it, then the paper was ripped in half. The pieces were off to the side of each other and kind of tilted in different directions. It's obvious what it is, but if you just took a quick glance, you might not immediately catch it. But it made it click."

"Made what click?"

Kneeling down at the side of the table, I spread out the stickers. "They look like they're just random red ink. Because they aren't individually anything."

I start to move the stickers around, maneuvering them to fit the image sketched in my head.

"But they are pieces."

I finish and turn my eyes to Sam. He meets them.

"I'll be damned."

CHAPTER EIGHT

I GET TO THE POLICE STATION BEFORE DETECTIVE MELTON THE NEXT morning. My travel cup filled with coffee in one hand and an aluminum container of six cinnamon rolls in the other, I stand in the lobby waiting. Edith at the front desk lifts her eyes occasionally from her computer to watch me rock back and forth on my feet. She doesn't say anything, but she briefly meets my eyes like she's anticipating me to speak. After nearly half an hour, I offer her a cinnamon roll.

"I baked them this morning," I tell her.

One eyebrow lifts as she looks at me, her fingers pulling one of the rolls from the pool of cream cheese frosting.

"This morning?" she asks.

"Yeah, I didn't get a lot of sleep last night," I tell her.

The door opens, and Detective Melton comes in.

"Morning," he says.

"Agent Griffin is here to see you," Edith says through a bite of cinnamon roll.

Melton looks at her for a beat. "Thank you." His gaze turns toward me, and he nods his head toward the door to the back.

"Thanks for the cinnamon roll," Edith says.

I shoot her a smile and follow Melton to his office.

"Did she say cinnamon roll?" he asks.

I set the container down on the table and take the top off again.

"Baked this morning while I couldn't sleep."

"I'll get some coffee."

"You're going to need it."

He pauses right before the door and turns to look back at me. "See, you say things like that and then expect me to just be fine with it. It scares me, Emma."

I look at him, expressionless. "Get your coffee."

He leaves, and I put my bag on the table, taking out the envelope I put back in last night. I pull out the stickers and put them on the table. When Melton comes back into the room with two cups of coffee, I'm arranging them.

"Oh," he says, noticing my travel tumbler on the table. "I…" He lifts both hands to indicate the cup in each. "It's fine. I'll just…"

His voice trails off, and he takes a sip from one cup, then the other.

"Saving time," I say. "Anyway, yesterday I told you I wanted to bring you a couple things I found at Denise Stein's house."

I tip the earring into my hand and hold it out to him.

"I found this in the grass in her front yard. It looked like it had been there for a bit. It could have been pulled out, but depending on when she wore them last, it could help narrow down when she was last at the house. Then there's this." I gesture to the stickers.

"Stickers?"

I nod. "We found them on the table in her living room. Her son said it wasn't something his mother would do normally. It didn't really mean anything to me, but I started thinking about it more last night when I was going over a different case. And I realized this."

I have the stickers arranged in a random line, but I move them around, overlapping them slightly and putting them in the order I discovered last night. When I'm finished, I step back so he can look at them.

"Oh shit."

"Couldn't say it any better myself."

He puts the cups of coffee down on the table and leans forward like he needs to get closer to the stickers to confirm what he's seeing. A few seconds later, he looks at me, his eyes dark.

"What do we do now?"

I look at the stickers, at the way the lines on them overlap to create the unmistakable symbol of the Game Master. My shoulders lower and square resolutely.

"We find her."

"Here it is."

"Thanks, Asher."

I take the freshly printed image from the officer and set it on the conference room table alongside the other three. I set the corresponding stickers from Denise Stein's living room into the corner of each image, leaving the rest in a stack off to the side.

"That's four," Detective Melton says.

A long breath escapes my lungs. "Three more."

I look at each of the images carefully. It's been almost two weeks since I realized Melton's first instinct was right and Denise Stein was selected as one of Game Master's players. The first thing I did was make sure that pictures of the stickers were released to as many law enforcement agencies as possible, including the Bureau, along with a brief explanation. The goal was to put eyes on the stickers and give them context. It's unlikely someone seeing them would give them a second thought. Just like when we saw them, it was their presence on the table—the uncharacteristic clutter—that was significant, not the designs themselves.

But if officers and detectives know what they're looking at, they are much more likely to notice them. A few days after releasing them to law enforcement, I arranged for a limited and highly controlled release to the media. They weren't given any details or explanation. I simply provided pictures of the stickers and had the news outlets show them. Viewers were told if they saw any of the stickers anywhere, they were not supposed to touch them but to immediately alert the police.

While we waited for either of those efforts to yield any results, I continued working with Rhys and Vivica as well as his brother, Guy, and sister, Lizette. We scoured every inch of the house again looking for anything that might give clues to her communication with the Game Master. With the help of the detective and other officers, I delved into the long and tedious task of going through every detail of her phone and financial records as well as everything on her personal devices as soon as warrants granted me access.

The last two weeks have felt like wading deeper and deeper into a swamp, but at least I can feel the bottom.

"We know her car left the airport the day after she left the hotel," Melton says. "But we can't say for sure if she was driving it. The footage we have isn't good enough to actually tell. It's from such an angle and so far away that all you can see is the shape of someone getting in."

"That's true, but the pictures on her phone show her wearing those earrings. She had them with her when she was at that hotel, which means she came back to the house after leaving."

"And that explains why her luggage is there," Melton says.

"Maybe, but it's just the luggage itself. Just the suitcase and carry-on. Rhys is adamant that there are pieces of clothing and jewelry she always had with her when she traveled that are not at the house. So my question is, did she go back to the house? Or just her earring and luggage?"

"What do you mean?"

"Her car isn't there. Her clothes aren't there. The location records on her phone show that she left the hotel but didn't go any farther than the airport for four days. Then it shows her a couple hundred miles away from her house. Then nothing after that. Nothing actually proves she made it back to the house," I point out.

"He put the luggage and the earring there to be found," he says.

"Could be." I look at the images again. "He knew eventually someone would figure out she wasn't at home or on her trip anymore and would go looking for her. They were put there to throw me off. Or just to screw with me. Honestly, I feel like they are equal opportunity possibilities at this point."

I tap my fingertips on the first picture in the lineup.

"This one was found second, but it may have been the first one to be left because it was in the area her phone picked up after leaving the hotel."

The picture is of one of the stickers attached to the side of a massive rock on the edge of a shallow stream. At first, it looks like it's in a really remote location, but I found out the spot is actually close to a walking trail on a piece of private property on a mountain. It's a few miles away from where Denise's phone last registered its location, but the area is well-maintained and easily passable by car or even on foot.

The owner of the property found the sticker while walking around the property checking for winter damage, something she does every spring. She didn't notice anything else that was strange on the trail or in the stream.

Footage from the trail cams set up in the area gives me the shred of hope I've been waiting for.

"The first camera showed Denise walking down the trail half a mile from here two days before the ping from her phone. She was wearing the same clothes as in one of the pictures on her phone."

"Which means she either still had her luggage at that point or he'd taken everything out to bring the luggage to her house."

"Right. Then the next camera caught her on a different trail the next day, wearing the same clothes. Which means either she was in there or was staying somewhere close and went there without changing, which doesn't really make any sense. The main issue I'm having, though, is, did she put the sticker on the boulder, or did somebody else put it there and she was looking for it? Maybe she had multiple sets and only took one to put in different locations, or these were sent to her and she was sent to look for other ones," I say.

"Sent to look for other ones, like that was one of her challenges?" Melton asks.

"That's what I'm wondering. We haven't been able to find anything in any of her personal devices that indicate any communication with the Game Master. Which means she has or had some way of communicating with him that we can't detect. A burner phone or an e-mail address nobody knows about. That isn't completely unprecedented. Remember, Terrence Brooks had a tablet nobody realized he had. So we don't really know when he selected her or what type of challenges he has been putting her through.

"It's possible this was the first thing she was supposed to do. Or he could have been messing with her for a long time. Nothing in her financial records suggested anything outrageous the way some of the other players did. She didn't make any really large purchases or withdrawals. She doesn't seem to have liquidated possessions. And while it's odd for her to be wandering around private property nowhere near her home, she didn't look injured or even all that distressed in the trail cam footage. She wasn't running. She wasn't looking behind her or trying to hide. I don't feel like she thought she was in imminent physical danger. At least at that point. Which makes me wonder what kind of experience she is having with the Game Master," I say.

"We have to remember, we don't know what kind of challenges he chooses for all of his players," Melton points out. "Even the ones we've talked to haven't been transparent with us about them. They're not always physical tasks. Terrence Brooks made that massive donation to the children's hospital, and there were donations to a few other places linked to other players."

"That's true. But I think the most important thing we have is the living players. Or at least the players who lived beyond their first several tasks. From what Terrence's family told us about some of the strange things he was doing, he probably got selected at least two months before he died. While he did ultimately end up dying, and the circumstances made it pretty obvious he was doing some sort of challenge, that's still a long time. Two months of him presumably being put through the game.

"But there were no signs of injury on his body other than what the medical examiner was able to attribute to that final task. No cuts, no scars, no healing bones. Nothing. Now, we don't know how long Denise was in contact with the Game Master. What's happening now could be her first task. I doubt it though. I really believe she was selected before the holiday season. Her son Guy told me she wasn't quite herself when they were home for Christmas. It was enough of a difference for him to notice it and have a conversation with her about it."

"But she didn't tell him anything," Melton says.

"No. Just like the others who didn't decide to come forward as soon as they were selected didn't tell anyone either. That's what he's banking on. He holds the information he has on them over their heads, and they have to decide what keeping it secret is worth to them. Are they willing to go along with everything this man tells them to do and not tell anyone? Or are they going to get help and risk exposure?"

"Which hasn't happened to all of the players," the detective says. "So far nothing has been released about Baron Johnson, Mike Morris, Paige Morrisey, or Denise Stein."

It's true. Of those four, two are missing, and two came forward as soon as they were selected. Nothing has been revealed about any of them. Among the other players, those who died during their challenges have been spared posthumous humiliation, with the exception of Terrence Brooks. But even his dark past was only uncovered because I spoke with the sister of his former lover. There was no viral social media post or video, no pages taken out in newspapers, no big public reveal of any kind, just as there wasn't for any of the other victims who lost their lives.

Some of the living players have not fared so well. Business empires have crumbled. Families have been shattered. People are facing criminal charges that could land them in jail for decades. From one perspective, it's harrowing. These are victims of a sadistic killer, and they're justifiably terrified of what's going to happen to them and to the lives they've built. But from another perspective, the dark secrets that went into building those lives are coming to light, and to some, the chosen players brought this upon themselves.

It's a harsh argument I could say is totally devoid of compassion and understanding. I could say it, but I won't. I do what I do because I want to help and protect people. That doesn't change regardless of who it is or what is happening. There have been many times in my career when I have stood in front of people who have done horrific things, putting myself between them and danger. I have shown mercy when I know there are plenty who would say I would have been justified in just walking away. I've been a voice for people who others told me should have been silenced.

I am an FBI agent because I carry the pain of my mother's murder going unsolved for more than a decade. Of my father's disappearance. Of the torture and loss of people I cared deeply about. I know what it is to see those things happen and for no one to ever be held accountable. That is a special kind of hell.

But in that time, I've also had the glimmer taken from my eyes. I haven't become jaded, but I have had to face a different reality and a different perspective than I used to have. I learned there is a difference between what someone deserves as a person and as a human. They are not the same. What I've seen in my years in the Bureau has taught me the cold, brutal reality that there are people who deserve the horrible things that happen to them.

As a person, they have done things that are reprehensible. Not unforgivable because it isn't my place to determine that. But gruesome and vile beyond description. As a person, they deserve retribution. They deserve torment, humiliation, misery.

As a human, it's another matter. By merit of being human, what they deserve transcends what they have done. We are repelled by what they are capable of doing, so we should be repelled at the thought of doing it to them as well. They should be given the same honor and respect as any other human being—if not for them, then for the rest of humanity. To keep our heads above the water of the dark whirlpools that are so easy to go down.

In that way, no one deserves what Terrence Brooks or Sean Coolidge went through.

Maybe the same shouldn't be said for the consequences of the truth coming out about a man whose multiple families spread across the world were finally revealed to each other.

Or the woman who put up a facade of ethics over her company only for the public to discover she was essentially using slave labor to make her products and squashing anyone who spoke out.

Or the contractor who knowingly used such cheap materials a massive department store he built collapsed with dozens of shoppers inside.

Finding out the gritty secrets in the lives of the victims makes the case easier for the public. Knowing what these people have done, and seeing what they've had to face because of it, makes it less horrifying for so many. And it also gives them a chance to feel reassured they aren't going to face the same fate. They aren't "those kinds" of people. They haven't done anything to put themselves in that position.

Or at the very least, they haven't done anything they believe anyone knows about.

But the variation in how the players are being treated is one of the things about this case that make it more complicated the longer it goes on. I can't convince myself it's arbitrary. Or that the man behind the name just had a change of heart about some of the players and not the others. The way he chooses the tasks and the punishments, including if their secrets are revealed, is deliberate. These things have to mean something.

And the fact that nothing has been revealed about those four players tells me that there's more to come for them. For Baron, the threat of consequences for his so-called "failure" has been hanging over him for months. Nothing has happened. He hasn't had any more communication. He hasn't been given any more tasks. And nothing has been exposed about him. He believes that the Game Master chose him because when he was a teenager, he witnessed his father brutally assault one of the house staff. He later watched his own father die and did nothing to save his life, knowing that his father was a monster. But even with that story, he told me that if the Game Master tried to blackmail him over it, he wouldn't even think of going along with it for a second. It makes me wonder if there's something he's not telling me.

I try not to think about that when I speak with him. I try to remind myself it doesn't matter what he's hiding, if anything. It's still up to me to protect him. And if the thought of protecting him feels like too much at any given moment, then I have to hang on to the reality that he's a witness. And those details could prove valuable to the investigation later. Keeping him safe keeps that information safe.

Paige Morrisey seems to be hovering in purgatory. The woman contacted me through Detective Melton several weeks ago to tell me she had been chosen. Paige is now being kept in a safehouse. But that's the extent of her presence in the case. She turned over the burner phone she found in her mailbox and showed us the messages from the Game Master. We arranged for her to be kept somewhere highly secure, and since then we've waited for any further communication. Nothing.

She was never given a task. She was never threatened for not responding or for getting me involved. He hasn't tried to connect with her again, and nothing has come out about her.

Just like Baron when he first came to us, she doesn't want to talk about her secret. She has her head firmly in the sand and is trying hard to just ride this out. She isn't as antsy as Baron was in the hotel, but every time I talk to her, she seems convinced everything is going to work out fine. She believes she'll be able to put this behind her and no one will ever find out anything. In her mind, she can move on with her life, and soon enough, she won't even think about this anymore.

I hope she's right. But I don't think she is. Just because she hasn't heard anything from him yet doesn't mean something isn't happening. The waiting feels like part of the torment, even if it isn't having the effect on Paige he might have expected.

My back is tightening up from standing hunched over the table, and I straighten, arching slightly to ease my muscles.

"Are you ready for a break?" Melton asks.

"No," I say, shaking my head. "I just needed a stretch."

"All right. Well, I need to not be in this room for a bit. I'm going to get something to eat. You sure you don't want to come with?"

"I'm sure. Thanks."

He shrugs and walks out of the room. I turn my attention back to the lineup of pictures. I look at the picture of the first sticker that was found, wondering how and when it got there. The timeline of Denise's movements after she left home for the vacation her children anticipated her taking is, as Sam would say, wonky. There's so much time unaccounted for and points that seem out of order. We know the flight she took and the hotel she checked into. The time she checked out of the hotel is confirmed through their computer system as well as video footage of her leaving the hotel. It is that footage, combined with pictures on her phone, that confirmed she was wearing the earrings.

There is still the question of why she decided to leave the hotel so quickly after arriving and without telling anyone. At this point, I am positive it is because of the Game Master, but I wonder if the entire trip was orchestrated by him or if she left the house in good faith only for him to interfere.

After her leaving the hotel, things start to get hazy. We've identified the flight she took back, but there is a huge gap in time between that flight and when her car was seen leaving the airport. Even with the massive number of cameras at an airport, we haven't been able to effectively track her movements. There is footage of her getting off the plane at the gate and heading for the baggage claim. She is alone and doesn't seem overtly distressed. We watch her pick up her bags, but then she moves further into the airport, and we lose track of her. The direction she is going almost makes it look like she was going to board another flight, but we haven't found any passenger manifests that include her name.

From there we have the trail cam footage of her walking around the private property on the mountain, but her phone actually didn't register the location there until days after that. There are no security footage or pictures that connect her to the first sticker that was found. It caught the attention of an officer arresting a man in an alleyway behind an abandoned business. He had seen the alert and noticed the sticker. It was identified before the one on the mountain, but I think it was put there later.

Her next verifiable location links her to the third sticker found.

I ran each of the stickers through an image search online and came up with a post from a travel vlogger's social media. The picture shows the sticker among other stickers and scribbled inscriptions on a plain, dark-gray background. Without tears or worn edges, it's obvious that the sticker was put there recently.

"Am I getting too old to understand graffiti tags?" the caption on the image read.

The post is from a touristy rest stop a few hours away from where the other sticker was found in the alley. We found out there were no cameras posted near the bathroom entrances, but scouring the internet for every post, picture, and caption mentioning that location around that time finally gave me what I was looking for. A group of friends on a road trip stopped at that rest stop to record a viral dance in front of one of the iconic signs, and in the background, Denise is seen walking by.

It's brief, but she's close enough to be unmistakable. It is definitely her. That places her in the area just hours before the vlogger posted the picture from the bathroom stall. And now we have the fourth picture.

The sticker was found this morning on the storm door of a house while the man living there was out for work. It wasn't there last night, which means someone came up onto his front porch in the middle of the night. That thought was enough to prompt him to call the police.

"Emma…"

Detective Melton comes back into the room. I glance over my shoulder at him, then look back at the picture.

"This house is only about twenty minutes away from Denise's house," I say. "Right back in this area. But again, did she put the stickers there? Or was she trying to find them? No one else was caught on the trail cams on the mountain, but there were other ways to access that spot. Depending on which one it is, this sticker being back in this area means either Denise was here last night or she could be on her way here."

The detective doesn't respond, and I turn around to look at him. His face is ashen, his expression drawn.

"What's wrong?" I ask.

"Have you checked your phone?"

"No, I have it on silent."

"I just got a text. You're going to want to look."

His voice is serious, and I immediately reach into my bag for my phone. I have missed a few notifications, but the one that stands out to me the most is an email from the park police I've been working with on the search for Mike Morris. The message contains two phrases and a picture. I draw a deep breath to try to fill my lungs, which suddenly feel hollow.

Found near Big Bear Ledge. Human?

The picture is of an uneven ring of rocks and a pile of ash. A burn pit. Among the debris, I can clearly see teeth and bone fragments.

CHAPTER NINE

Nadia

NADIA PUT THE LAST STYROFOAM CUP OF MICROWAVE NOODLES on the bottom shelf and turned it to face forward. She liked keeping the shelves neat and organized. Maybe no one noticed when they were bending down to scoop up a midnight snack or quick lunch, but she knew. It still made her feel good to do her job the best she could. Even the little parts.

She stood up and turned to go back to the counter, nearly walking into someone looking at the next display.

"Oh! I'm sorry," she said.

The man smiled at her and shook his head. "No worries, I don't mind at all."

She'd seen him in the store a couple times before. They'd never exchanged names, and she wouldn't immediately jump to calling him a regular, but she recognized him.

"Can I help you find anything?" she asked.

"No, I'm good. You're new around here, right?"

Nadia nodded. "I started here a few weeks ago. My daughter and I just moved into the area."

The man mirrored her nod. "I knew I would have noticed you before. How are you liking it?"

"It's great."

"Good to hear." He looked like he was about to say something else, but a ring from the front counter cut him off.

Nadia flashed him an apologetic smile. "I've got to get that."

She walked around him and went to the phone connected to the number posted on the outside of the motel office. The man continued his stroll through the aisles while she answered.

"Mel's Corner Market and Motel," she said brightly.

"Yeah, I need to check in but there's nobody at the desk."

"No worries—I'll be right there to help you," she said.

It had already been a busy day. Joseph, the guy who usually worked the motel, called in sick, and Christy and Maren couldn't fill in until later. They'd both needed to take off for different reasons, which sounded great at first, since it would give Nadia some extra hours. But now it meant she was hopping all day trying to juggle the stream of customers in the convenience store and the motel.

She couldn't just walk out of the store to go help the person at the hotel with the man still inside. But she also didn't want to leave somebody standing at the motel office for too long. A wave of relief washed over her when the door opened and Maren came in.

"I'm so glad you're here," Nadia said. "I need to run out to the motel real fast. Be right back."

Maren nodded as she slipped out of her jacket and stepped behind the counter. Nadia grabbed the keys to the motel office and went outside. She jogged around the side of the building, but when she got to the back, she noticed there was no one near the office. There were no cars parked in front of the motel or behind the convenience store. She looked around and didn't see anybody. It had only been a couple of minutes. Just to make sure, she walked around the back of the motel, but there were only the same few cars that had been there since people checked in the night before.

Confused, she went back to the store and hung the keys back on the hook under the counter.

"That was weird," she said. "Somebody called right before you got here and said they wanted a room. But there's nobody there. I literally hung up with them thirty seconds before you walked through the door."

"That is weird," Maren said. "I didn't see anybody leaving when I got here."

The man walked up to the counter with a few snacks and smiled at Nadia. Maren rang up his purchases, but he barely took his eyes off Nadia. When Maren handed him his bag, he thanked her but gave a wider smile to Nadia.

"I guess I'll see you around," he said. "Maybe next time I will think of something you can help me find."

He walked out of the store, and Maren turned to her with raised eyebrows and a sly smirk. "What was that all about?"

"Nothing," Nadia said. "I walked into him after putting some stuff onto a shelf and asked if there was anything I could help him find. That's it."

"That's it?"

"He asked me if I was new, and I told him I've been working here for a few weeks."

"Uh-huh," Maren said, a smile coming to her lips.

"What?"

"He was flirting with you."

"No, he wasn't."

Maren scoffed. "Yes, he absolutely was. No one warns a convenience store cashier that he's going to need help the next time he comes in. He was trying to be cute."

Nadia busied herself straightening up the impulse buy display on the counter so she didn't have to make eye contact with Maren. She could feel her cheeks burning and willed them to cool.

"Well, I'm flattered, but not interested."

"Why not?" Maren asked. "He was cute."

"I'm just not in that place. I'm still dealing with so much nonsense from my divorce and everything. I've got to figure out my own life before I even think about dating again. I just want to focus on me and Amelia."

Maren held up her hands like she was surrendering. "Hey, if that's what you want. New life, new you, I get it."

"What about you?" Nadia asked, deflecting the focus of the conversation onto Maren instead of her own self-imposed romance hiatus. "How is everything going with Ron?"

Maren's face broke out in a massive smile, the kind that was completely involuntary but showed just how happy something made a person. She sighed and leaned her hip against the counter.

"Amazing. He's… everything. Trust me, I know that's a giant cliché, but I don't even care. That's how incredible this guy is. I am perfectly fine being a gushing pool of goo when it comes to that man."

Nadia cringed. "Maybe think of a better way to put that."

"Yeah," Maren said, her own face contorting. "It sounded a lot better in my head."

The women laughed as more customers came into the store. Both of them greeted the family and turned back to their conversation.

"When is he coming back?" Nadia asked.

Ron had been traveling for work for the last two weeks, and Maren had been very vocal about how much she missed him.

"Next week," she said. "Tell me, though, who in the living hell would want to set up a hotel somewhere that looks like this?"

Maren took her phone out of her pocket and pulled up a picture, turning the screen toward Nadia so she could see. The image showed a man in heavy winter gear standing in front of a snowy background. One thickly gloved hand held out to the side seemed to show off the mountain behind him. Beneath a pair of large, polarized goggles in the recesses of a faux fur-edged hood was a big smile topped with a thick, dark mustache. A few snowflakes cling to the mustache, making Nadia suddenly crave a cup of hot cocoa.

"People who like skiing?" Nadia asked.

Maren looked at the picture. "Oh, that's true. I hadn't thought of that. Anyway, he's coming back, and I really hope I can convince him to come out with us one night soon. He's so sweet, and I know he wants to meet you guys, but he's just gun-shy. It's only been a few months, and after the really nasty end of his marriage… I guess you can understand that."

"I definitely can," Nadia said.

She was still at a place where she couldn't fathom dating, but she knew even if she were, she wouldn't be going public with anybody until she was really sure. It wasn't a knock on anybody she might potentially date. It was a matter of protecting herself and her daughter. Anyone who had the potential of getting close to either one of them in the future was going to have to accept going very slow.

"It might be hard to believe, but he's also pretty shy," Maren said.
The door opened, and Christy breezed in.
"Unlike somebody else I know."
Christy gave her a look. "Are you talking about me?"
"Yes."
"What did I do?"
"She was saying that Ron is shy."
"Oh yeah, no, not me," Christy said with a laugh.
"Or any of the guys you're dating."
It didn't take long after Nadia started working at the store for her to learn all about Christy's storied dating life. She was the poster child for not taking things seriously. Even the word *relationship* gave her the shivers, though she did maintain ongoing "connections" with a few men.
"I don't know. Garrison is pretty reserved," Christy says.
"Garrison is a librarian who caused a public freakout when he pushed to have an illustrated erotica section in the library, and he performs in a heavy metal band on the weekends," Maren pointed out.
"I still can't believe that a person like that exists," Nadia said. Though, having met him, she knew he did.
"Well, he's a lot better than Lyle," Maren muttered.
That took the conversation to a darker place. It had been a bone of contention between the women for the last couple of weeks. When Christy showed up at the store with the new guy she had just met, Maren was immediately resistant. They weren't friends, but she knew of Lyle and the reputation he had. He was known for not exactly being the kindest man to the women he dated, complete with quite a few run-ins with law enforcement and some time behind bars.
Christy was defensive about Maren's rejection. She felt that her friend was being judgmental and not giving Lyle an opportunity to prove himself. She insisted that he had changed. Maren said that was strange for her to say, considering she hadn't known him when he was younger and was only taking what he said at face value. Nadia wasn't looking forward to hearing yet another argument about him.
She tried to stay out of it. She didn't want it to cause friction between herself and her new friends, and she really didn't think that she knew enough about Lyle to come to a real conclusion about him. At the same time, the things that Maren had told her about him were concerning. He definitely didn't sound like the type of guy that Christy should be spending a lot of time with. But it was not her monkey or her circus. She decided that was a good moment to take off.

"Well, I've got to go pick Amelia up," she said. "I'll talk to you guys later."

She got her jacket and purse from under the counter and walked out of the store. She had parked around back, and as she turned the corner, she noticed someone standing near the motel office. They were on the side of the glassed-in area, their hands in their pockets and the hood of their sweatshirt pulled up against a rain-laced wind.

"Can I help you?" Nadia called out. "Do you want to get a room?"

"Yeah," a voice called back. It sounded muffled, like maybe the person was wearing a scarf over their face.

She waved. "Give me just a second. I'll have somebody come help you."

She went back to the door and popped her head in. "Hey, there's somebody at the motel who wants to get a room. I don't know why they didn't call, but could one of you go help them?"

Christy wasn't technically clocked in yet, but Nadia hoped she would keep an eye on the register while Maren went to check the new guest in. She didn't want to be late getting to Amelia's school to pick her up.

Maren grabbed the keys and followed her out. They walked around to the back, but the person was gone.

A slight chill went down Nadia's back.

"They were right there," she said. "They answered me when I talked to them. Where did they go?"

"Did you see a car?" Maren asked.

"I really wasn't paying attention," Nadia said. "I just saw the person. This is the second time today that's happened."

"It's fine," Maren said. "Don't worry about it. Just go get Amelia."

Despite her friend's reassurance, Nadia felt uncomfortable as she got into her car and headed for the school.

Amelia had stayed after to rehearse for a play her class was doing. She was excited about the new friends she was meeting, and Nadia was happy to see how well she was settling into her new school. She pulled into the pickup loop just as the doors were opening and the teacher and assistant were bringing the children out. Nadia got out of the car and went toward Amelia, who was walking alongside two other girls, giggling about something.

"You really need to pay better attention."

The snapping voice caught Nadia off guard, and she turned around to see a man glaring at her from a few steps away.

"Excuse me?" she asked.

"You cut me off. You could have made me hit you."

Nadia was confused. She hadn't noticed any cars anywhere near her when she was pulling into the loop. At the same time, she was distracted thinking about the strange person at the motel, so maybe she really hadn't seen him.

"I'm sorry, I didn't see you," she said.

"Yeah, that's freaking obvious. Maybe you should actually pay attention when you're operating a motor vehicle. Get your face out of your phone, and don't put other people's lives at risk."

At this point, other parents were watching, and the children were staring at them. Nadia felt heat crawling up the back of her neck and her stomach tightening. Too many memories were trying to force their way out of the vaults she worked hard to force them into after leaving Brent.

"I wasn't looking at my phone," she said calmly. She was hoping if she didn't rise to his level, maybe it would make him settle down. "In fact, it was in my bag. I'm sorry if you think that I cut you off. It certainly wasn't intentional."

"If I think?" the man asked incredulously, now nearly growling through his clenched teeth. "If I *think*? Are you saying I'm a liar? Or maybe I'm stupid?"

"Is everything all right here?"

The principal walked across the sidewalk toward them. She was clutching a walkie-talkie in her hand like she was ready to call for help if the situation warranted it. The man's arm flailed in Nadia's direction.

"She almost caused a crash," he accused. "I was trying to pull into the loop, and she came flying up and cut me off."

"Flying?" Nadia asked with a baffled scoff. "I was going the speed limit. And again, I didn't see you."

The man took a step toward her, and the principal got in between them. She held a hand up toward the man's chest.

"Mr. Pruett, you need to take a step back. I can see that you're upset, but everything is fine. There was no accident. No one was hurt. There's no need for this to go any further. Let's just settle down."

He glared at her with obvious disdain but didn't say anything else to either of them. He looked beyond the principal at where the children were gathered.

"Lacey! Come on," he shouted.

Nadia looked over and was horrified to see the little girl standing right beside Amelia scurry forward. Amelia slunk toward her mother, obviously upset. They got in the car, and Nadia looked in the rearview mirror at her daughter.

"Why did you do that?" Amelia asked.

"I didn't do anything, honey. That wasn't me."

"Lacey is my friend. She's my best friend. Now you made her daddy angry."

Her arms were crossed tightly over her chest, and she turned to stare out of the window.

"I didn't do anything wrong," Nadia said. "He is the one who wasn't acting right."

The reasoning didn't seem to affect Amelia. She continued to stare through the window and didn't say a word for the entire drive back to the house.

CHAPTER TEN

A WEEK LATER, NADIA WALKED INTO THE STORE FOR HER SHIFT and was surprised to see Mel himself standing at the counter talking to Maren. The namesake and owner of the string of convenience stores and motels, Mel was friendly and personable with all his employees. But he also had high standards for performance and was known to be strict with keeping up with those standards. Even though Nadia felt like she was doing a great job, always on time and doing her job well, she felt a nervous twinge in her stomach.

It didn't get any better when Maren looked over at the door. "There she is," she said.

Nadia tried not to let the immediate shock of fear show up on her face. She had gotten so comfortable working here at the store and was saving up for a place for her and Amelia. Everything seemed to be going well, and now she was afraid that it was all about to be taken away from her.

"Hi," she said.

"Hi, Nadia," Mel said. "I was just looking for you. I wanted to have a talk."

She kept her eyes firmly on Mel's rather than looking at Maren. If her friend knew something about this, she didn't want to see the pity in her eyes.

"Sure," she said.

"Come on back to the office with me."

They walked into the back of the store, and he closed the door of the small office behind them. There was just enough space for a desk, a couple of chairs, and a couch up against the wall. He gestured at the couch as he sat down in the chair next to the desk.

"How have you been getting on since getting here?" he asked.

"Good," Nadia replied without hesitation. "I really love the area, my daughter is happy at school. I love working here."

She hoped she didn't sound too desperate, like she was campaigning to keep her job.

"I'm glad to hear that," Mel said. "I've been paying close attention to your performance, and I have to say, I'm really impressed."

That took a second to process, but when it did, Nadia felt her muscles release a bit.

"You are?"

"Absolutely. You have been a fantastic employee. You always go above and beyond with all your responsibilities. Customers love you. Maren and Christy have both commended you on your flexibility and willingness to pick up extra shifts—stay late, I might even add—and that you're here bright and early every day. You are everything that Maren promised me you would be and more. I am very happy to have you on my team."

"Thank you," Nadia said with a relieved exhale. "I'm really glad. This has made a really big difference in my life. And Amelia's."

Mel smiled. "Well, I was hoping that I could make a bit more difference."

"What do you mean?" Nadia asked.

"I know you make the drive in from Dogwood Valley every day. I have a store that is closer there. It's pretty much just like this one. Just without the motel. The manager who has been working there for years is moving, and I need to find somebody else to take over that store. It isn't quite as busy as this one most of the time, but I am hoping to make some improvements and expansions in the coming months to generate more traffic to it. I need somebody at the helm who I can trust and know is going to be able to handle it."

"Oh," Nadia said. "I think Maren would be really great in that position. I'll miss working with her, but I can absolutely help pick up the slack here."

Mel laughed. "I know she would be great in that position. Which is why she has it here. I'm not having her move to that store. I wanted to give it to you."

Nadia stared at him. She blinked. She couldn't believe what she was hearing. "Me?"

"Yes. You've done so well and really proven yourself. The location would be easier for you to get to, and I can offer you higher pay and benefits. It's a big undertaking, so I understand if—"

"Yes," Nadia said, the word bursting out of her before he could even finish what he was saying. "Yes... I mean, I would love that. Thank you."

"Great," Mel said with a chuckle. "I was hoping that's what you were going to say, so I brought along some paperwork. Read over it, and then come to the store tomorrow morning, and I'll get you oriented. I'm really glad you're taking this on. I think it's going to be fantastic for both of us."

"I knew you were going to do big things," Maren said later when they'd filled Christy in about the promotion.

"Thank you," Nadia said. "I wouldn't be here if it weren't for you."

Maren did a dramatic curtsy, earning a laugh.

Nadia turned to Christy and said, "You're sure it's okay with you? I know you've been working here longer than I have, and..."

Christy held up her hands to stop her. "I already told you, it's fine. It's great. You're perfect for this job and I'm super happy for you. Don't you worry about me. I wouldn't want to do it anyway."

Nadia couldn't help but grin. She was over the moon about her promotion. It was a huge compliment and self-esteem boost for Mel to recognize her hard work. And it really would make a huge difference. The store was much closer to Jeff and Lisa's house, so the commute would be much easier. Not having a motel attached to the property also made the responsibilities much easier, even if she was taking on more by being the manager. The increased pay and benefits, though, were what she was really excited about. It was a dramatic raise. Enough that she and

Amelia could have their own place months sooner than she thought. Everything was finally going well.

"We have to celebrate," Maren said.

"Yes!" Christy said. "We're taking you out tonight."

"No," Nadia said. "You don't have to do that."

"Of course, we don't have to," Maren said. "We want to. This is huge. You deserve to be happy and celebrate. Besides, when was the last time you did something that was just for fun?"

"I brought Amelia to the church carnival a couple weeks ago," Nadia said.

Christy belted out a laugh. "Okay… that is one of the saddest things I've ever heard."

"No, it isn't," Maren said. "I'm sure Amelia had a fantastic time. But what I mean is, when was the last time *you* did something just for fun that didn't involve cotton candy or children screaming?"

"I honestly don't remember," Nadia said.

"Exactly. Which is why we are going out tonight."

It wasn't a question or an offer. It was a statement.

"I'll have to see if Jeff and Lisa can take care of Amelia."

When she checked with them, Jeff and Lisa were almost as adamant about Nadia going out as Maren and Christy were, and Amelia was excited at the promise of ordering pizza and having ice cream sundaes while she was gone. It had been so long since Nadia had actually gone out with friends that she felt a bit nervous as she was trying on outfits that evening. Lisa came in and eyed the pile of clothes on her bed.

"Is this one of those bars where you have to do costume changes every twenty minutes?" she asked.

Nadia looked at her. "Is that a thing?"

Lisa laughed and shook her head. "No… At least not around here."

"I feel like I'm trying to get ready for my first middle school dance. I don't even know what to wear. Haven't gone out in so long I don't even think I have boots that would work."

"Well, you aren't going to a dance. You're just going out for a couple of drinks with some friends. And you absolutely deserve it. You got an amazing promotion, and you are absolutely killing it with this whole 'new life' thing. I bet if somebody told you six months ago this is what would be happening, you wouldn't believe it," Lisa said.

"That's true. I wouldn't have believed any of this. Six months ago, I had no idea what I was going to do. I felt like my life was crumbling around me, and there was no way to get out of it."

"Exactly. And yet you put on your big-girl panties and figured it out. And not only are you getting by—you are thriving. And it's just getting better. You deserve to celebrate that. And you deserve to think about yourself every now and then. Everything is always all about Amelia. And you are a great mom. She is beyond lucky to have you. But even great moms need to take a breath and remember that they are people too. Seeing you happy is the best thing you can do for her," Lisa said.

Nadia felt surprisingly emotional as she pulled her friend in for a hug. "Thank you," she said.

"Anytime," Lisa said. "And speaking of time, you're already ten minutes late. Put on the black dress and go."

Nadia laughed and did what she was told. Maren and Christy had a table when she got to the bar. They both waved enthusiastically and gestured for her to come over. Nadia noticed a few pairs of eyes watching her as she crossed the crowded room. It was an unfamiliar feeling to be so obviously appreciated. She hadn't gone on a date since before she got married, and it had been a long time since her ex-husband made her feel like he saw her as anything but a maid and personal assistant who happened to live in the house. It felt good and somewhat unnerving at the same time.

"Finally," Maren said when she slipped into the booth across from them.

"We thought you had punked out on us," Christy said.

"Sorry," Nadia said, "I had some trouble figuring out what to wear."

"Maren grinned. "I guess it was worth the wait. You look amazing."

Nadia looked down at herself. "Thank you."

"All right, girlies," Christy announced. "Drinks! What is your cocktail?"

"I have no idea," Nadia said with a laugh.

"Not a problem, I'll surprise you." Christy waggled her eyebrows and got up from the table to go over to the bar.

"So how do you feel about your promotion now that you've had some time to think about it?" Maren asked.

"Excited. Nervous," Nadia admitted. "I want to do a good job. I feel like it's such a big deal that he even thought of promoting me. I'm sure there are other people he could have chosen. It's a huge opportunity, and I feel like if I screw it up, I'm going to be throwing away everything."

"Then you have to stop thinking like that," Maren said. "Mel chose you because you are good at what you do. He knows you can handle it. And I do too. You're going to do a fantastic job, and that's just all there is to it."

"He wants me to come in tomorrow to see the store and have an orientation," Nadia said.

"That won't be a big deal. It's pretty much the same as our store. No motel to deal with though. But essentially, the same layout. A little bit bigger and newer, but it's not a big difference. You're mostly just going to have to get used to some of the new responsibilities of opening and closing, dealing with vendors, that kind of thing. I'm sure you can do it."

"Nope," Christy said, coming back to the table. "No talking about work. We are here to have fun, and that's what we're going to do. Cocktails all around!"

She set several brightly colored drinks in the center of the table. For the next couple of hours, the three laughed and talked. They got up a few times to dance. It took Nadia some time to warm up and get comfortable, but by the time Maren announced she needed to dip into the restroom, Nadia was having more fun than she could remember having in a long time.

"I'll go with you," Christy said. "Nadia?"

"I'm fine. I think I want to order some snacks."

Maren pointed at her. "The mozzarella sticks here are the best in town. Don't miss out on them."

"Noted," Nadia said, chuckling as she reached for the menu while the other two women headed for the restroom.

She browsed through all the food offerings, and out of the corner of her eye, she saw a waiter step up to the table.

"Hi," he said.

"Hi," she said, still looking at the menu. "I think I'm going to go with a couple of these appetizers. Definitely the mozzarella sticks. I heard they're the best in town." She looked up and saw a man not wearing the bar uniform smiling at her. "Oh."

"They are pretty good. Unfortunately, I don't work here, so I can't bring you any." His light-green eyes sparkled with amusement.

"I'm sorry," Nadia said, squeezing her eyes closed in embarrassment.

"No reason to apologize. If it helps, I might be about to get very awkward too. I noticed you as soon as you came in. I haven't been able to keep my eyes off you all night."

She smiled and looked down at the table, hating the way she blushed. "Thank you."

"See? Awkward," he said.

Nadia laughed. "I guess we're even."

"Lennon," he said, extending his hand.

"Nadia."

He swept a piece of dark-blond hair away from his forehead. "I know you're here with friends, and I don't want to be that guy, but—"

Nadia's phone buzzed.

"Oh, sorry. I have to check that. My daughter is home with sitters."

She took her phone from her bag and glanced at it. She had a notification of a text. It was a relief since she knew Lisa wouldn't text her if there was something wrong. Thinking it might be one of the girls texting her from the bathroom or even from the other side of the bar to see if she needed to be "rescued" from the man, she opened her inbox.

She didn't recognize the number the message was from. Curious, she opened it.

You look incredible. I'll be thinking about you all night.

Nadia's heart started pounding in her chest. She felt hot.

"Everything okay?" Lennon asked.

Nadia looked up at him, unsure what to say.

"No," she said, shaking her head. "I actually need to go."

"Oh. Well, it was nice to meet you," Lennon said. "Maybe I'll see you around?"

Nadia already had her bag in her hand and was getting out of the booth.

She nodded. "Yeah, maybe."

The cool night air felt good on her cheeks when she got outside, but she didn't want to stand there. She felt exposed and just wanted to get in the car.

"Nadia," Maren called after her when they burst through the door behind her. "Wait."

She stopped and waited for them to catch up to her.

"What's going on?" Christy asked. "Did something happen?"

"We came out of the bathroom, and you were already hightailing it to the door," Maren said. "Sorry it took a while. There was a long line."

Nadia shook her head. "No, that's not it." She cringed and covered her eyes with her hand. "Shit, I look crazy."

"To us?" Maren asked.

"No, the guy."

They exchanged glances, then Christy looked back at her. "What guy?"

"He must have already walked away. A man came up to talk to me while you were gone from the table. I basically just ran away from him."

"Why?" Maren asked.

They'd crossed the parking lot and made it to Nadia's car. She showed them her phone so they could read the message.

"Who is that from?"

"I don't know. I don't know that number."

"Honestly," Maren said, "it's weird, but I wouldn't put too much thought into it. Because you don't know the number, it could just be a mistake. Maybe somebody is on a first date and was trying to send a flirty message and just put the wrong numbers in."

"Really?" Nadia asked.

"Have you given anybody your number recently?" Christy asked.

"No," Nadia admitted.

"Then that's what it has to be. Come on, let's go back inside. I have a taste for those mozzarella sticks, and you can show us that guy."

"No," Nadia said. "I really think I need to call it a night. Thanks for doing this for me. I really appreciate it. I had a lot of fun. But I think I need to ease into this a bit more."

"Are you sure?" Christy asked.

"I'm sure. I just need to go home and get some sleep."

"Message me when you get there," Maren said.

"I will. Good night."

CHAPTER ELEVEN

N ADIA'S FIRST WEEK AT THE NEW STORE WAS A LOT. IT WAS VERY similar to the other one, but the list of new responsibilities now that she was managing the location was long, and Nadia wanted to put every bit of effort she possibly could into doing well. That meant going in early and staying late. Jeff and Lisa took on more time watching Amelia, and more than once, Nadia got home after her daughter was already in bed, just to leave the next morning before she got up. It was hard, but she reminded herself of why she was doing it. This was what was going to get them to the next place they wanted it to be in life. All this time, effort, and exhaustion was going to pay off.

She was feeling more like she had gotten into the groove when Mel came to check on her. He looked around at the store and gave her an approving smile and nod.

"This place looks fantastic. You are definitely keeping up with everything," he said.

"Thank you," Nadia said. "I'm doing my best."

"Well, keep it up. I did have one thing I needed to update."

"What's that?" Nadia asked.

Mel pointed to the corkboard on the wall behind the counter. There were various pieces of paper pinned there. Licenses and legal documents. Pictures of people who were no longer welcome at the store for one reason or another. A couple of advertisements from vendors. Right in the center was a piece of paper with the name of the former manager and his phone number. Nadia had noticed it the first time she came to the store, but it was just a piece of the backdrop, and she hadn't really put any more thought into it.

"Oh," she said. "Right, I guess you would want to change that."

"Me and Oscar," Mel said. "Apparently, he's gotten a couple of calls from people wanting to know why we don't carry certain flavors of drinks and when we're going to get one of those skill games."

"Is that something I need to order?" she asked. "I'm sorry they bothered him."

Mel waved her off with a chuckle. "Nothing to worry about," he said. "I will never get one of those games, which is what I have told that same customer for the last ten years. And the flavor of drinks that the other customer called about three times doesn't exist. Probably better for him to have dealt with them anyway. But he did ask that I take his phone number down so he doesn't get any more calls."

He produced a new piece of paper with Nadia's name and phone number on it. Walking around behind the counter, he pulled down the one with Oscar's information and put hers up in its place.

"Now I feel very official," she said with a grin.

"Good. Anything you need from me? Anything I can do?"

"I don't think so," she said. "I've got everything taken care of."

"You were a good choice, Nadia Holmes."

She waved as he left the store. There were no customers at the moment, and she busied herself with cleaning and reorganizing, but her eyes kept moving back to the piece of paper with her phone number on it. It gave her a strange feeling to have that information posted that way. She thought back to the text message she got the night she went to the bar with Maren and Christy. It had to have been a wrong number. Other than filling out her application and giving her number to Maren, Christy, and Amelia's school, nobody else knew it. She had changed it before they moved.

Shaking her thoughts clear, Nadia grabbed her clipboard and went to the cooler at the back of the store to do some inventory while she had the time.

A little while later, she was ringing a customer up when the door opened and Maren and Christy came in. She waved at them and finished the transaction. Another customer stepped up to the counter before they could, and it was several more minutes before the store cleared out and she could talk to them. Maren came up and leaned against the counter.

"Well, I guess we know who the popular girl is now," she teased. "I think a couple of those people used to come into my store, and now they're driving out of their way to come here and see you."

Nadia flashed her a look and shook her head. "I highly doubt that. Except for Mr. Higgins. He said my store has better doughnuts."

Maren threw her hands up in the air dramatically. "That's it, I'm retiring."

Nadia laughed. "How is the store? I know it's only been a week, but I miss it. Is that weird? I mean, I'm doing pretty much the same thing. But there is actually a part of me that misses the craziness of the motel."

"Funny you should mention that," Christy said, cutting her eyes over to Maren.

Nadia looked at Maren, then back to Christy, then back to Maren.

"What?" She asked. "What was that about?"

"Just a couple of weird things have happened in the last few days," Maren said.

"Weird like that day when two people wanted to get rooms but both disappeared before we were able to check them in?" Nadia asked.

"Weird like somebody calling to ask for fresh towels to a room where nobody was staying," Christy said. "Twice. On two different days."

"And also weird like three different guests reporting somebody knocking on their door in the middle of the night," Maren added.

"All right, I rescind my sentiments," Nadia said. "I do not miss the motel."

They laughed.

"We're actually pretty used to it," Maren said. "It's not like it happens all the time, but these are definitely not the first weird experiences we've had with that place. I think it's just a reality of an old roadside motel. I mean, we keep it nice, but it's still a bit of a throwback. And it does attract some of the more interesting members of society."

"That's putting it mildly," Christy said. "We get the travelers. And travelers are a weird bunch. Sometimes it's perfectly normal families in their little sedans headed to vacations. And sometimes they're absolute banana nut muffin crazy on some sort of spirit quest."

"Not to mention the truckers. And the hitchhikers left behind by truckers. And the people we think are hitchhikers who gave up because they just walked up to the motel," Maren said. "Where could they possibly be walking from?"

"You two certainly know how to make a girl feel excited about what she's going to encounter in her new career," Nadia said with a smile. "All right, catch me up on everything else. How is Ron?"

"He is wonderful," Maren said. "But I am not."

Nadia frowned. "Everything okay?"

Maren shook her head. "I think there's something inside my head that is just determined to chase off anything that could possibly be good in my life because I decided to completely emotionally unload on him yesterday. And it was over the stupidest thing. We were watching TV, and a commercial came on. It reminded me of my ex. I've barely even thought about that man in months. But for some reason, that commercial just triggered everything."

"Maren was dating this other guy forever, before Ron," Christy supplied. "And he sucked. No offense."

Maren gave an acknowledging nod. "Ron knew that, but I had never really given him the entire story. Until last night. It's like I had a blackout and just couldn't control the words spilling out of my mouth. When I was finally done, I figured he was about to run for the hills. But he didn't. He reassured me and gave me his own breakup story."

"Seriously?" Nadia asked.

"Yep. And she sounded like a real peach, let me tell you. They met in college. She was on the track team, and so was his roommate, so they met through him. He watched her meets. He helped her train. The whole thing. But she was always checking out other guys and paying more attention to them than to him. Then she ended up going on spring break and ghosting him."

"Ouch," Nadia said.

"Yeah."

"College?" Christy asked. "How old is this man?"

"It was a while ago," Maren said.

"And that was his last breakup? You don't think that's a little strange?"

"He didn't say it was his last breakup. Just one that was particularly bad. He was commiserating with me because I told the whole story about Anthony."

"And you?" Nadia asked, pushing past what was building up to be bickering between the two women. "How is your... everything, Christy?"

She laughed. "Everything's good, but it almost wasn't. You should have seen it. Yesterday at the store, Garrison came in to surprise me. Then, literally as he was leaving, Lyle walked in. He held the door for him!" She laughed again, her head falling back like the whole situation was hilarious. "And then when he went out to pump gas into his car, Brick came in!"

"Brick?" Nadia asked.

"He's new," Maren said.

"And his name is Brick?"

Maren shrugged, her eyes fluttering closed briefly.

"What are the chances of that?" Christy asked. "All three of them coming to the same store within, like, five minutes of each other. It was crazy."

"Do they not know about each other?" Nadia asked.

She'd always just assumed the men in Christy's life were aware of the other ones. It seemed far too risky, not to mention time-consuming and confusing, to try to balance multiple connections without any possible overlap or mention of the others.

"No," Christy said. "I mean, they don't *not* know about each other. But they don't know about each other."

"How does that work?" Nadia asked.

"None of us have ever had 'the talk.' I mean, we never said we were exclusive. I've talked about having other plans when they've asked me to get together. And I have certainly never called any of them my boyfriend. They don't know specifically about each other, but I've also never said I wasn't seeing anyone else. So it's not like I'm lying to them." Her phone chirped in her pocket, and she glanced at the screen. "I've actually got to take this. Be right back."

She walked out of the store to take the call, and Maren looked at Nadia. Nadia lifted an eyebrow at her.

"Yeah, it's good decision-making all around. I've tried to talk to her about it, but it really hasn't sunk in yet. Look, I don't care if she doesn't want to be exclusive with anybody. If she has no interest in settling down and just wants to have fun, more power to her. Go ahead and let her freak flag fly. But I just think she needs to maybe be a little smarter about it.

"Lyle just makes me so uncomfortable, and the fact that these guys aren't legitimately aware of each other seems like a recipe for disaster. But it's not up to me. She's an adult. All I can do is be there for her when things get rocky and hide her behind displays of potato chips when multiple guys that she's dating at the same time are in the vicinity."

"Who hasn't been there?" Nadia asked.

They were still giggling when Christy came back in.

"And what's funny?" she asked.

"Nothing," Nadia said.

"I need to get going. I'm really glad to see how well you're doing here."

"Thank you for coming by to see me," Nadia said.

"We should get together for dinner sometime soon."

"Absolutely."

She waved, and the women left. Nadia missed working with them, but it really felt like they had settled into a true friendship.

A steady stream of customers filled the next couple of hours before another lull hit. Everything was quiet, and she was back to doing her inventory when the phone behind the counter rang. She jogged over to it and answered.

"Are you finally alone?" a voice asked from the other end of the line.

"What?" Nadia asked.

"Are you finally alone?" the voice repeated.

Her heart tightened in her chest. She didn't recognize the voice, but the words were chilling.

"Who is this?"

"I've been waiting for you to be alone for a long time. A lot of people come in there, don't they?"

"I'm not alone," she said.

"Don't lie to me. You haven't had a customer in fifteen minutes."

Nadia felt like she couldn't breathe. Her hand tightened around the phone. She looked through the glass at the front of the store, but she couldn't see anybody.

"Who are you?" she asked again.

A car suddenly pulled into the parking lot, and a woman got out of the driver's seat.

"Bye for now," the voice said.

The call dropped, and she hung up. The sound of the door opening made her jump even though she knew the woman was coming inside. She was relieved when two more customers followed. The phone rang a couple more times, but she ignored it as she helped the customers. She told herself it would be bad customer service if she stopped to pick up the calls. As the final customer of the small wave left, her cell phone rang in her bag under the counter. Nadia scrambled to pick it up when she saw that it was Mel calling.

"Nadia, what's going on? I've been calling the store and haven't been able to get in touch with you," he said.

She cringed. "I'm sorry. We had a whole lot of customers, and I didn't want to make them wait."

"Okay, that's a good reason. I just want to make sure you understand that you need to be accessible all the time."

"I know," she said.

When he said he needed her to be accessible all the time, she knew that he meant it. During her orientation, he made sure she understood the expectations. Since this store was her responsibility now, she needed to be available to handle any issue that arose, and he needed her to be reliable to come to the store whenever she was needed or to fill in at the other locations if necessary. It sounded like a heavy expectation to take on herself, but Nadia wasn't going to argue. The benefits of this job were far too good for her to argue something like being accessible by phone.

"Thanks, I appreciate it. I was just calling to make sure the delivery came in today. I know it had to be scheduled because of that storm. But I've had some trouble with that vendor recently and wanted to make sure everything was okay."

"Yep," Nadia said. "It actually got here twenty minutes earlier than they quoted. Everything is intact and exactly as I ordered it."

"Awesome. Let me know if you need anything."

She hung up and was starting toward the stockroom to get one of the newly delivered boxes to unpack when the phone rang again. Thinking Mel must have forgotten to tell her something, she grabbed it. "Mel?"

"How long until your shift is over?" It was the same eerie voice.

"Leave me alone," she said, slamming the phone down.

It rang again almost immediately. Trembling slightly, she considered ignoring it, but she couldn't.

She picked it up and answered it cautiously.

"What the hell, Nadia?"

"Brent?" she asked, shocked to hear her ex-husband's voice through the phone.

"Do you know how much it pisses me off to have to call you at some convenience store because I can't get a hold of you?" he demanded.

"How did you get this number?" Nadia asked.

"I've been trying to call you, but your cell isn't working," he said.

"It's working just fine. You just don't have the number," Nadia pointed out.

"Which is bullshit. You have my daughter. I shouldn't have to go on social media and find out where you work so I can get in touch with you."

"What do you mean you got it from social media? My profile is private."

"And we know a lot of the same people, Nadia," he said. "All kinds of people who were more than happy to report to me that you are working in some hole in the wall on the roadside somewhere and that's supposed to be good enough."

"It isn't a hole in the wall," she defended. But then she closed her eyes and took a breath. She reminded herself that she didn't have to give in to him anymore. "What do you want, Brent?"

"We need to talk about Amelia."

"What could you possibly have to say about her?" Nadia asked.

"I want to see her. You need to send her back here to stay with me for a while."

Nadia laughed bitterly. "You can't be serious. You haven't seen her in… how long? We were living five minutes down the road from you, and you never even bothered to come by to say hi to her. You could have picked her up from school and spent all afternoon with her anytime you wanted. You never did. Now all of a sudden, you think I'm going to drive her all the way back there and leave her with you?"

"You can put her on the bus," he said.

"I'm not going to put my nine-year-old on a bus by herself."

"The train then," he said.

"Because that's so much better. You are being ridiculous. She's not going there, and you aren't having her stay with you for any amount of time. Remember, the court gave me full custody. They granted me permission to move and didn't give any restrictions or conditions."

"I pay child support," he said.

"Only because you're forced to. You didn't for almost two years."

"Well, I do now, and that means you owe me," he said.

"I don't owe you anything. If you want to choose a place halfway and see her with me there, fine. We'll plan something, but that's what you're going to have to deal with."

"No. She's my daughter. I'm not going to be supervised by you to see her."

"You don't have a choice."

"You did this, you know," Brent said. "You destroyed our family. She doesn't have two parents in her life because of you. We could have been happy."

The familiar sad, manipulative sweetness that made her stomach feel sick was back in his voice. It took so long for her to see through that and not let it twist her emotions. So many times that very voice brought her back into his clutches. Not anymore.

"No, Brent. You did this."

She hung up, her hand still shaking when she let it drop from the phone.

CHAPTER TWELVE

THE NEXT MORNING NADIA OPENED THE STORE BEFORE GOING
back to the house to pick up Amelia. She'd have to return for the
evening shift, but it was worth it to be able to be here for Amelia's
big day. She drove up to Amelia's school with her daughter in the back
seat holding her costume for the play being performed that day. She'd
been so excited she had trouble eating her bowl of oatmeal that morning, and Nadia had slipped some extra snacks into her bag to make sure
she wouldn't get too hungry later.

She stopped in front of the school and turned to look into the
back seat.

"Okay, baby. I'll see you in there," she said. "Good luck!"

"Mama, you're not supposed to say that for a play," she said.

"I'm sorry. Break a leg," Nadia said.

"I don't want to do that either," Amelia responded.

"All right. How about… do your best?"

"Okay!"

Nadia smiled as Amelia opened the door and scurried out, rushing toward the teacher's aide waiting there to supervise the students arriving. She waved through the window at the woman and then drove toward the entrance to the parking lot. She still had a few minutes before she was supposed to go inside for the performance, so she scrolled through her phone sitting in the parking spot.

Opening her social media page, she noticed a friend request from someone she didn't recognize. Like she always did, she rejected it. As she looked over the posts, Brent's words came back to her mind.

She had maintained her social media page after leaving for Dogwood Valley because she felt like she needed to stay connected to some people in her life. And if she was being really honest, she did it out of spite for Brent. He had spent so much of his life controlling her and trying to make her live exactly the way that he wanted her to. He was involved in everything that she did and was constantly trying to influence what she thought, what she said, and what she did. That extended to her social media.

He read everything she posted and made sure to comment, interjecting himself into any conversation she got into. When he decided to start signing in with her password so he could read all her messages and make posts on her behalf, she stopped using it altogether. Keeping it and starting to post again after their divorce was a way for her to reclaim her autonomy and show that he didn't have that control over her anymore. But now she was looking at it differently.

While she regularly interacted with a few people, she realized now she couldn't truly trust anyone there. Just like he said, they all knew him too. And obviously, their loyalty hadn't gone with her. Now that she'd really stopped to think about it, she realized there wasn't a single person in her connections list who had her new phone number or who had reached out in any effort to see her or really check in with her since she moved. Everything there was surface level, staying in touch for the sole reason of consistency.

She looked through the pictures still posted there. She had never wanted Amelia so publicly and readily accessible, so it was a strict rule of hers that her daughter's face was never shown in any of the pictures. That meant nearly every image was just of her. Everything that had Brent in it had been stripped away. But now that she was looking at the images again, she realized that he was still there. With the exception of the new pictures she had put up of the store, Dogwood Valley, and her with Lisa, every single one of the pictures she looked at brought up a memory of her time with her ex-husband. Even without his face actually in them, she knew he was there.

Nobody in her new life was connected to her here. It was just a strange way she was clinging to the past. Knowing she needed to do it now or she was going to talk herself out of it, she deactivated the page. There was a brief moment of anxiety, a sense of something being cut away and now missing.

But after a couple of breaths, the relief came. Weight was taken off her shoulders. She saw clearly now and knew that Brent was still controlling her even without her realizing it, and this was a way to end that.

Nadia went inside and sat in the combination cafeteria and auditorium to watch the play the children had worked so hard to prepare. It was adorable, and she found herself tearing up in pride. When it was over, the chairs were moved aside, and tables full of refreshments were brought out. She waited for Amelia to come back into the room, and when she did, she scooped her into a hug.

"You did such a good job," she said. "Did you have fun?"

"Yes!" Amelia said. "Do you want to meet Lacey?"

She recognized the name. This was the girl who Amelia called her best friend during the uncomfortable encounter with the man who accused her of cutting him off. But she couldn't say no to meeting a child. Especially one who had made her own daughter so happy. She kept her smile on her face and nodded.

"Absolutely," she said.

Amelia scuttled away and came back a few seconds later holding hands with the blonde little girl.

"This is my Mama," Amelia said. "This is Lacey."

"It's really nice to meet you," Nadia said.

"Lacey and I want to have a slumber party," Amelia said.

It made Nadia's heart jump a bit. Amelia had never been invited to a sleepover. An actual one, not just the two of them eating snacks in a hotel room. None of the friendships she had back in their old neighborhood had ever gotten that deep.

"That sounds like fun," Nadia said.

"I'll ask my dad," Lacey said and took off before Nadia could stop her.

It was obvious that the girls had put the entire encounter between their parents out of their minds. As awkward as it had been when it was happening, neither of them seemed concerned about it anymore. Which meant that moments later, Lacey came back pulling her father by his hand. He was smiling until he saw Nadia. His expression fell, and she offered a tight smile and a small wave.

"Hello," she said.

"It's you," he said.

"Yes, it is," she said. "And it's you."

"Lacey, I…" he started, but the little girl interrupted him.

"Daddy, this is Amelia's Mama. She said that it sounds like fun for us to have a sleepover."

"Oh, she does, does she?" he asked.

"It seems our girls have gotten pretty close," Nadia said. "So maybe now is a good time for us to actually meet. I'm Nadia Holmes."

"Jonathan Pruitt," he said after a few seconds of hesitation. He looked at Lacey. "Honey, I've got to head to the office now. I'll see you when I get home tonight."

Lacey looked visibly disappointed that he wasn't staying for any more of the reception the teacher had set up for the parents, but she didn't express it. Nadia had a feeling this was something that she was accustomed to.

"And we'll do a slumber party soon?" she asked.

Smart girl. She had learned to take situations like this and turn them to her advantage.

Jonathan's face softened. "Yes," he said. "We will talk about it tonight."

Both little girls cheered and clapped their hands together gleefully. It was enough to make Nadia laugh, but when she looked at Jonathan, hoping to clear the air a bit more by sharing the cute moment, he only glared back at her. Obviously, the water wasn't fully under the bridge yet. He walked out of the room, and Nadia forced herself not to give him any more thought and instead focus on Amelia.

For the next half an hour, her daughter walked her around, introducing her to other people and showing her things like where she sat for lunch and the piece of artwork that was on display among others from her class.

When it was time for the children to get back to class, she left and headed for the car. Before unlocking the door, Nadia felt an uncomfortable sensation coming over her. It was like being watched.

She glanced around the parking lot and back toward the school but didn't see anybody. The sound of an engine turning over startled her, and she watched a car drive out of the lot. Taking a breath, she got in her car. She took out the to-do list she had made for herself for the day. She had to go to work that evening, but she wanted to take advantage of the next few hours by getting some errands done. She hadn't yet left the parking lot when a text came into her phone.

Do you really think that's the kind of dress you should be wearing in a school?

A sharp breath shivered into her lungs. She reached over and locked the doors before peering out of her window. Other parents were trickling out of the school and getting in their cars, but none of them seemed particularly interested in her. One mother she'd met noticed her sitting there and waved at her. Nadia waved back and started the car. She wanted to get away from the parking lot as quickly as possible.

She went back to the house and changed into a pair of jeans and a sweater. She put her hair up into a ponytail and considered washing off her makeup but stopped herself. In the kitchen, she checked the refrigerator and cabinets, making notes on her phone of what she and Amelia needed. She was planning to make dinner for everybody on her next day off in a couple of days as a way to thank Jeff and Lisa for being so kind to them, so she needed everything for that too.

At the grocery store, Nadia was roaming through the produce section when she got another text. She navigated away from her grocery list to read it. Her stomach sank when she saw that it was from the same unknown number as the others.

You really shouldn't have deactivated your social media. People might be offended.

She quickly swept back to her list and forced herself to focus on it completely as she continued through the grocery store. But even as she was debating between two brands of canned tomatoes, she couldn't help but look around her suspiciously. Everybody who turned into the same aisle as her or seemed to look up when she approached seemed slightly ominous. Finally, she finished shopping and went back to the house to put the groceries away.

It felt more secure there. The feeling of being watched went away when she was there, and she checked the time to see how long she had until she needed to go to work. There were a couple more things that she had planned to do that day, but instead, she stayed at the house and kept herself busy in the kitchen. By the time Amelia got off the bus and came through the front door, Nadia had three meals cooked and cooling to be put in the freezer.

She only had a couple of hours with her daughter before she needed to go to work, and Nadia spent them helping with her math homework and reading another book. Finally, it was time to leave, and she reluctantly put on her work clothes and headed for the store. When she pulled into the parking lot, she stayed in her car for a few seconds to make sure nobody was following her. She looked at each of the cars at the gas pumps to see if any of them looked familiar. When she couldn't wait any longer, she went inside.

Devon was finishing up with a customer and smiled at Nadia when he noticed her walk inside. She waved at him and went into the office. Stashing her bag, she sat in the chair behind the desk and took a moment to breathe. She hated this feeling. It reminded her far too much of everything that she had been through already. She fought hard to escape feeling like this, and now it was coming back.

She heard a knock on her door.

"Come in," she said.

Devon popped his head into the office. "I got everything taken care of for the end of my shift. Do you mind if I take off now? I'm sorry for the rush, but my sister has a school dance, and my mom has to work, so I said I would bring her."

It made Nadia's heart ache to think about a mother having to miss out on something so precious to her daughter and relying on her other child, who was already working to help the family. She knew all too well what it was like to have to make those kinds of sacrifices.

"Go ahead," she told him. "Thank you. I'll see you tomorrow."

He took a step to leave the doorway, then hesitated. His eyes narrowed slightly.

"Are you okay?" he asked.

"Oh yeah, I'm fine. Just a little bit of a headache. Nothing to worry about."

"Soda and potato chips," he said. "I swear by it. Works better than a pill any day."

She managed to smile. "Thanks, I'll try it." She stood up. "I'll head out there with you."

She shut the office door and went out to the counter. Devon left, and she glanced around. Just like he said, he'd already taken care of everything on the list that must get done before clocking out. It was one of the first things she implemented when she took over the store. Organizing what needed to be done at the beginning and end of every shift of the day and night helped keep everyone on track and ensured the store was always running smoothly.

She was worried about presenting the idea to the employees at first since she'd just started, but they took to it easily. There were only three other people who worked at the store, so it wasn't too hard to get everyone on board.

The shift went fine for the first few hours. She greeted a familiar stream of customers who came in around this time just about every

THE GIRL ON THE RUN

day. She delighted one by showing him they had finally gotten a new shipment of his favorite frozen burritos, and he promptly put two in the microwave. A few new people came through, and she was able to help one with directions by explaining GPS systems got confused by a certain turn in a road nearby. Relaying the same information given to her when she first started, that there used to be another road there but it had been blocked by an abandoned construction project a few years ago, made her feel strangely good. It was like she was really starting to be a part of the area.

But it didn't last.

Two customers were in the store when she got another text message. Nadia kept her phone with her during her shifts in case Amelia wanted her. She'd given her the number to the store, but her daughter still called her phone first. Nadia didn't want to risk the little girl really needing something and she wasn't there. She looked at the message.

Remember when I said I was going to think about you all night? I still am.

Another message came through before she could close the first.

I just want to have you all to myself.

She turned her back so she was facing away from the main floor of the store and called the number on the texts. It rang several times, but there was never any answer. She tried again, but there was still no answer. Another customer came into the store, and she heard someone stepping up to the counter. Brushing her face to make sure there were no tears, she turned to them with a smile.

"Did you find everything?" she asked.

As she rang that customer up, she noticed a regular come in. She already knew he was there to buy fifteen dollars of gas, two packs of gum, and a pack of cigarettes and to walk past the beer cooler a few times. He wouldn't buy any of it. He would just look at it. Sometimes he stopped in front of it and seemed to examine each of the labels carefully. Once his hand lifted just enough to look like he was going to open the door, but he stopped before he did. It seemed like the actions of someone who had serious problems with alcohol at one point and still battled the temptation.

She also knew him being there meant he was going to hit on her.

As surprising as it was to get attention from the man she ran into when she first started at the other store, Nadia had since gotten used to it. There was a bit of a feeling of conceit in admitting that, but she couldn't ignore it. People flirted with her on a daily basis. Some she never saw again. Some she knew she would see the next day. She'd come to the conclusion that for most of them, it was just loneliness. Truckers and business travelers who spent the majority of their lives looking at a steering wheel rather than another person. They liked any chance they got to exchange a smile and a few friendly words with another human being.

But then there was this man. She knew his name was Emmett because it was on the credit card he always used. She never called him by it. He, on the other hand, plucked her name right off the tag on her shirt the first time he saw her and tossed it around with abandon. He seemed to particularly like greeting her with it when there were other customers within earshot. It was as if he thought it gave him some kind of extra cred.

He came up to the counter, and she reached for his preferred brand of cigarettes.

"Hey there, Nadia," he said. "How you doing tonight?"

"I'm doing fine, thanks. How are you?"

"You certainly look fine."

She tried not to flinch. She tried to carefully construct her conversations with Emmett to avoid anything that seemed to be an invitation to flirt, but she hadn't been quick enough with that one.

"Fifteen dollars?" she asked, starting to set up the gas pump.

"When are you going to let me take you out to dinner?" he asked, leaning on the counter.

Nadia lifted her eyes to look over him and see who else was in the store. A woman she recognized was browsing the baked goods, and a man was standing at the soda cooler.

"It's very kind of you to offer, but I am really busy right now."

"You have to eat. No matter how busy you are, you have to stop at some point to have a meal. Why not have it with me? I better know some good restaurants you haven't been to before. I know you're new around here," he said.

Her jaw tightened, and her hand stopped over the keys of the computer.

"Why would you say that?"

He gave a bit of a mocking laugh. "Because you just started working at this store. And you said you came from the other one that you started working at right after moving into town."

"Right," she said, remembering mentioning that to him the first time they spoke—before she had grown wary of him.

"See now? You're not even thinking clearly. Probably because you're hungry. That just means you've got to take me up on bringing you out. What time do you get off?"

"I appreciate the offer," she said. "But no, thank you."

His face darkened. One hand slammed onto the counter. "Come on, Nadia! Why are you playing hard to get? I come in here all the time, and I have been nothing but nice to you. You can't just reciprocate by letting me take you out?"

"Let me just get your gas set up for you," Nadia said.

"I know you're lonely," Emmett said. "Nobody your age is working all the time then sitting around at the house alone and not thinking about what they are missing out on. I could take care of all that for you."

He leaned further across the counter, and Nadia took a step back. A hand dropped to Emmett's shoulder. The contact made him whip around, and Nadia saw the man who had been at the cooler standing right behind him.

"Get off me," Emmett snapped.

"I believe she said no," the other man said.

"Back off. Nadia and I know each other."

"She said no. And she was a lot more polite about it than I'm going to be if you don't take your cigarettes and your gum and move along." He reached into his pocket and pulled out a couple of bills. He set them firmly on the counter and slid them toward Nadia. "There. Taken care of. You can go now."

Emmett looked like he was going to say something else, but he noticed the woman now standing at the end of one of the aisles with her phone. It was obvious she was recording what was happening, though she was trying to be subtle about it. He angrily adjusted his jacket and glared at each of them before stomping out of the store, not even bothering to take his purchases with him.

Nadia let out a breath and put the pack of cigarettes back.

"Thank you," she said to the man. "I really appreciate it."

"I hope I didn't damsel-in-distress you or anything," he said.

"That's perfectly fine with me. I'm not going to turn down getting somebody like that away." She looked at the money still sitting on the counter. "You really didn't have to do that."

"It worked," he said with as shrug, picking the bills back up. "And if he had taken the stuff, I would have just considered it a down payment on that drink I wanted to buy you."

Nadia was surprised by the words. She looked at the man fully. It took a second to process, but she realized it was the man she met when she was at the bar with Maren and Christy.

"Lennon," she said.

Lennon smiled. "I'm sorry. That was probably really inappropriate of me to say, considering that whole situation."

She shook her head. "No, I'm just surprised to see you."

"I'd like to say it was serendipity, but I have a confession to make. One of my buddies was with a girl that night, and she recognized you from the other store. She saw me talking to you and said you worked there. Then when I built up the courage to go in there and talk to you, I found out you're working here now. And now that I'm saying that out loud, I realize how creepy it sounds." He sighs. "Wow, I'm swinging for the fences with you, aren't I?"

"I'm sorry I didn't realize who you were."

"That's okay. You're seeing me without the ultra-flattering neon bar lights."

Nadia laughed. "We all know those are everybody's best look."

Lennon smiled at her gently. "I don't know. I like how you look in these lights." His eyes widened slightly. "Wow, again. Okay, I'm going to go before this whole thing ends up posted on a shaming site somewhere."

"It was good to see you," Nadia said.

"You too. Maybe I'll try it again sometime."

He walked out, and the woman with the phone stepped up to the counter.

"You didn't record all that, right?" she asked.

The woman shook her head. "I stopped when the other guy left. I already deleted it."

"Okay, thanks."

"He's a cutie," the woman said as she took her bag from Nadia. "You should go for it."

"Have a good night."

She pursed her lips a bit, but there was a smile in her eyes as she walked out of the store. Nadia was alone for a matter of seconds before her phone buzzed. She looked at it for a long moment before opening it.

When I have you all to myself, will you be a good girl, or will I need to lock you up?

Her blood went cold. She shot back a message.

Leave me alone.

Not wanting to wait for a response, Nadia blocked the number and shoved her phone away again. The store phone rang behind her, and she shook as she picked it up.

"Hey, Nadia,"

Her shoulders relaxed. "Hey, Mel," she said.

"Do you think you could do me a favor tomorrow?"

"What do you need?"

"Joseph quit, and Maren is going to be out of town for a couple of days. I've got Christy, but she obviously can't work the whole day. I have a guy coming up to the store to look at that back freezer that hasn't been working. He's doing it as a favor to me, so he's coming after hours. I can come up there and be there for the evening and night shift if you can go up to the old store and work that one."

"The late shift?" she asked.

"Is that okay? I can pay you overtime for the inconvenience."

"I can do that."

"Thank you, you are saving me," he said.

"What happened with Joseph?" Nadia asked.

"I don't know. He's been dealing with all those health issues recently, and he said it was just causing him a lot of stress. I feel like there was something else, but he wasn't going to say it. All I know is right now, I've got to find somebody to take his place. I guess I can't wait for another transplant in town to show up and have their car break down in the parking lot."

Nadia chuckled. "I think you probably get a one-time shot with that."

"Oh well, I guess it worked out for me. Thank you, thank you, thank you again," he said.

"You're welcome. Talk to you soon."

She hung up and hesitated, waiting for it to ring again. It didn't.

CHAPTER THIRTEEN

BLOCKING THE MYSTERIOUS NUMBER DIDN'T DO ANYTHING. THE next morning Nadia woke up to two messages from a new number. She blocked that number too, only to get three more messages within an hour. After Amelia left for school, she got dressed and headed to the police station. They had to be able to help her. There had to be some way they could figure out who was doing this and stop them.

She waited to speak to a detective for almost an hour, and it took less than five minutes for her hope to be completely crushed.

"I'm sorry, but there's really nothing we can do about this," he said, sliding the phone back across the table to her.

"What do you mean there's nothing you can do?" Nadia asked incredulously.

"It's text messages, and I get that they are making you uncomfortable, but that isn't a crime."

"Harassment is a crime. So is stalking."

"I don't really think this qualifies as either one of those," the detective said.

"How could you possibly say that? I just showed you four messages with distinct threats in them."

"One asked if he would need to lock you up. One asked how long you thought you could handle being blindfolded. And two mentioned waiting for you to be alone."

"Yes, thank you for the recap," Nadia said sarcastically. "How can you see that and say it isn't harassment?"

"Honestly, to me, it sounds like something else."

Nadia was disgusted by the implication, and somehow it was even more skin-crawling because the detective couldn't even bring himself to say the words.

"You think I'm enjoying this? That this is some sort of kinky sex game?"

"I'm just saying, there isn't anything in those messages that is directly threatening you. I get that unwanted messages are annoying…"

"And illegal."

"In extreme circumstances. It has only been a couple of weeks and a handful of messages and phone calls. You said yourself, you don't recognize the number, and there's a strong possibility we wouldn't be able to identify the person anyway. Somebody swapping numbers that fast is using burner phones or text apps. Right now, the best thing you could do is just wait for it to blow over. Keep blocking the number if you keep getting texts. Don't answer if he calls."

"That's it?" Nadia asked.

"If anything else happens, feel free to call," the detective said.

"So I need to wait until I am actually physically harmed before you'll take any of this seriously?" she said. "Outstanding. Way to protect and serve."

She got up angrily and stormed out of the police station. She was shaking and felt tears stinging in the corners of her eyes. She went in for help, and not only did they not take her seriously, but the detective had all but mocked her. It was infuriating and deeply disheartening.

Nadia was glad about the busy shift that evening at the old store. More customers were coming in than usual, but she welcomed it every time the door opened. It meant somebody else was inside the store with her. It was good to see a few familiar faces of people she used to talk to when working there. They checked in with her, and she was happy to feel the time passing. Finally, though, the customers tapered out, and the usual, quieter, time of the night settled in.

She busied herself the ways she usually did: tidying up, stocking, making sure everything was as it should be. She looked around for the deck of cards Maren played with but realized she probably had them with her. The door finally opened again, and she looked up. A woman who looked close to being asleep on her feet stood in the doorway.

"Is there somebody who could help me at the motel? You are taking more guests, right?"

"Absolutely."

Nadia took the keys and followed the woman out. She locked the door to the convenience store, and they walked around the back of the building.

"I tried to call the number that was on the door, but it wouldn't go through," the woman said.

"It wouldn't?" Nadia asked.

"No, it just didn't connect."

"That's really strange. It should redirect straight to the store. I'm glad you came in though. I can get you into a room."

"Thank you. I've been driving all day. I am completely exhausted," she said.

Nadia noticed her looking down the row of rooms on the front of the motel.

"Is housekeeping cleaning at this time of night?" She asked it like the thought made her second-guess wanting to stay at the motel.

Nadia couldn't blame her. She wouldn't want to try to sleep through rooms being cleaned on either side of her either. It was only eight thirty, but that was still late enough for something like that to be disruptive.

Nadia followed her gaze and noticed one of the room doors standing open and light from the TV flickering out onto the sidewalk.

"No, the rooms are cleaned in the mornings. That's probably just a guest wanting some fresh air. Or maybe they're looking for the vending machines and didn't want the door to lock behind them," Nadia said.

She unlocked the office and went inside, flicking on the light as she went.

"Where are the vending machines?" the woman asked.

"We don't have any," Nadia said, walking around behind the registration desk. She flashed the woman a smile. "But that doesn't stop people from looking for them."

She got the woman registered and walked her around to the back of the motel to her assigned room. As she came back around to lock up the office, she saw the open room again. Curious, she walked up to it.

"Hello?" she called out as she approached the door.

The darkness around her started to feel thicker as she walked down the sidewalk. She was suddenly acutely aware of being by herself out in the parking lot. Her breath became shallower, and she reminded herself that she wasn't really alone. There were guests in these rooms. Allison Black, the woman she just registered, at the very least was there and still awake.

Nadia got to the room but stopped short of stepping in front of the open door. Just in case there was a guest inside trying to air themselves out, she didn't want to just pop up in the middle of their relaxation. She didn't know who the room was registered to. It had to have been rented when she wasn't there, and she didn't check the computer. So she didn't know who to expect to be there.

"Hello?" she called out again, knocking on the window with one knuckle. "Are you all right?"

There was no answer. She wanted to just go back to the store, but she couldn't just leave the room open like that. She knocked one more time, and when there was no answer, she stepped into the room. As soon as she did, her stomach dropped to her feet, and a wave of dizziness rushed over her. The bed was soaked in blood. Spatters covered one wall and stretched across the ceiling. Bloody fingerprints smeared around the corner of the wall, as if someone grabbed at it in a desperate bid not to be dragged into the bathroom.

There was no way in hell Nadia was going into that bathroom.

She took off running to the store. She went inside and locked the door, flipping the sign over to "Closed." Yanking her phone out of her pocket, she went behind the counter to call 911. Before she could dial, her phone rang.

"Hello?"

"Don't make me mad, Nadia."

The lights in the store went out, making her scream in surprise. Nadia ran for the door and yanked on it. It wouldn't move. She pulled on it frantically until she remembered she'd locked it. She went back to the counter for the keys and got out of the store, running for her car and jumping into the driver's seat. There, she called for help.

The dispatcher kept her on the line as she waited for the police to arrive. They kept asking her questions she didn't have answers to. They sounded almost surprised she hadn't gone all the way into the room to see if there was anyone in the bathroom. It almost sounded like they thought that meant she knew more than she was saying.

When the police got there, she immediately told them she needed to call Mel and tell him what was going on. They made her wait until she told them everything that happened and brought them to the room. An officer stood with her as she called the store owner. Sounding horrified, he told her he would be right there. The officer ushered Nadia over to his car, and they sat in it together until the first officer came around the building to them. He gestured for her to get out.

"Who did you rent that room to?" he asked.

Nadia shook her head. "I didn't rent it to anybody."

"So it should have been empty? Didn't you find it strange that a room that was supposed to be empty was open and had the TV on?" he asked.

"I didn't say it was empty. I said I didn't rent it to anybody. I don't usually work at this location. I came in to fill a shift tonight, but that room must have already been rented out to somebody. I just gave a room to someone else, and the system assigned her a room in the back, which means all of the ones in the front were either already full or reserved."

"Can you find out who was staying there?" he asked.

"I can check the computer."

"I'll go with you."

He wasn't giving her any information, and that made Nadia feel even more uneasy. They walked to the office, and she checked the bookings.

"It says it was rented out yesterday to someone named William Jennings."

"Do you have a contact number for Mr. Jennings?" the officer asked.

Nadia gave him the number listed on the registration, and he immediately dialed it. He immediately lowered the phone.

"Not in service. Is there another number?"

"No, that's the only one that was given."

"Did the credit card he paid for the room with have his name on it?"

Nadia looked at the computer again. She scrolled to the payment information section and shook her head.

"He didn't pay with a credit card. He paid cash," she said.

The officer's eyebrows shot up. "Cash? Somebody just walked in here and paid cash for a room without any kind of credit card verification or copying their ID or anything?"

"That's the policy of the motel. It has been since it opened. Most of the time, people pay with credit cards, but Mel still accepts cash."

"Nadia!"

She could hear Mel yelling outside. The detective walked with her back across the parking lot, and she saw the store owner try to run toward her. An officer stopped him, not allowing him to get closer to the motel. They walked up to him, and the officer beside Nadia reached out to shake Mel's hand.

"Officer Bertinelli," he said.

"Mel Olsen. I own this place. What's going on?" He looked at Nadia. "Nadia, are you all right?"

"I'm fine," she said. "Just shaken up."

"What happened?" he asked, looking back at Bertinelli.

By now, all the other guests of the motel had come out of their rooms and were watching the drama unfolding. Nadia saw Allison Black off to the side. She'd already changed into pajamas and was tugging the sides of a lightweight robe close around her. As they watched, Nadia couldn't help but notice that no ambulance had arrived.

"Let's get everybody back in their rooms," Bertinelli called over to the other officer.

The younger man immediately went to action, shooing the guests back inside and making sure all their doors were shut. Of course, this didn't stop them from pulling open their curtains and peering out to watch.

"Officer, I need you to tell me what's going on. Nadia said there was blood in the room. Did something happen to one of my guests?" Mel demanded.

"We don't know," Bertinelli said. "There isn't anyone in the room."

"No one?" Nadia asked, shocked.

"No. We searched the entire thing. The bathroom is pristine."

Nadia was sure they were going to find a body in the bathtub. She was glad there wasn't, but at the same time, it was alarming to wonder what happened to whoever was in that room.

"The room was registered yesterday to a William Jennings, but no identification was taken," the officer said.

There was a tone in his voice that almost sounded like he was testing Mel, like he wanted to see if what Nadia told him about their policies was accurate.

Mel was unfazed by what the officer told him and simply nodded, "All right."

"Did you check him into the room?"

"No, that would have been my employee, Christy."

"Hey, Bertinelli?"

One of the officers who had gone into the room was crossing the parking lot toward them. He had a confused expression on his face and a gloved hand held out in front of him. Nadia saw him rub his fingertips together as he approached the officer.

"What is it?" Bertinelli asked.

"That's kind of my question. Look at this."

Bertinelli took the flashlight from his pocket and shined it on the other officer's glove. It illuminated what at first looked like blood on his fingertips. After looking at it for a second, though, Nadia saw that it was not the right consistency and was a strange color. Admittedly, she wasn't exactly well-versed in the appearance of human blood. Especially after it had been smeared and spattered across a hotel room. The way the lead officer was looking at it, though, told her he saw something strange about it too.

"CSU should be here any minute. Have them check."

The crime scene investigation team arrived within minutes, and it didn't take long for them to come back with an answer.

"It isn't blood," a woman with a short ponytail and bright blue eyes said, coming over to them where they still stood at the edge of the parking lot. "We sprayed the whole place down with luminol. There was some reaction like you'd expect from any motel room, but not the red substance itself."

"If it isn't blood, what is it?" Mel asked.

"I'd say corn syrup and food coloring," she said.

"Fake blood?" Nadia asked. "All of that was fake?"

"Yep," the woman said. "Do you rent your rooms out to indie horror movie makers by any chance?"

"No," Mel said.

She shrugged, looking like she was trying not to laugh as she turned away. "You might want to check up on that."

"Did you have something to do with this?" Bertinelli asked.

His expression was not as jovial as the CSI.

"Me?" Nadia asked. "No, I'm the one who called 911, remember?"

"You wouldn't be the first to call in a prank."

"She wouldn't do that," Mel said.

"No, I wouldn't," Nadia said tersely. "And it isn't just the room. What about the lights in the store? And the phone being disconnected? Are you going to tell me those are pranks too?"

"I don't know what's going on with the lights. Or the phone. What I do know is that it's a faked crime scene. And I would really like to know who did it because we just wasted time and effort coming out here for nothing. You say you were working here for the last few hours?"

"Yes."

"And you didn't notice that door open? You didn't see anything or hear anything?"

"No, I was in the store working until Allison Black showed up to check into a room. That's when I came out here and saw the door open," Nadia told him.

"Officer, I get that this is an unusual and unfortunate situation, but I'm telling you, Nadia didn't have anything to do with it. If she says she didn't hear or see anything, then that is the truth. She was obviously terrified when she called me. I don't know what happened in that room, but you can't deny that the power is out in my store and the phone is disconnected. I think it would be a good idea for you to stop focusing on what this isn't and figure out what it is."

Officer Bertinelli looked distinctly unhappy with being told how to do his job, but Nadia was grateful for Mel standing up for her.

"Do I have to stay here?" she asked.

"We won't be able to open again tonight," Mel said. "Can she go home?"

"Yes," the officer finally said. "But leave me your contact information so I can get in touch with you if I need to ask you anything else."

Nadia gave him the information, and Mel walked her to her car.

"I'm so sorry," she said. "I really don't know what happened."

"You have nothing to apologize for. Like I told him, if you say you didn't have anything to do with it, I know you didn't. We've had some weird stuff happen in that motel before. Maybe not quite like this, but it's a story," he said. "Are you sure you're okay?"

Nadia thought about telling him about the phone call, but something stopped her.

"Yes, I'm fine."

"Good. You go on home. Get some rest," Mel said.

He put both hands on her shoulders and gave them a squeeze. She gave him a tight-lipped smile and got in her car to go home.

Jeff and Lisa had made plans for a date night before Nadia was called in for the later shift, so she'd hired a babysitter to come give Amelia dinner and put her to bed. The young woman was sitting cross-legged on the couch in the living room with college textbooks spread around her when Nadia went inside.

"Hey, Ms. Holmes," Jennifer said. "You're home early."

"It's Nadia. Yeah, my shift got cut short. Don't worry, I'll still pay you the full amount. How did everything go?"

"Great. Amelia was an angel. She had dinner and played for a while, then took a bath and went to bed without any issue."

"Thank you."

"No problem. Call me anytime," Jennifer said, collecting her books.

"I will."

The babysitter left, and Nadia checked the time. It was long enough after Amelia's bedtime that she would be fully asleep by now. She didn't want to wake her up by going into her room, but she stopped by the door to listen. Only the gentle whirring of her sound machine came through the door.

Nadia turned off the lights in the living area, then went to her bedroom to get undressed for a shower. She tossed her clothes into the hamper and went into the bathroom. The hot shower felt amazing, and she stood under it for far longer than she needed to.

She would have stood there longer if the sound of her phone didn't pull her out of the blissful relaxation. Wrapping a towel around herself, she went into the bedroom where she'd left her phone. Another message from another unknown number filled her screen.

You look better with your clothes in the hamper.

Nadia gasped, and the phone fell from her hand. Her eyes snapped to the window, and she saw the blinds open. She hadn't even checked before getting undressed. Wrapping the towel tighter, she rushed over to the window and closed the blinds, yanking the curtains closed. She put on pajamas as quickly as she could. Even with the window covered, she felt like eyes were on her.

Outside the room, she heard footsteps. She went still. They were coming down the stairs onto the lower floor. Her stomach twisted, realizing they would pass by Amelia's room first, and her door was unlocked. Nadia wasn't going to let anything happen to her daughter. Despite the fear growing inside her, she grabbed the only thing within reach—the umbrella leaned against the wall—and ran out of the room. With a shout, she brought the umbrella down toward the man coming toward her in the dim light from only the night-lights along one wall.

"What the hell?" Jeff shouted, ducking out of the way.

"Jeff?"

"What is going on down there?" Lisa asked.

The rest of the lights came on, and Lisa rushed down the stairs.

"I'm sorry," Nadia said. "Jeff, I didn't realize it was you. What are you doing?"

"I came down to get something out of the bar. I knocked upstairs, but you didn't answer. I figured you were asleep, so I didn't want to turn on the lights and wake you up."

"Did you go after him with an umbrella?" Lisa asked.

A sudden crush of emotion came down on her, and Nadia sank to the couch. Lisa came over to sit beside her and looked at her husband, who backed away.

"I'm going upstairs."

Lisa put her arm around Nadia. "What's going on?"

Everything about the messages and the phone calls came spilling out. Lisa looked horrified when she was finished.

"Why didn't you tell me any of this sooner?" she asked.

"I didn't want to worry you. And I didn't want you to not want me here anymore. And I guess I felt like an idiot because I didn't know how to stop it," Nadia said.

Lisa held Nadia's shoulders firmly. "Listen to me. I would not toss you away. Never. Especially when you're dealing with something like this. You don't have to worry about that. You hear me?"

Nadia nodded. "Yes."

"Good. And you are not an idiot. Things like this happen. That's why there are laws about it. You need to talk to the police."

"I already did," Nadia said. "I went to them and told them exactly what was going on, and they didn't take me seriously. They essentially said it was nothing and I was overreacting."

"Did you show them the messages?" Lisa asked.

"I did. And they still said there was nothing they could do about it. Because I don't know who it is and nothing has actually happened to me, they don't think there's anything to be done."

"Nadia, do you think this could be Brent?"

"I don't know. I know he is more than capable of something like this. When he called the other day, he was trying hard to convince me to come back..." She let out a heavy sigh and ran her fingers back through her hair. "But I don't know. Brent has always been very direct in his threats. Slimy and manipulative, but when it came to trying to scare the hell out of me, he didn't cut corners. I don't know if I see him doing something like this. What would be the point?"

"To see you squirm," Lisa said. "And maybe..."

Her voice trailed off, and Nadia searched her face. "And maybe what?"

"And maybe to try to make it look like you aren't a safe parent for Amelia," Lisa said.

Nadia drew in a shuddering breath. "I can't let him take her. I can't let her be with him."

"We aren't going to let that happen. We're going to figure this out."

CHAPTER FOURTEEN

Emma

"No, Emma. This is Doughn't You Forget About Wheat. With the white ribbon." Xavier touches the ribbon tied around the jar of sourdough starter like a bow tie.

"That's right. I'm sorry," I say, realizing I mixed up the names of two of the babies who made the trip to visit me this week. I point to one with a blue crochet cozy. "And that one is…"

"Toastmaster Jay."

"Yes, he is." The timer goes off, and I glance over at it. "The dough is ready to roll out."

Xavier goes over to the freezer and pulls out the large balls of dough we've had chilling. Each will make several dozen sourdough crackers, but with the speed at which Sam and Dean go through them, the three batches are not excessive. He puts the dough on the table and pushes up his sleeves in preparation for rolling them out. Each batch of crackers will be a different flavor. One's being kept simple, just plain with a sprinkle of coarse salt at the end. The second is garlic and rosemary, and the third is Xavier's favorite—poultry seasoning.

"Did I tell you there are now five empty rooms on the third floor?" Xavier asks as he works one of the balls to a thin sheet.

"You didn't. That's fantastic." I work my own dough for a second, then pause. "Which rooms did the stuff go into?"

Xavier gives me a withering look. "Oh, ye of little faith." He keeps rolling. "It's in a storage unit."

"Ah."

"But just a small one. I can't even lie down in this one."

I happen to know that isn't something he's guessing. I've witnessed this measuring technique in several spaces.

"Then I still say that's fantastic. I'm proud of you."

"Thank you. The farmhouse is coming along too. Dean and I stopped by on the way here to check out the progress."

The farmland Xavier bought is by no means "on the way" between Harlan and Sherwood. But since he sometimes has a hard time telling what's on the way between our house and a few streets away, I give him a pass.

"How are the cats handling the construction?" I ask.

"They do not seem thrilled. I tried to reassure them it will be very nice when it's finished and I'm around more often. Only time will tell how long it takes for them to forgive me."

"I'm sure it will work out," I tell him.

The large colony of surprisingly friendly feral cats living on the property was one of the biggest selling points for him. In addition to the farmhouse being built there, Xavier has also designed an elaborate shelter and climbing structure for them. I understand him wanting to give them a comfortable, safe place to stay warm and dry during bad weather, but I'm unsure why cats living on predominately wooded land would need a climbing structure.

"Why does a sky that's predominately water need bubbles?" was his answer, and that ended that conversation.

I hear my phone on the counter and go to check the notification. It's an email from the forensics lab. Wiping my hands on a kitchen towel, I open the e-mail.

"Something interesting?" Xavier asks.

"The results came back for the tests on the burn pit," I say. "Damn. Inconclusive. They weren't able to extract enough DNA to get an accurate profile. So we still can't prove if those are actually Mike Morris's teeth and bones. The area is going to have to be excavated. We need to find any other remains that might be there. There could be a chance at getting a profile."

It's going to take work to get that done. The burn pit is in a national park, which makes this ordeal a logistical nightmare. It's not easy to get the approvals and permissions necessary to do any extensive work like that within a protected park. And even if everyone is cooperative, getting the necessary equipment to the remote location within the park is going to be a massive challenge. Most likely, we'll end up with mostly shovels and manpower. But it will get done.

My phone rings. I expect it's Eric calling about the results. Instead, it's an old friend of mine: Lisa Cambridge.

"Lisa?" I answer.

"Hey, Emma," she says. "I'm so glad you answered."

"Of course, I did," I say.

"I know you're really busy now," she says.

I laugh. "I've been really busy for about fifteen years. It's never stopped me from talking to you. I'm glad you called. It's been a while. We need to plan another visit."

"We definitely do," Lisa says. "And I wish that's why I was calling. But it's not."

I can hear in her voice that whatever motivated the call is serious.

"Is something wrong? Are you all right?"

"I'm fine. Jeff is fine. We're good."

"Thank goodness, you had me worried. What's going on then?" I ask.

I go back to the table to return to rolling. Xavier has already progressed through the poultry seasoning ball and has moved on to the plain.

"I have a friend who is going through something, and I was hoping you could give her some advice."

"I'm not sure if I'm the best person in the world to be doling out advice, but I'm happy to listen and see if there's something useful I could say."

Lisa tells me about her friend Nadia and the disturbing messages and phone calls she's been getting. Even hearing it through Lisa rather than Nadia herself, I can tell how terrifying the situation is for her.

"And you said she talked to the police?" I ask when she's finished.

"Yes. After the first few messages. They would barely even talk to her about it," Lisa says.

"Unfortunately, that's not much of a surprise. Laws have come a really long way when it comes to things like harassment and cyber-stalking, but there's still a lot of work to be done. It can be really diffi-cult to define those kinds of things in a way that can be legally applied. It's obvious to the person it's happening to, but it's not always so easy to just put that into action. And without anything actionable to go on, it gets looked over," Emma says. "I promise not all law enforcement is like that."

"I know," Lisa says. "Sam is wonderful."

"I'm pretty partial to him. But he's not the only one."

"So what is she supposed to do?"

"Right now, the most important thing she needs to focus on is safety. For herself and for her daughter. This person is obviously getting in very close proximity to her. That might be the extent of it. It might not be. She needs to take whatever steps she can to keep herself and her daughter secure. That might mean she needs to leave your house," I say.

"Leave my house? Wouldn't that just be putting her in even more danger? She'd be on her own. At least here she is living with other peo-ple and we can help protect them," Lisa says.

"That's true. But he knows where you live. He knows that's where Nadia is. I can't tell her, or you, what to do, but I would consider moving somewhere without telling anyone. If it would make both of you feel better, you could stay with her for a while. I don't know how Jeff would feel about that, but it would mean she wasn't totally alone.

"She also needs to really brush up on her personal safety skills. She needs to be aware of her surroundings all the time. Try to avoid going places in the dark unless she can park close to the entrance, somewhere well lit. Keep track of any communication. And as an extension to that, now might be a good time to consider changing her phone number. I know that's a hassle, but since she doesn't know where this person got her number, but he clearly has it, this will end the stream of contact," I tell her.

"Thank you, Emma," Lisa says.

"You're welcome."

"We really do need to get together again soon," she says.

"You just tell me when."

We get off the phone, and I feel a tinge of guilt. I don't know what she was hoping I would do or say, but that was the extent of my ability to help in that kind of situation. What she told me is eerie and frighten-ing, to put it absolutely mildly. But it also isn't unique. Unfortunately, things like this happen pretty frequently. There's a reason the old trope of the anonymous obscene phone call or scary letter exists. People enjoy upsetting and scaring each other, and they will go to pretty creative lengths to do it.

The other explanation is more unsettling. Not stemming from a desire to scare anybody, constant, unwanted contact like this can also just be the compulsion of a mind desperately searching for connection. Devoid of the ability to foster a real relationship with the person, or sometimes living in the delusion that they already have, the stalker bombards their victim with communication. There are times—more often than not, in fact—when this fixation doesn't go any further than messages and phone calls.

Even if they try to make plans to see their victim or threaten to come physically close to them, it never actually happens. They are safe behind their screen and aren't going to step over that line to do anything in real life. When this isn't the case, though, and the stalker is capable of taking that step beyond the screen, the results can be devastating.

That night I have a big wooden bowl filled with crackers sitting beside me as I work. The bowl belonged to Sam's mother. According to him and a couple of hazy memories from when I was much younger, she used to make salad in it. She would take a clove of garlic and rub it on the inside of the bowl, then make her dressing right inside it before adding any of the vegetables. My serving of a mix of the different flavors of crackers looks meager at the bottom of the large bowl, but I like using it. It makes me feel more connected to my mother-in-law.

Even though I knew her when I was a child, I never had the opportunity to make a real connection with her as an adult. She didn't live long enough to see me come back to Sherwood and reconnect with Sam. I never had the chance to call her my mother-in-law. I never even got to bicker with her on Thanksgiving for asking me to make a certain side dish and then going behind my back and making one as well. Sam got rid of or put away the vast majority of his parents' belongings, but using a few treasures I've kept really helps me feel closer to them.

I grab a few more crackers and pop them into my mouth. The combination of flavors is a lot, but they work well together. I brush my hands together to get rid of crumbs or little bits of clinging herbs, then pick up the large envelope I got in my PO box today. Inside are three standard mailing envelopes. A folded piece of paper comes out with the envelopes, and I pick it up. It's a note from Lavinia McDonnell, explaining what she sent me.

These are the original notes I received in the mail.

I look at them carefully. None of the envelopes has a return address, and the address of the McDonnell house on the front is printed rather than handwritten. It eliminates a point of comparison and shows more deliberate planning than someone just scribbling out an address. I take note of the postmarks on the envelopes. They are not the same. These notes were mailed from three separate locations. This immediately strikes me as strange. These are not three different counties or towns in the same general location that would still differ in their postmarks. The three places are vastly far apart.

This brings to mind the question of whether it was the same person who mailed all three of the envelopes, or if they had other people do it for them. But it also makes me wonder why those places specifically. If the notes were mailed by other people, they could be completely random locations that mean absolutely nothing. That would be a highly effective way of scattering the evidence trail and making it far more difficult to track who is responsible. On the other hand, they could very well be far more significant than that.

While it seems that a person who would go to such great lengths to cover up their identity would not send mail from places that could be connected to them, that isn't always true. For the most part, human beings are creatures of habit. We like what is comfortable and familiar. Even people who think of themselves as restless adventurers and adrenaline junkies have their touch points. Favorite clothes, a preferred hotel chain, a particular pillow or stuffed animal, favorite destinations. These are their comfort zones—just like a neighborhood, home, or even work location.

Without putting any thought into it, people tend to default to these comfort zones. It doesn't occur to them when they return to the same things over and over. This often proves especially true for criminals. They are already doing something inherently out of the norm. They tend to soothe themselves or make themselves feel less at risk by staying close to what makes them comfortable. Which means these postmarks could be a critical key to tracking down who sent these notes. And what happened to Sebastian McDonnell.

CHAPTER FIFTEEN

Nadia

NADIA UNDERSTOOD THAT EMMA GRIFFIN WAS A WELL-RESPECTED and skilled FBI agent. She had dealt with many different kinds of cases throughout her career and had probably seen more stalkers like this than she could count. But Nadia couldn't bring herself to fully follow the agent's advice. She changed her phone number the next day but stopped short of looking for a new place to live.

Jeff and Lisa's house had been the one place where she really felt safe since all this had started. And even though she knew that had changed, she still couldn't face the idea of leaving. Whoever was sending those messages had gotten close to the house. They had looked through her bedroom window and seen her getting ready for the shower. That was a terrifying and sickening thought, but so was being completely alone. At least there she had other people in the house with her and her daughter.

There were two other adults, and that made her feel more secure there than the thought of moving somewhere new and having no one.

Lisa didn't argue with her. Nadia knew she thought they should follow Emma's advice, but she had also committed to Nadia and Amelia staying with them for as long as they needed, and if Nadia felt safer and more comfortable being there, then she wasn't going to force her to leave.

Together they added extra locks to the windows and doors and put a camera at the front and back. Magnetic alarms that let out a loud, shrill tone if the two halves were separated by a window or door opening made moving around the house somewhat more challenging, but at least they gave them peace of mind, knowing that if somebody tried to come in, everybody inside the house would be alerted immediately.

Things were quieter for a few days, and she was starting to feel better until she got an email from Brent's attorney. She hadn't had any contact with him since the end of the divorce, and she felt her heart start to pound as soon as she saw the email address.

"He's planning something," she told Christy later. She poked at the salad that her friend had brought her with her plastic fork. "I don't know exactly what it is, but I know he's planning something. I'm so scared that he's going to try to take Amelia away from me. The way he was talking the last time..."

"All the attorney asked for was your phone number?" Christy asked.

"Yeah. The message just said that immediately changing my phone number without properly informing Brent and the courts was unlawful and went against our co-parenting agreement, so I needed to rectify it immediately. Honestly, I don't even know if that's true. As far as having any co-parenting agreement, the courts granted me full custody of Amelia. He didn't even get visitation. Not formal visitation anyway. He can come and see her if he arranges it with me first."

"You don't have to talk to him about any decisions that you make for her? Or make sure that he is kept up to date with what's going on in her life?" Christy asked.

Nadia gave her a questioning look.

"My parents got divorced when I was a kid. I was a little bit older, so it didn't apply to me as much, but my brother was ten years younger than me, and there was a lot of contention about him. I remember a lot of the things that the lawyers said and stuff my mom had to do just to keep my dad from melting down," Christy explained.

Nadia bobbed her head in understanding. "I guess I did agree to that. I just wanted it over with and was so glad the judge was seeing things my way that I was willing to accept the terms. I know he's angry that I really moved on with my life. Even though we've been divorced for a few years, he still had so much of a sense of ownership and control over me. Before Amelia and I moved out here, some people thought we were still married. As in, they had talked to Brent and he called me his wife. He never accepted that it was over. He always just assumed that I would come back."

"Do you think the calls and messages could be from him?"

Nadia had finally broken down and told her friends about what she was going through. They were surprised she'd kept it to herself for so long but were there to support and comfort her. It felt better to talk about it in some ways, but it also made her feel even more vulnerable in a way. By talking about it, she was admitting that she didn't know what to do. She wasn't just telling them that she was getting these messages and calls; she was saying that she hadn't been able to stop them. That there was nothing that the police could do to protect her.

"I don't know. I don't feel like he would be this elaborate just to scare me. Especially going so far as what happened at the motel. I just don't see him coming all the way out here and doing something like that. But he has always been manipulative, and maybe this is a new way that he's found to control me."

"The police still don't know anything about the fake blood in the motel room?" Christy asked.

"Not as far as I know. They tried to get fingerprints from the smear on the wall, but it turned out that whoever made it was wearing gloves. They definitely didn't want to be found. I'm sorry the store is still closed so you aren't getting any hours."

Christy shrugged. "It's all right. Mel is taking care of us. And he said it should only be for another couple days at the most. They had to fix the cut wiring, and he's taking the opportunity to do a few renovations."

"Well, if nothing else, this might push Mel to finally update the security around here," Nadia said.

Christy chuckled. "That would be something to behold. If there is one thing that I know about Mel, it's that he has very specific ideas about how things should be. And he is very adamant about people having their privacy and not interfering. That's why he still lets people rent rooms with cash and no credit card verification. He says people have stories, and you never know what somebody's story is. Sometimes it gives them a reason to not have a credit card or not want to be seen on camera."

"He doesn't think that maybe the stories that made these people not want to do those things are the exact reason why they should? Shouldn't he be concerned that somebody doesn't have a credit card? Or that they don't want to be on camera?" Nadia asked.

"I don't know. There are all sorts of reasons. Not all of them make a person untrustworthy. I don't know all the details, but I have a feeling Mel has some stories of his own. And that makes him sympathize with these people." She took a bite of her own salad. "I don't know. I know you said the police don't necessarily think that the fake crime scene had anything to do with the calls and messages, but I think that's ridiculous. I wonder if your ex-husband isn't trying to scare you just to scare you."

"What do you mean?"

"If he is behind this, maybe it's his way to get you back. If he is so shocked that you actually moved away and are living your own life, he could want to make that seem unsafe. He could think if he scares you enough, he could then swoop in and save you," Christy said.

"He has never been the rescuing type. But my phone number... I really don't know what to think."

A car door slammed just outside, and Christy straightened from where she was leaning against the counter to look through the door.

"It's Maren," she said. "She doesn't look good."

Maren wrenched the door open and stomped inside. Her face was red, her eyes puffy like she'd been crying.

"Maren?" Nadia said. "What's wrong?"

"He's seeing somebody else."

"Ron?" Christy asked.

"Yeah. I was wondering why he was going on yet another business trip when he just came back from one. He said that he travels a lot, and I understood that, but this just seemed strange. So I did some digging, and I found out that he wasn't going on a business trip. He was going on vacation with this other woman that he's dating. I confronted him about it, and he tried to talk himself out of it of course. He is a man after all. They will do anything if it keeps them from admitting they're wrong.

"But he finally told me that she isn't the other woman. Technically, I am. He was dating her before he met me, but things got complicated, and he didn't know what was going on in their relationship. When he met me, we clicked, and so he just went with it. But then things started working out with her again, and so he was just seeing both of us. But here's the kicker. You know what he meant by 'things got complicated'? She's married. She is cheating on her husband with a man who is cheating on her with me. And I'm over here like a complete dreamy-eyed imbecile thinking I found my Prince Charming."

"I'm so sorry," Nadia said.

"Who's this other woman? What's her name?" Christy asked.

"I don't know," Maren said. "He didn't tell me. I don't want to know. It isn't her fault. I mean, her having an affair is her fault. But her having an affair with a man who turned around and started a relationship with me isn't." She let out an aggravated sound that was something close to a growl. "How could I be so stupid?"

"You didn't do this," Nadia said. "You had no way of knowing. You trusted what someone told you, and that doesn't make you stupid. It just makes you hopeful."

"Yeah, well, I think a lot of the time those two words mean the same thing," Maren said.

"What are you going to do?" Christy asked.

"I already told him I never want to see him again. That he should not call me or try to come see me. Nothing. I want to pretend I never met him and move on."

"Good for you," Nadia said.

Maren scoffed bitterly. "Yeah, I really feel like throwing a parade for myself right now."

"It's going to work out," Christy said, rubbing Maren's back. "Everything is going to be fine."

Nadia was a little surprised at the way Christy was reacting. She thought she was more likely to tell Maren that this was what she got for getting herself into what she thought was a committed relationship.

"Thanks," Maren said with a teary half-smile.

"You know what? We should go out tonight."

Maren shook her head. "No."

"Come on," Christy said. "We should go out and blow off some steam. You can be pissed off at Ron. I can be pissed off at Lyle and Brick. Nadia can be pissed off at this piece of shit who is bothering her. We'll have a couple of drinks and dance like we're the only people there."

"Great. Then no one will ever want to date us," Maren said.

"And we can get a triplex and live out the rest of our lives together," Christy said. "What do you say?"

Maren looked at Nadia. Neither of them was totally convinced, but Christy's enthusiasm was contagious.

"Let's do it," Maren said.

"I'll see if Lisa will watch Amelia," Nadia said.

"Perfect. Can't wait." Christy gathered the trash from lunch. "I've got a mountain of laundry waiting for me to haul to the laundromat, so I'm going to live it up on my day off. I'll see you girls tonight."

"I'm coming too," Maren said. "I made a dentist appointment. Because apparently, I needed a cherry on top of this day."

"Message me and let me know when to meet you," Nadia said. "Thanks for lunch, Christy."

"A triplex?" Maren asked as they walked out the door. "Is that even a real thing?"

Nadia chuckled and went back to work. She was filling out an order form for the week when the door opened. She looked up to greet the customer, and her eyebrows pulled together from confusion. The pen in her hand dropped to the counter.

"Steven?"

Steven Web was a man she and Brent had known since high school. He'd never been good at hiding the fact that he had a crush on her. She couldn't think of a single reason he would be in this area.

"Hey, Nadia," he said with a bright smile. "It's been a while."

"Yeah, it has," she said. "What are you doing here?"

He gave her a quizzical look. "Really? That's how you're going to greet me?" He threw open his arms. "Come give me a hug."

Nadia hesitated, still confused about him being there, but finally, she walked out from behind the counter and stepped into the friendly hug. He gave her a little squeeze, then stepped back. His eyes moved up and down her, giving her a slightly uncomfortable feeling in the pit of her gut.

"You look great. Being out here has done you good."

"Thank you," she said. "Steven, what are you doing here?"

"Oh!" he said like he'd completely forgotten he hadn't answered the question. "I met a girl online, and we've been talking for a while. We finally decided to meet up. We figured out Murphy is halfway between us, so we're going to meet up there. Brent told me you were working out here, and I thought I'd swing by for a little road snack and see you. How have you been?"

Nadia tamped down the flare of irritation at Brent's name and smiled. "I've been good. You met a girl online?"

"Yeah, can you believe it? I spent my whole life looking around the same town and the same pool of women I went to school with, trying to find the right one. Then I finally catch up with the times twenty years behind everybody else, and there she is," he said.

"I'm happy for you," she said.

"Well, I couldn't just keep waiting around for you," he said. Steven laughed, and Nadia forced herself to laugh along with him.

This situation was strange. She knew it wasn't unusual for people her age to find partners online, and if they were at a distance, they would meet halfway. She had known Steven for essentially her entire life, so him stopping by to say hello after not seeing her for a long time made sense. But something felt off. She hadn't told Brent she changed stores, and her social media was still deactivated, so there wasn't anything posted there. Murphy was closer to the other store than this one, so it would make sense for Brent to mention that one to Steven if he found out he was meeting a woman there.

So how did Steven end up here?

"What's her name?" Nadia asked, trying to sound casually interested.

"Lila," he said. "She's really amazing. At least she is through her messages and on the phone. I hope she's just as amazing in person."

"This is the first time you're meeting her in person?" Nadia asked.

"Yeah. We've been talking for a while and decided it was about time to take it into the real world."

Out of the corner of her eye, she saw someone lumbering toward the door. She turned toward it just as Lyle slammed the door open with enough force for it to hit the window. His eyes were flashing angrily, and his hands were clenched by his sides so hard the veins were visibly popping up from his skin.

"Where's Christy?" he demanded.

"Lyle, what's going on?" she asked.

"I want to know where the hell Christy is."

His voice was a fearsome growl deep in his throat, and Nadia felt it rattling in her bones.

"She doesn't work here. She works at the other store. You know that."

She was trying to sound calm and reasonable to bring down the intensity of whatever was coursing through him in that moment.

"The other store is closed. That means she's here," he insisted. "Tell her to get out here."

Steven stepped forward, holding both of his hands up like he was waving beside his chest. He tossed a polished salesman smile at Lyle.

"Let's just all settle down and talk about this," he said. "There's no reason to be so worked up."

"Get out of my face, little man," Lyle said. "You're not a part of this."

"You don't need to talk to him like that," Nadia said.

"I want to see Christy. She's not answering my calls. She tossed my shit out in the front yard. I've got people telling me she's going around with some other dude. I need to talk to her."

"She isn't here," Nadia told him. "Like I said, she doesn't work here. The other store is closed, but she's not picking up shifts at this one. I'm sorry about whatever's going on between the two of you, but I can't help you."

He looked around the store like he thought she might be hiding in one of the aisles, then met Nadia's eyes again.

"When you hear from her, you tell her I want to talk to her." He spun on his heel and left with the same explosive force as he came in.

Steven looked at Nadia with wide eyes. "What the hell was that all about?" he asked.

She let out a sigh and walked back around the counter. "That would be a guy a good friend of mine is dating. Or seeing. Or was seeing. I'm not fully clear on the specifics."

"I don't think he is either," Steven said. "Are you okay? Is he going to come back?"

"I'm fine," Nadia said.

"Okay." He looked at his watch. "I should go. It was really good to see you. I hope we'll see each other again soon."

She noticed his eyes flicker up above her head and linger for a second. Then they came back to her face, and he smiled wider.

"Have fun with Lily," she said.

He didn't correct her.

Steven left, and Nadia turned around, looking at the piece of paper on the board with her new phone number on display.

That night Christy rolled her eyes when Nadia told her about Lyle coming to the store.

"He just can't take a hint."

"By 'hint,' do you mean throwing his stuff out in your front yard?" Nadia asked.

"Possibly."

"Why did you even have his stuff at your house?" Maren asked. "I thought you were strictly noncommittal."

"'Noncommittal' doesn't mean non-involved," Christy said. "Just because I don't want to limit myself to one person doesn't mean the connections I have with men aren't important to me. I know you don't understand it, but I do care about them."

Maren leaned into the corner of the booth, her head resting sullenly on the wall. She didn't respond to Christy's assertion. She'd been quiet and withdrawn since they got to the bar. It was obvious how much her breakup with Ron was affecting her. As much as it seemed like she wasn't having a good time, Nadia couldn't help but think it was good for her to be out with them rather than alone that night.

"Was Lyle living with you?" Nadia asked Christy.

"No, I don't do living with men. I have my roommate, and that's plenty for me. But usually, he'd spend the night once or twice a week, so some of his stuff ended up migrating to my house and just kind of stayed there. I wanted it out, so I got it out."

"He doesn't seem like the kind of man you should piss off," Maren said.

Christy rolled her eyes again. She picked up her drink and took a long swig.

"I'm not scared of Lyle. I wasn't scared of him when I first started seeing him, and I'm not scared of him now. He can fee-fi-fo-fum his ass around town all he wants. It's not going to get my attention."

Maren didn't even crack a smile. She just stared into the distance.

CHAPTER SIXTEEN

"SO IT TURNS OUT THE FAKE CRIME SCENE WAS FOR AN INTER-net prank," Mel said the next day.

"An internet prank?" Nadia asked, continuing to stock a shelf of candy while he stood beside her.

"Yeah, it popped up on that site all the kids use. The one with the books and the dances. I don't know these things."

Nadia laughed. "I know what you're talking about."

"Apparently, there's an account on there that posts videos of crazy pranks and people doing ridiculous things to get a rise out of other people."

"I think there are a lot of those accounts," Nadia said.

"Well, this particular one put out a challenge for people to fake a crime and record the aftermath to see who could be the biggest and most convincing. The video of the room all done up like that was tagged with that challenge."

"I can't believe someone would do something like that just for the hell of it," Nadia said. She put up a few more pieces of candy and something clicked. "You said they recorded the aftermath. Does that mean I'm in the video?"

"Yeah."

"Shit," she said, dropping her head. She looked at Mel. "Sorry."

"Nope. I think this definitely qualifies as a 'shit' moment. If it helps, I saw the video. You can't even tell it's you. The part that shows the room is up close, but then the rest was taken from a pretty far distance. All you can see is a person going to the room and then running to the store. Then it cuts to the police being there. There aren't any close-ups of your face or anything."

"So it's just the people who know I work here and can piece that information together who would know it's me," Nadia said.

"Yeah."

"Great." She shook her head. "This is messed up. Do they not realize what they're doing is illegal in like ten different ways?"

"Either they don't know or they really don't care," Mel said. "With VPNs and throwaway accounts, it's next to impossible to actually track down who has those accounts. And there's nothing in the video to give it away."

"VPNs? You know more than you're letting on."

"I don't know about social media and video-sharing sites," he said. "I do know British TV and that I can only watch my shows if the TV thinks I'm in England."

"Fair enough. What about cutting the power and phone lines? That has to be considered serious enough to put more effort into following up on it."

"That's the thing. They don't think whoever made that video did the lines," Mel said.

"Why not?"

"It wasn't included in the video. The whole point of the video was to fake a crime and show how people react to it. Cutting the power and phone lines is a real crime, even more so than vandalizing the motel room. But beyond that, they didn't show any of it. If they were going to go to the effort of cutting those as part of this prank, it would have shown up in the video. So they don't think it had anything to do with it."

"They think it's a more reasonable explanation that someone was recording a faked crime at the same time that another person was committing a real crime in the same location?" Nadia asked, incredulous.

"Sounds like that's what they're going with," Mel said.

"And somehow that's supposed to reassure me?"

"Honestly, hon, I don't think they know what it's supposed to do."

"Fantastic," Nadia grumbled.

"I've got to get going. They're doing some work on the other store today, and I want to check in on it."

"Have a good day."

Nadia went back to stocking the shelf. As Mel was leaving the store, she heard him greet someone.

"Hi," she called out to the customer. "Be with you in just a minute."

"Should I stay clear so you don't run into me again?"

Nadia looked up and saw the man from the other store that had been flirting with her. He chuckled and waved.

"Hey," she said, standing up. She made a show of carefully stepping aside like she was trying to avoid him. "I think you're safe."

"I didn't realize you were working at this location now. I just went to the other one and saw it's still closed, so I came here."

"Gas card?" Nadia asked.

"Hot dog loyalist," he answered. "Mel's always has the best around."

"Ah. Well, let me get that for you."

They walked across the store to the grill, and she plucked one of the fresh hot dogs from the rollers.

"What all happened at the other store? I saw on the news that there were police and stuff there the other night and they were investigating something, but it didn't say."

"It was just a bunch of nonsense," Nadia said, not wanting to get into any detail about what actually happened. She put the hot dog in its bun and handed it over to him. "The store is still closed because Mel is making some improvements. It should be open soon."

"That's good to hear."

She heard the door and looked over to see Lennon come inside. He noticed the man standing at the counter and went over to the beverage cooler without saying anything to her. Nadia gestured at the condiments.

"Help yourself."

As he loaded up the hot dog, she walked over to Lennon.

"Hi," he said. He reached into the cooler for a bottle of juice. "Am I interrupting something?"

She glanced over at the man, then casually shook her head. "No."

"How's your day been?" he asked.

"Not bad. It was really busy this morning. I don't know what was going on, but it seemed like everybody was heading somewhere. I had to make twice the amount of coffee I usually do and sold out breakfast before eight." She smiled. "The thrilling chronicles of my life."

"Well, you can't always be living it up in the flattering bar neon lights."

The other man cleared his throat, and Nadia saw he was standing near the register. She headed over and started scanning his selections.

"Sorry," she said.

He shrugged, no longer smiling the way he had been. She finished up, and he took the bag from her.

"Thanks."

He walked to the door, and before he left, he glanced over at the board behind her. Lennon went over to the counter.

"Does he know I wasn't interrupting anything?" he asked.

Nadia sighed. "Maybe not. Speaking of the bar neon lights, I was actually there again last night."

"Look at you, living it up," he said. "Celebrating something else?"

"Not exactly. My friends, Maren and Christy, the same ones who were there with me the first time, are both dealing with some… unfortunate relationship issues."

"Ah, that doesn't sound nearly as festive."

"Not particularly, no. But Christy thought it would be a good opportunity to blow off some steam. I don't think it worked for Maren, but I did finally get to try the mozzarella sticks."

"Check that right off the bucket list," Lennon said.

"They were pretty good, I must admit. I looked around for you. I thought you might be there."

"You did?" he asked.

Nadia nodded.

"I'm sorry I wasn't. Maybe you should let me make it up to you by coming to dinner with me."

She hesitated but then smiled. "There's a teacher workday the day after tomorrow, so my daughter is having a sleepover at her friend's house tomorrow night. I'm available then," she said.

He smiled back at her. "Not anymore, you're not." He shook his head. "Good lord, I'm just going to stop talking."

He walked out of the store as Nadia laughed.

The light feeling didn't last long. Less than an hour after Lennon walked out, a woman came in from the parking lot with an uncomfortable look on her face. She didn't say anything to Nadia but went to the display of packaged sandwiches and sides where she stared at the offerings. Nadia finished with the customer she was helping and started the next transaction. The woman glanced back at Nadia, but she only approached her when the second man was finished and had left.

"Are you all right?" Nadia asked. "Do you need help?"

"There's a man out there," the woman said.

"Outside?"

She nodded. "Near the gas pumps. He's walking around and looks really suspicious. I was just going to come in here and get a drink, but I don't want to go back out there while he's there."

Nadia walked around to look through the door at the gas pumps. At first she didn't see anyone who seemed unusual. One of the men who had just come through the store was at the pump filling his tank. Two people were standing between their cars talking as they ate the lunch they picked up. She thought maybe the woman saw someone just passing by, but as she was about to turn away, she saw the two people between the cars pause. They looked slightly behind them, toward the far end of the parking lot away from the store, and then back to each other. Nadia noticed their expressions shift. Their body language became tight, and they stood up straighter, like they were preparing to make a move.

Suddenly, a large figure stalked across the lot toward the gas pump again. It was Emmett. He took long, heavy strides as he crossed behind the pumps, then turned and came in front of them. His head was turned toward the store, his eyes trained on the door. Nadia stepped back.

"Stay here," she said to the woman and walked around the counter to the phone.

"Who is that?" she asked.

"Just stay inside. If he starts toward the door, tell me."

She grabbed the phone and called the police.

"I need an officer at Mel's Corner Market on Poppy Bridge Road. There is a very angry-looking man walking around the parking lot intimidating my customers," she said to the dispatcher.

"Do you know who this man is?" the dispatcher asked.

"Yes, he is a regular customer."

"Have you had problems with him before?"

"Yes. Not like this, but there have been issues."

"Does he have any weapons on him?"

Nadia tried to keep her breath steady and not lash out at the woman she knew was just doing her job.

"I don't know. I'm inside the store with a customer who felt threatened by him. He's outside. I guess he could have a weapon, but I don't see anything," she said.

"I'll have officers out to you as soon as possible."

They didn't come fast enough. By the time the squad cars pulled into the parking lot, Emmett had already left. The two men standing between their cars talking had tried to tell him off, but it was threatening to call the police that got him moving. He didn't know Nadia had already called them. She was thankful they were trying to help her and was relieved he was gone. At the same time, she wished he had been there so the police could've confronted him.

The officers still took her statement, but it was obvious they were less inclined to take it seriously when they realized who she was. One of the officers had been there that night at the staged crime scene. Listening to the other customers describe Emmett's behavior seemed to make them more compassionate, but all they said was to call them again if he came back, and then they left.

Nadia was glad to have the day off the next day and pushed away her frustration and anger while getting Amelia ready for her first slumber party. Her daughter was so excited she didn't even seem concerned that it was going to be the first time that she would be sleeping away from her mother in her entire life. She just kept talking about all the fun things that she and Lacey would be doing and trying to figure out how many of her toys and stuffed animals she could stuff into her duffel bag to bring along with her.

After sending Amelia on her way, Nadia got dressed and took her time lingering over makeup and styling her hair. She had insisted on driving herself to the restaurant and smiled when she saw Lennon standing outside the door waiting for her when she arrived. He let his eyes move over her admiringly.

"You look gorgeous," he said.

"Thank you. You look really good yourself."

He did. In a pair of fitted slacks and a lightweight sweater, he looked sleek and put together without seeming fussy. He offered her his arm and escorted her into the restaurant. She was worried that she would feel awkward or out of place, but they fell into an easy, comfortable conversation as soon as they sat down. They laughed their way through appetizers and dinner and were waiting for their dessert when Nadia's phone buzzed. She didn't want to pick it up. She was too happy just enjoying her time with Lennon. But she was very aware of Amelia being at the sleepover and was worried that something might have happened.

"Go ahead," he said. "Your daughter comes first."

Her heart warmed, and she took the phone out of her bag. Opening it, she saw she had another text message.

Who is the guy you're with? What does he have that I don't? Let me show you what you are missing.

Another popped up on the screen.

I'm going to, whether you like it or not.

Nadia's mouth fell open, and she started shaking slightly.

"Nadia? Is everything okay? Is something wrong with your daughter?"

"No."

"What is it? What's wrong?"

She couldn't bring herself to answer until finally, Lennon reached across the table and took the phone from her hand. He looked at the screen, and his jaw hardened.

"What the hell is this? Who sent you this?" he asked.

"I don't know," she finally answered. "But it isn't the first time."

"What?"

The waiter came to the table with their dessert.

Lennon looked up at him and said, "Would you mind boxing these up to go please? And I'll take the check."

Nadia focused on her breathing, trying to get a hold of herself while he paid the bill. The waiter came back with their desserts, and Lennon stood up, coming over to her chair and taking her hand. Nadia let him help her out of the chair and lead her out of the restaurant. They walked around to the parking lot, and he brought her to her car.

"They put plastic forks in the bag. Do you want to sit in your car and talk?"

Nadia didn't want to say anything. She was overwhelmed, and part of her was even embarrassed. But she felt like she couldn't hold it in anymore. The center of her chest ached like it was going to crack open, and she just needed to get it out. They got in the car and opened the paper boxes with their desserts. As they ate, she told him the whole story. He stopped eating partway through, his eyes locked on her.

"And nobody's doing anything to help you?"

"The police said there wasn't anything they could do. I don't know who it is, and until something happens, they're kind of stuck," she said.

"That's bullshit," he said. "You shouldn't have to be worried for your physical safety before somebody comes in and stops this jackass."

"That's about how I feel too. I just don't know what I'm supposed to do. I have blocked every number that he messaged me from. I even changed my own phone number. Not that it does any good since my number is posted right there in the store for anybody to see."

"It is?"

"Yep. Right there on the board behind the counter. My manager posted it there when I took over the store. And when I changed my number, he changed the sign."

"That's asinine. Why would he do that?"

"He said I need to be available at all times because I'm responsible for the store. I need to be able to talk to vendors or customers. Anybody who needs something having to do with the store comes to me. Having my number there is a way to foster trust and show our commitment to the community," Nadia said.

"Then he needs to be providing you a work phone. There's no excuse for your personal contact information to be out in public like that. It's dangerous. You need to tell him what's going on and that you aren't going to have your number out in front of people like that." He took a breath. "I'm sorry. I shouldn't be telling you what to do."

"That's all right. You weren't saying anything that I don't know is true. But I can't bring myself to say anything to Mel. I am just really getting back on my feet after my divorce. Amelia and I went through so much with my ex. I was barely getting by, and things were really bad. But now I'm here, and I finally feel like I have a chance at some kind of life. And so does Amelia. I don't want to jeopardize that."

"I don't think you would lose your job because you would tell him that someone is harassing you."

"But I could. And it wouldn't just be losing my job. My ex is suddenly pushing to get my daughter. This is a man who has had almost nothing to do with her, but suddenly, he wants to play family man. And I would appreciate that sentiment. Really, I would. If I thought it was genuine. But I know him. And I know all he sees is a prop he can use to boost his reputation and be more appealing to family-focused companies he wants to do business with.

"And what scares me is he could walk into court and the judge could see him as a much more suitable parent. He has an extremely high-paying job. A gorgeous house. He has a family who lives close by. Compare that to living in a friend's basement and getting fired, and who do you think the courts would say she would be better off living with?" Nadia asked.

"That isn't going to happen," he said. "We're going to figure this out."

"I just feel like I can't take any more. It's too much."

"No, it's not. You're strong. You can handle this." He stopped for a second like he was thinking. "You know what? I'm gonna take you somewhere that is going to help you get all of that out."

Nadia could have kissed him. She very nearly did. "Thank you."

CHAPTER SEVENTEEN

ADIA LET OUT A PRIMAL SCREAM AND SWUNG THE BAT AS HARD
as she could. It came into contact with the tall, baby blue vase with
a satisfying smash. As she watched the shards rain down on the
floor and stomped down on them with one heavy boot, she turned and
walked up to another plinth. This one held a delicately curved floral
porcelain bowl. It shattered beneath the impact of her bat, and she felt
another rush of tension escape her body.

When everything in the room was in crumbled pieces on the floor,
she pushed the goggles back on top of her head and walked out. Several
rage rooms heavily stocked with extremely breakable objects and bats
were arranged around a circular room at the center of the building. Each
of the rooms had an observation window with an optional curtain that
could be pulled across it so the person inside could smash in privacy.

She had hers open, and Lennon was applauding when she walked
out. She leaned the bat up against the wall and took off the goggles.

"Looks like you understood your assignment," he said. "Do you feel better?"

Nadia kicked out of the heavy protective boots and unzipped the thick coveralls the company required her to wear.

"So much better. I had no idea places like this even existed," she said.

"They are a pretty good invention. I think everybody goes through times when they just want to smash the living hell out of something. This place lets you do it. There are even rooms here where you can bash up a car."

"That sounds like fun. Maybe next time," Nadia said.

Her phone rang in her bag, and their eyes met.

"Do you want me to answer it?" Lennon asked.

When she didn't answer, he picked up the phone and pressed the button to answer.

"Hello? Yeah, this is Nadia's phone. Who is this?" His eyes slid over to Nadia. He held the phone out to her. "It's Christy."

There was something in his voice that made Nadia nervous. She took the phone and walked over to the side of the room away from the others in the lobby.

"Christy? It's me. What's going on?"

"Who is that?" Christy asked.

"That was Lennon, the guy I met at the bar."

"Oh. Have you heard from Maren?"

Nadia knew the situation must be serious. Christy barely even reacted to the idea that she was out with a man.

"No. Not for the last couple of days. Why?"

"I haven't either. She was supposed to come over to my place last night, but she never showed up. I couldn't get her on her phone, and she never responded to any of my texts. Then she didn't come to work tonight. Mel hasn't heard from her," Christy said.

A shock of fear rushed through Nadia. She hurried back over to where her shoes were tucked into a cubby and shoved her feet into them.

"Are you still at the store?" she asked.

"Yeah. There isn't anybody else to work the shift. The store just reopened, and Mel hasn't replaced Joseph yet."

"Send me Maren's address. I'll go to her place and check on her."

She hung up, and Lennon gave her a questioning look.

"Maren? Your other friend?"

"Yeah. No one can get a hold of her and she didn't come in to work today. That isn't like her at all. I told you she's going through a rough time right now, and I am really worried about her. I need to go to her house and make sure that she's okay," Nadia said.

"Do you want me to go with you? I don't think you should go by yourself."

"I really appreciate it, but with what she's going through, I think she would really need to just see a familiar face."

"Are you working tomorrow?"

"Yes, I have the late shift."

"I'll come by and see you if that's all right," he said.

They were out of the building, and Nadia stopped with her hand on the car door handle.

She smiled at him. "I'd like that."

"Okay, I'll see you then. Be safe," he said.

Nadia got in the car and checked her messages. Christy had sent the address, and she put it into the GPS.

It was a ten-minute drive. She got there in seven. Within fifteen, the police were standing on Maren's front porch.

It was a chilly night, and Nadia hadn't brought a thick enough coat. She stood with her arms wrapped around herself, rubbing her shoulders, trying to get some heat to go through her body. Even if the friction had produced enough to warm her, she didn't think it would make a difference. Her blood was like ice.

The lights from the police cars swept across her face and cast an eerie glow on the front door of Maren's little white house. She answered their questions the best she could, but there was little for her to say. She didn't know Maren's family or any of her friends other than Christy and Smith. They never connected on social media, so she didn't even know if she had a page she kept up with regularly. She assumed either she didn't or there wasn't any information on it, because it would've been something Christy knew about and would have mentioned.

Christy arrived at the house an hour after Nadia did. Mel came in to cover for her so that she could leave, and she came right over. The police took her aside. Nadia guessed they were asking her the same questions. Looking over at her, all she saw was Christy shaking her head and occasionally wiping tears from under her eyes.

She had to stand there in the cold while they searched Maren's social media and Christy called every person she knew who would have had any contact with her. Nadia tried to help by calling Smith, the mechanic. He didn't know anything but offered to call her parents.

Finally, Christy reached into her purse and pulled out a key. "Look, I have a key to the house. She gave it to me when she was going out of town so I could keep an eye on it. Can I just go in?"

"An officer has to go with you."

"Fine."

Without waiting for anybody to go ahead of her, Christy rushed up to the front door and unlocked it. She stepped inside, and Nadia braced herself, not knowing what she was preparing for, but she didn't want to think any further than that. Nothing happened. She didn't hear a scream or any other reaction. Two more officers followed them inside, and a few minutes later, they all came back out.

"Nothing. She's not in there," Christy said.

"How about her phone?" Nadia asked.

"It's not there either."

"Which means she is probably off somewhere on her own accord," one of the officers said. "You both told me she is going through a rough breakup. She probably just needed to clear her head and wanted some time by herself."

"Her car is here," Christy pointed out.

"So she got a ride from somebody. This is an adult we're talking about. Adults are allowed to come and go as they please. They don't have to answer to anybody."

"But this isn't like her. She doesn't just miss work," Christy said.

"Maybe that's exactly why she's doing it. Because it isn't like her. She's going through a rough time and feels like her life is a mess. So she escapes it for a little while. Does something totally unexpected, just because she wants to. I get that you are worried about your friend. But right now, we just have a grown woman who isn't where people think she should be. Keep calling people she knows. Maybe visit some spots she likes. If you still don't hear from her in a couple of days, call us back."

Nadia went to bed that night feeling empty and afraid. She didn't feel any better the next morning or when she went to work. All day she waited for her phone to ring. She wanted it to be Maren explaining where she had gone. Or Christy saying that she posted something and everything was fine. But those calls never came. She had been at work for a few hours, going through the motions of her day, when she noticed a police car pull into the handicapped spot right in front of the door.

Officer Bertinelli walked in, his expression stern.

"Are there any customers here?"

Nadia pointed to the back of the store where a few people were milling around picking out snacks.

"As soon as you finish with them, you need to lock up the store and come with me."

Nadia blinked a few times, trying to process what he just said.

"Come with you? Why?"

"I'll explain then."

She got through ringing up all the customers, and as soon as the last one was through the door, she got her bag. She locked up but paused before following the officer to the car.

"I need to call Mel and let him know," she said.

"He already knows."

He opened the passenger side door for her, and Nadia climbed in, relieved that she wasn't in cuffs or sitting in the back. She didn't know what was going on, but at least it didn't seem like she was being brought into custody.

Nadia looked over at him after a few moments of driving in silence.

"Are you going to tell me what's going on? Where are we going?"

"To the hospital. Christy Carpenter was attacked."

CHAPTER EIGHTEEN

Emma

L ISA COMES OUT ONTO THE PORCH TO MEET ME BEFORE I EVEN GET out of the car. I hurry up the sidewalk toward her, and she comes down to gather me in a hug.

"Thank you so much for coming."

"Of course. It sounds like the situation has gotten a lot worse," I say.

"I'm really scared. I couldn't get her to agree to move somewhere on her own, but she did change her number. It didn't stop the messages. And now one of the women she worked with, the one who got her the job, is missing, and the other is in the hospital a bloody mess. I don't know what to do."

"You did what you could do. You called me," I say. "Can I talk to her?"

"Come on in."

We go into the house, and she leads me to the living room. The woman is sitting on the center cushion of the couch, bent over so her elbows are rested on her thighs, as she holds a mug between her palms. Her eyes are wide, unblinking, as she stares ahead of her like she is somewhere else.

"Nadia, Emma is here." Lisa looks over at me. "Can I get you a cup of tea?"

"That sounds good. Thanks."

She heads into the kitchen, and I walk over to the couch. I sit beside Nadia and tilt so I can look into her face.

"Nadia? I'm Emma. I think Lisa has told you about me."

Nadia's head bobs just enough for me to notice the movement.

"You're the FBI agent. You found her friend who went missing in college."

"She was my friend too," I say. "Still is. But I'm here to try to help you. Lisa explained what was going on with the calls and messages, but now she tells me that someone is missing and another friend of yours was hurt. Can you give me the details about that?"

Lisa comes back into the room with my tea as Nadia is telling me about her friends Maren and Christy. She starts to loosen up, and soon I can hear all the emotion in her voice. She is obviously stressed, overwhelmed, and afraid about what's happening. I listen closely so I can pick up every detail she's offering me.

"Tell me more about Maren's boyfriend," I say. "You said they were going through a rough breakup."

"They weren't going through it. She had cut him off at the knees. I really don't know much about him. I never actually met him. I know that his name is Ron, but she never mentioned his last name. I saw him the first night I was in town. It was across a parking lot, so I didn't speak to him or anything, but they looked really happy together. And I know she was completely wrapped up in him.

"She always talked about how wonderful he was and how good he was to her. He was even willing to listen to her talk about her ex and told her about the time some track runner in college ghosted him and totally broke his heart."

"So she was still dealing with feelings for an ex?" I ask.

"I don't know if I would exactly say it was feelings. More like just everything that comes with a breakup. She had gotten out of a long relationship I guess a few months or so before she met him. I think that made her even happier about feeling like she was in a good place. But she was also kind of cautious," Nadia says.

"What do you mean by that?"

"Maren was ready to get more serious than he was. She really wanted to introduce him to us and, I guess, make their relationship more public. It's not that it felt like it was a secret, but they weren't hanging out with each other's friends and meeting family or anything. She said he was just hesitant about taking things too quickly because of his own past relationships, and she was willing to respect that. Even though it got to her a little bit, she didn't want to rock the boat at all. And I think part of her was really aware that the relationship could be seen as a rebound."

"So if things were so good between them, what happened?" I asked.

"She found out he was already in a relationship when he started seeing her. Not only was he in a relationship, but that woman was married. So the whole time he was commiserating with her about broken hearts and relationship drama, he was cheating on her with a woman who was cheating on her husband. It really got to Maren. It just crushed her."

"Did she mention how he reacted to her breaking up with him?" I ask.

"Apparently, he tried to explain and was playing the victim card. It didn't impress her."

"But he wasn't violent or threatening?"

"Not that she mentioned," Nadia says.

"What have you been able to find out about your other friend?" I ask.

"Christy? Almost nothing. Her roommate found her on their back patio. She'd been beaten so badly that the roommate thought she was dead when she saw her. Apparently, the paramedics did too, and they were really surprised when they realized she was still breathing. They got her to the hospital and did surgery. She made it through and is in the ICU."

"No evidence of who it was?" I ask.

"If there was, they didn't mention it to me. I have to assume they think that it's connected to Maren."

"Why?" I ask.

"When Christy and I reported her missing, the police immediately tried to brush it off. They did the whole 'she's an adult and can go wherever she wants' thing. Her car was at her house, but her phone wasn't. They took that as evidence she'd gotten a ride somewhere and was just off somewhere dealing with the breakup and would be back when she felt like it. But then when Christy was attacked, an officer came to my work and took me to the hospital. He was asking me about Christy and if I knew anything about what happened to her, but it felt like he was keeping an eye on me. If they didn't think her attack had anything to do with Maren, why would they think it had anything to do with me?"

"That's a good point," I say. "It sounds like there might be something they aren't saying right now. I'll talk to the investigators and see if they will share with me as a professional courtesy. It doesn't mean I'll be able to tell you, but it might help me better understand what's going on. But you don't know any other details? Did you talk to her roommate and find out anything else?"

"She just said that she came home from work and couldn't find Christy in the house. She noticed the back sliding door was open and went to close it, but she saw Christy on the ground with blood everywhere. She didn't see a weapon, and there was no sign of forced entry into the house. The door was open, but it wasn't broken, and the lock was still intact," Nadia says.

"So maybe it was someone she knew," I say.

"Lyle," Nadia says.

"Lyle? Who is that?"

"A guy she had been seeing who she wasn't seeing anymore. He was not happy about it and actually came to my store really angry trying to find her. Another customer—the man I'm seeing now, as a matter of fact—had to tell him to leave."

"And you are seeing this man now?" I ask.

"We met before that happened," she tells me.

"Okay. And you don't know if the police have talked to Lyle?" I ask.

"I don't. I told them to. Even Christy's roommate told them to."

"You went to the police about the phone calls and messages you were getting, right?"

"I did, but nothing came of it," she says.

"Did you tell Maren and Christy about them?"

"Yes, after a while."

"After I talked to you," Lisa says. "And I called you as soon as she told me."

"Other than Lennon, they are the only ones I told. And I only told him because I got one of the texts while I was out to dinner with him, and it kind of pushed me over the edge," Nadia says.

"Is there anything else? Did Maren ever talk about places she especially wanted to visit or people she wanted to see? Did Christy have other men she was seeing who could have been violent?" I ask.

"The only person Maren really ever talked about other than Ron was her aunt who taught her to play cards. And Smith. He's a mechanic in the area, and they've been friends their whole lives."

"And Christy?"

"She's always seeing men. More than one. Maren warned her about Lyle and said he had a bad past, but she didn't seem worried about the other ones. Her roommate and I told the police everything we knew about the other guys in her life," she says.

"All right. I appreciate you telling me all of that. I'm going to go talk to the investigators and see what else I can find out. I'll be back later. Again, I can't promise I'll be able to tell you anything, but I promise that anything I can tell you, I will."

Lisa walks me to the door, and I hand her my empty mug.

"Thank you again for doing this," she says.

"Don't thank me quite yet. I haven't done anything other than drive here. I don't know if there's anything I can do. But I'm going to try."

"That means a lot."

CHAPTER NINETEEN

"**A**GENT EMMA GRIFFIN," I SAY, HOLDING OUT MY HAND TO THE detective who comes out to the lobby to meet me. I notice he's carrying a slim stack of folders with him.

"Detective Hawke. Glad to meet you, Agent. Come with me. We'll go talk in the back."

He doesn't seem surprised that I'm here or ask why, which makes me curious. Usually, police officers are more interested when a federal agent shows up at their department. I follow him down a long hallway, and he gestures into a fluorescent-lit lounge.

"Coffee?"

"I'm okay, thanks."

"Mind if I grab a cup? I'm not running on a lot of sleep," he says.

"Go ahead."

I wait in the hallway while he pours himself a cup of coffee and adds a long stream of sugar. Swirling a stirring stick around in the cup, he comes back out into the hallway and continues walking. I follow him to a room furnished with a couple of sofas and well-worn armchairs.

"I don't have an office of my own, but I like to claim this spot for when I talk to people," he says.

"It's a good one."

"Go ahead and have a seat. I know the chief talked about getting some help with this case, but I didn't realize you were going to get here so fast," he says.

I narrow my eyes at him, even more confused now.

"I think I must have missed something," I say.

"The Bureau didn't send you?" he asks.

"No. I am an FBI agent, but I came because a friend called me asking for help. I was hoping to find out what you can tell me about Maren Honeycutt's disappearance and the attack on Christy Carpenter."

A strange smile comes to the detective's lips, and he tosses the folders down on the table in front of the couch where I'm sitting.

"The Bureau might not have sent you, but maybe somebody's guardian angel did. Take a look."

I pick up the top folder and open it. A picture of a smiling young woman attached with a paper clip to the documents inside has a name across the bottom.

"This is Maren Honeycutt," I say.

"Yes, it is. She's the case I thought you were here to help with," Detective Hawke says.

"I don't understand," I say. "She only went missing a few days ago. I just spoke with Nadia Holmes, and she told me the official word right now is that she left on her own."

"That isn't the official word. It's just what she knows. And that is what the officers thought right after she was reported missing. Until yesterday, when her body was found in the desert."

I look further in the folder and find a series of crime scene images. They show the woman from the first picture. She's no longer smiling. Her body is sprawled in the dirt, her face unrecognizable.

"Geez," I say.

"Someone beat her head in with something hard. Possibly a tire iron or crowbar. She's covered in injuries, including a fracture in her ankle and her arm. The medical examiner found gravel in some of the scrapes. Not consistent with any of the dirt around her."

"She rolled across the road," I say.

He nods. "Blood was found on a nearby road. There were two sets of footprints in the area. As injured as she was, she ran for her life. This crossed state lines and shows all the hallmarks of an abduction."

"So we *are* in Bureau territory now," I say.

"If you're willing. Give me the word, and we're on board."

"Let me make a call."

Eric is not as immediately enthusiastic about the idea of me getting involved as I hoped he would be. Not that I actually thought he would be, but I choose to maintain hope sometimes.

"Do you have any idea how much work you are already doing?" he asks.

"Um, yes. Funnily enough, I am aware of the amount of work I am dealing with."

"Then why would you want to add something else? I already had to promise Sam I would call you at regular intervals to make sure you are doing things like drinking water and touching grass."

"I already have Xavier for that," I say.

"No. You have Xavier to call you at regular intervals to make sure you are doing things like getting your daily hydration by catching snowflakes on your tongue—while trying to figure out what crystalline form they have—and touching ancient relics that threatened to get you thrown out of national museums."

"He only did that once, and the security guard chose to look the other way," I say.

"My point is, there is already so much on your plate."

"I know. But I'm waiting for things like test results and records. Camera footage. I'm essentially in a holding pattern until something else comes up. And right now, this case needs me."

"Give me a brief overview—and I mean genuinely brief," he says.

"You are in a salty mood today," I say.

"Yes, I am. I just had an agent decide he was going to try his very best to be James Bond by falling for a woman who was just so very fascinated by his big, manly job she wanted to hear every detail about his eighteen-month-long undercover investigation."

"I'm not sure what that has to do with James Bond. Serious problem though. Did you manage to save it?"

"Yes, but it left me salty. Brief overview. Go."

I'm able to tell him enough about the case in three sentences for him to give me the go-ahead. I know him well enough to know he is not thrilled about it. But he knows me well enough to know I won't let it go.

Those are the perks of working with one of the best friends you have had your entire adult life.

I go back to the room with Detective Hawke and sit down.

"You've got me. Tell me everything you know."

We move into a conference room where I can settle in and spread out. Hanging my jacket on the back of the chair, I open the folders he gave me and scan them quickly. I notice one of them is for the attack on Christy.

"Nadia Holmes told me that she and Christy's roommate both mentioned a former boyfriend of Christy's who could be somebody to look at in her attack."

"Lyle Turner. He was the first person both of them mentioned. But he couldn't have had anything to do with her attack. He was in jail at the time."

"Well, that'll do it. What was he in for?"

"Assault," the detective tells me.

"Not a great look, but if the timing doesn't line up, then he's out of the running. Was any other evidence gathered from the scene? Fingerprints on the door or anything?"

"The only fingerprints on the sliding glass door belonged to Christy and her roommate. At first, that did seem strange because Christy apparently had men over pretty often, and Maren Honeycutt had also been there recently. But apparently, they had cleaned the house that morning before the roommate went to work. That included cleaning the door. Which means Christy's fingerprints got on it when she opened the door to go out to the patio, and her roommate's got there when she went outside looking for Christy."

"And I suppose it would be too much to ask for there to be security cameras on the back of the house?"

"You can always ask, but in this case, no. We've surveyed the neighbors, and none of them have doorbell cameras either."

"So no fingerprints. No pictures or video. No eyewitnesses. And yet, it's here right alongside Maren's file. Is that because you believe they are connected?" I ask.

"Even without specific evidence, the fact that these two women were close friends and worked in the same place and one ended up murdered and the other nearly there… I don't think it's a leap to connect the two."

"Not at all. What about Nadia Holmes? She was friends with both women. Worked with both of them. And she is on record reporting harassing and threatening phone calls and text messages to officers."

"As far as anybody knows, neither Maren nor Christy had any kind of communication like that. Right now, the issue we're running into is there aren't many links among these women. Other than each other and their workplace."

"Which opens up a long list of links," I point out. "Have you looked into Smith? Nadia didn't give me his last name. He's a mechanic who Maren knew well. I would think that means it's likely Christy also knew him."

"I talked to him about Maren's disappearance before her body was found. He was completely cooperative and really upset about the situation. He provided receipts to show that he was working around the time the medical examiner believes she would have been left in the desert. There's no way he could have gotten that far out and back and still done all those jobs. I haven't talked to him about Christy."

"When were you planning on releasing the information about Maren's death?" I ask.

"Because she has no surviving family, there was no next of kin to notify. I made a strategic decision to keep her death confidential for now in hopes of getting more information from potential suspects."

"That can work," I say, "but it's not something that you can drag out. A statement needs to be made as soon as possible. Details about the cause of death can and should be kept confidential, but if you don't announce her death, you risk coming across as shady or like you're trying to cover something up. I'm assuming you have been in contact with the police department with jurisdiction over the place where she was found?"

"Yes. We have agreed to work in conjunction with each other. I can get you the contact information for the detective in charge of the case there. Sloane Collins."

"Thanks."

He gets me the information for the other police department, and I keep going over everything he gave me about Maren's death. She went through something horrific. From the injuries identified on her body and the way she was found, it looks like she suffered a prolonged, torturous ordeal. She would have been in excruciating pain and terrified. Abrasions on her skin different from the ones caused by skidding across the pavement are consistent with carpet burns. This is a strong indicator she spent some time in a trunk.

This file doesn't contain anything about her phone or financial records, so I'll have to ask the detective in the other department about it. I'm hoping they've already started the process of requesting the information so it can be accessed sooner. It may contain critical details that could help create a timeline of her movements and narrow down who could be responsible.

"The only information you have in here about the man she had been dating is his first name," I point out later.

"That's all we know about him. We can't seem to find any other information. Not even his last name."

"I guess that's one way to stay under the radar when you're palling around with a married woman and have another girl on the side," I say. "Stay as anonymous as you can. I know how his college girlfriend broke up with him, but not his last name."

"Want to order some lunch? It's getting kind of late."

"Thanks, but I'm going to see if I can get in touch with Detective Collins and find out what I can from her. Then I need to talk to Nadia some more about the messages and phone calls she was getting. Even if that's not connected to the other two women, whoever is behind it needs to be stopped."

CHAPTER TWENTY

Detective Collins offers to video call with me, and I take her up on it. I don't have my computer, so I'll have to do it on my phone, but the awkwardness of holding the phone and the weird closeup visual is worth getting more information more efficiently.

The call connects, and a striking woman with chestnut curls framing her face waves at me.

"Agent Griffin, nice to meet you," she says.

"Emma," I say.

"Sloane. I have to say, I'm really excited to have the opportunity to work with you."

"Thank you," I say. "It's always nice to see another woman in law enforcement."

"Yes, it is."

"I've gone over what Detective Hawke had regarding Maren's murder. Are there any other details you have that you can share with me?"

Sloane describes how scavenger birds in the area caught the attention of a passing motorist. They stopped to investigate and discovered the body. Due to the extreme nature of the injuries to her head, there was no way to immediately identify her. The medical examiner was only able to conclusively find out who she was by the serial number on a plate in her jaw. Without giving any specific details about the victim or what happened to her, the police did a press release asking for any information anybody might have.

"A lot of tips came in that didn't have anything to do with the murder at all. Either they were totally made up for the thrill of giving information or people saw things they misinterpreted. There was only one reliable tip."

"Who did that come from?" I ask.

"A 911 dispatcher."

That's not what I was expecting to hear.

"A 911 dispatcher?"

"A call came in from what sounded like a young woman in serious distress. She couldn't say where she was and wasn't able to give any clear information about what was happening to her. But the dispatcher knew she was in extreme danger. They weren't able to trace the call, and it dropped. They tried to call back, but it wouldn't connect. Since they weren't able to determine where the call was coming from, they didn't know where to send officers.

"As soon as I heard that, I knew what she was talking about. Several cars were sent out to different areas to try to find an unknown caller in mortal danger. They did everything they could to try to figure out where she could be based on the things she said and what the dispatcher heard, but they didn't find anything. One pair of officers was almost there. They were in the vicinity. But because the body was so far off the road and hidden behind a pile of brush, they didn't know.

"No one involved in the search, the dispatcher or the officers, knew what to think. The dispatcher said it seemed completely legitimate. The woman sounded terrified and like she was in really serious danger. But because they weren't able to find anything or get back in touch with the caller, there was the possibility it was a hoax. When she heard about the body being found, though, she knew that it was the caller. Making that connection provided us a clearer window of the time of death."

"And confirmed she was being hunted when she died," I say. "The injuries on the body are consistent with impact on pavement at speed."

"Right. She was either pushed or fell from a car," Sloane says. "While it was moving."

"The trunk," I specify. "I noticed carpet burns noted on the postmortem."

"Those could have come from being captive in a carpeted room."

"The type of burn was more indicative of a very dense pile. Not the kind of carpet that is found in houses. It could be industrial carpeting like in an office building, but because the report specifically said that the burns looked fresh and had fibers embedded in them, I think it's a lot more likely that they happened within very close proximity to the other injuries.

"Add to that the scrapes on her hand and arm, and my theory is she broke out a backlight and reached through it. Then she released the trunk and jumped out. But the impact itself didn't kill her, and she wasn't beaten immediately after. The call to emergency services proves that. She was trying to get away from whoever had her. There was a chase, then she was bludgeoned. The crime scene picture of her body didn't seem to show enough blood to justify the type of injuries she had. She was killed somewhere else and then dumped behind the bush."

"Damn," Sloane says. "I heard you were good, but that was incredible."

"Thanks, but I wasn't just having a Sherlock moment. That was all for a purpose. You said some of the officers who went out looking for the caller that night got close to where Maren's body was found. She was clearly not dead when she made that phone call, and the blood that showed where she fell out of that trunk was not anywhere near where her body was found. Which means that there was a fairly long pursuit. The person who had her did not just kill her quickly and get out of the area.

"Did the officers who got close to where her body was found, or any of the other officers, encounter anybody that night? Did they do a traffic stop or a suspicious activity check? Did they speak to anybody while they were looking for the woman who made that call?"

I can see the gears turning in Sloane's head.

"Can you give me just a second?"

"Sure."

She gets up and disappears from the frame, leaving only an empty chair. It takes a few minutes, but then she's back with a new folder in her hand.

"Yes," she says. "They did. But it was never connected to the situation. The officers who were in the area closest to where the body was found talked to a man at a truck stop about two miles away from where she was found. He was sitting out at a picnic table, which is what got their attention at first because it was the middle of the night. But they realized he was eating, and he explained he'd been on the road all day and night. They asked if he saw any cars traveling in that area or if he'd noticed anything unusual. He said he hadn't in the time since he stopped."

"Did they check his ID?" I ask.

"No."

I drop my head back. "Great."

"But they did take a picture."

I look at her again. "Of the man?"

"No. Of a car they saw in the parking lot."

She moves papers around in the folder and takes out a picture. Holding it up to the camera, she shows me a sedan without license plates. One of the backlights is broken out.

"How quickly can you get security footage from that truck stop?"

Detective Hawke comes back into the room shortly after I finish my call with Sloane. He's carrying a white paper bag and a takeout cup.

"I know you said you weren't hungry, but I couldn't resist showing off my favorite restaurant in town. Do you like roast beef?"

"Not as much as my husband does, but I am pretty convinced no human likes roast beef as much as my husband does," I say.

"Try this. You will be right up there with him."

I take the bag and pull out a wax paper–wrapped sandwich. It does smell incredible.

"Thank you." I take a bite and nod. "That's really good."

"Told you."

"I know I said you need to report Maren's death as soon as possible, but I'd like the chance to tell Nadia before it hits the news. She deserves to find out from someone personally rather than having to hear it on TV," I say. "I know she's working tonight, so I'll talk to her in the morning. It can be on the news tomorrow night."

He nods. "I'll put together the release."

CHAPTER TWENTY-ONE

Nadia

I T DIDN'T FEEL RIGHT BEING AT WORK. WITH MAREN MISSING AND Christy lying broken and battered in the hospital, fighting to survive the brutal attack, Nadia felt uneasy and out of place. She did everything she could to fill the time. She was thankful for every customer who came in and talked with her. It was obvious who paid attention to the local news. They were the ones who looked at her with something bordering on pity in their eyes.

They knew about the disappearance and the attack. They knew something was going on with the women who worked at Mel's, and each of them looked at Nadia like they were waiting for what was going to happen to her. There was sympathy from some of them. She didn't know if it was sympathy because of what she was going through with her friends or because they had already come to the conclusion that she was next. Others looked at her almost like she was a novelty.

She waited for Lennon to get there from the time that she walked through the door. It took far longer than she would have wanted it to, but finally, he came through the door. She surprised herself by rushing around the counter and wrapping her arms around him. He reciprocated, pulling her close and resting his head against hers when she burrowed her face into his neck.

"Did you hear anything else about Christy?" he asked.

Nadia shook her head and stepped back from him. "No, she's still the same."

"She's going to be all right. They're taking good care of her."

"What about Maren? She's still missing. What if something happened to her? What if the same person who has been..."

He took her by her shoulders and tilted his face enough to look her directly in the eyes. "You can't let yourself think that way."

"It won't stop. I blocked the numbers. I changed mine. The messages keep coming. It's like the harder I try to make them go away, the more they come. And I can't turn my phone off because I have to stay accessible. And now both Maren and Christy..."

Lennon drew her into another hug. "It's going to be fine."

She wished he could stay all night, but soon the customers started showing up again, and he needed to leave. She promised to message him when she got home to let him know she was safe, and he left. As the night wore on, the number of customers dwindled, and as much as she appreciated the voices and presence of other people when she first got to work, it was a relief when it was over. There was still another hour or so before she would close up for the night, and she started her list of tasks to finish the day.

The sound of her phone ringing startled her.

She rushed over to it, hoping that maybe this was what she had been waiting for. Maybe something about Maren or an update from Christy's doctor. Instead, when she took her phone out of her bag, she saw the number for the motel on the screen.

"Hello?"

"Hi. I just got this number from the motel office. I hope I'm calling the right person." The voice sounded gravelly, like the man speaking had a sore throat.

Nadia realized this was one of those times when she was supposed to be readily available.

"Yes. I am working at the other store location tonight, but can I help you?"

"I just want a room for the night. Is there anything available?"

"Yes," Nadia said. "I'm sorry no one's there to help you right now. I can head over, but it will be a little bit of a wait."

"That's perfectly fine. I'm just exhausted and glad I found a place to stop for the night. I'll just wait in my car."

"I appreciate it. I'll be there soon."

There was still some time that the store should be open, but Nadia closed it up. She wasn't going to go all the way to the motel and check this person in and then come back here for just a few minutes. It was late, but she still called Mel on the way to the store.

"I thought you cleared out the motel," she said when he answered sounding groggy.

"Nadia?"

"I thought that when you closed the store because of Maren and Christy, you had the motel guests leave," she said.

"I did. But I can't just have most of my business shut down for some indeterminate amount of time. I still have to make a living. And there are people who need somewhere to stop at night. So I decided to open back up. Just the motel for now," he said.

"Were you going to tell me? I'm currently hauling ass over there because I just got a call from somebody wanting a room."

"I told you that you needed to be accessible whenever you were needed. That is part of the responsibility of being a manager. You said you could handle it. Now, I know you're going through a difficult time. But you still need to take care of your daughter. And maintaining the business is good for both of us," he said.

For the first time since meeting him, Nadia felt a wave of disgust toward Mel. He was acting like he was struggling, like these two were his only stores and it was a major hardship to have one closed. She was sure he had noticed the reduced revenue from having the original shutdown, but he had plenty more businesses to keep him afloat.

She ended the call and pulled into the parking lot. Even though it was closed, the lights were on inside the store. Nadia had spent enough time working at a grocery store as a teenager to know that keeping the lights on even in a closed business was an important security measure. Often insurance companies required it. Despite knowing that, there was still a little part of her that looked through the windows, half expecting to see Maren and Christy inside.

Driving around to the back of the store, she looked for a car. She didn't see one, and the familiar creeping feeling started up her spine. She drove around to the back of the motel and finally saw a small, dark-colored vehicle parked in the corner. She rolled her window down and waved. The other car's window rolled down.

"Come on inside, and I'll get you registered," she called.

She drove back around to the front of the motel and pulled into the first spot. There was a key to the motel office on the same ring that had the keys to her store, and she went inside. She was bent over the computer trying to get it started when she heard the door open.

"Give me just another second. Sometimes this computer has a bit of trouble waking up."

"Don't we all?"

It was the same voice she heard over the phone, but the rough tone was even more pronounced. She lifted her head to smile and caught a glimpse of dark eyes and a thick mustache before the man's hand flicked the light switch down.

The sudden darkness was such a shock Nadia didn't know what to do.

"Could you turn that back on?" she asked.

The man didn't answer but advanced toward her. There was no time to react, nowhere to go. The desk was positioned in a way that only created one entrance to the space behind it, and before she could try to get out, he was blocking her way. She tried to scramble up onto the desk to go over it and head for the door, but he lunged forward and grabbed her around the waist.

Nadia cried out as he yanked her down from the desk and tossed her against the wall like a ragdoll. The glass was designed not to break, so she just slammed into it and dropped to the floor. Rather than standing up, she tried to crawl in the direction of the door. The man was too fast for her. He scooped her up and threw her again. There was enough light coming from outside for her to see the shapes of the objects inside the office. She knew she was right next to the full-length mirror.

When he came at her again, she pulled her bent arm forward and smashed her elbow into the glass. This time she heard the sound of shattering. A piece cut into her elbow, but she didn't stop. She grabbed the biggest shard from the floor and bounded to her feet. He seemed surprised by her sudden boldness and wasn't prepared for the hard kick she planted into his stomach. He bucked forward, and she weaved around him to head for the door.

His hand clamped around her hair and flung her to the floor. Nadia clutched the glass tighter and swung it, trying to make contact with him any way she could. He still had his hand tangled in her hair and used it to slam her head into the ground. The pain was dizzying, and Nadia tasted blood. For a few stunned seconds, she couldn't move. A sharp sensation in her side broke through the haze. In a surreal moment that almost felt like she wasn't in her own body, Nadia realized the man had stabbed her.

She wasn't going to give him the satisfaction of going gently.

With every bit of strength she could muster, she kicked up with both legs, making contact with his chest. He stumbled back, hitting his head on the desk. It stunned him long enough for Nadia to run. She got out of the office and dived toward her car. He was right behind her. She couldn't get the door closed before he wrenched it from her hand and pulled it open. Nadia kicked him away, but she knew she wasn't going to be able to get the car started in time. He was already trying to pull her out.

She crawled across the car and out the passenger door. Her legs nearly buckled under her as she started to run, but she managed to stay on her feet. As she ran around the side of the store, she grabbed the keys out of her pocket. She unlocked the door and darted inside. She ran for the office and threw herself inside, locking the door behind her. She heard his hands slam against the door an instant later.

Nadia shoved the couch until it was across the door and dropped down to the floor, crawling under the desk and curling into a ball. She felt for her phone in her pocket and realized it was gone. It had fallen out at some point. The sound of his hands pounding on the door in her ears, she reached up for the phone on the desk. When she brought it to her ear, there was nothing. The phone was dead.

She pushed herself further back into the corner, still clutching the glass. It had cut deep into her hand, and blood was running down her wrist and onto the floor. Headlights washed through the window above her head. The pounding stopped, and she heard footsteps retreating from the door. Moments later, she heard a woman's voice calling from inside the store.

"Hello? Is anyone here?"

Nadia wanted to answer. But she couldn't bring herself to move from the corner. She couldn't force her own voice out of her throat. She knew it was ridiculous, but she willed the woman to come find her. To call for help. At the same time, the thought of the woman being in the store with the man still close by made her feel sick. Nadia clutched the glass tighter.

Run.

CHAPTER TWENTY-TWO

Emma

'M STILL AWAKE AT THE HOTEL WHEN LISA CALLS. I'M SHOCKED TO see her name on the screen. I've never known her to be this much of a night owl.

"Lisa?"

"I'm sorry to call you so late," she says.

"No, it's fine. I'm still up."

"I'm really worried. Nadia didn't come home from work."

My heart gives a hard pound in the center of my chest.

"When was she supposed to be there?" I ask.

"Over an hour ago. I tried to call her, but she wasn't answering. I called the store, but she didn't answer there either. I'm really scared," she says.

"Do you have the number for the owner of the store?"

"I can find it."

"Call him," I say. "See if he's heard from her. I'm going to head for the store."

I put on a pair of leggings and a sweatshirt after my shower earlier, and I don't bother to change out of it. I just shove my feet into my boots and run out of the room. I am a few minutes down the road when Lisa calls me again.

"She went to the other store," she tells me. "The other location. Somebody called looking for a room, and she went to check them in. Mel said he's going to go up there."

"No. Call him back," I say, turning around to head for the other store. "Tell him not to go. I'm heading that way."

I end the call and immediately call Detective Hawke.

"I'm sorry to call you so late," I say.

"I think technically, it's early," he says, sleep still trying to hold onto him. "What's going on?"

"I'm requesting backup. I wanted to contact you directly."

I fill him in on the situation, and he tells me he's going to get officers to meet both of us there. It's only a few minutes further to the store, and I know I'm going to get there before the detective or officers. I pull into the parking lot and don't see any cars. Driving around to the back, I notice a car sitting by the motel office. The lights are off in the office, unlike the store, but it's the doors of the car standing open that set me on edge.

To make sure I am fully aware of my surroundings, I drive around the rest of the motel. There are no other cars parked in the lot. Going back to the front of the store, I park and take out my gun before climbing out. I walk up to the door and try it. It isn't locked. Stepping inside, I call out to Nadia.

"Nadia? Are you in here? It's Emma."

I notice a few crumpled bills lying on the counter. It looks like someone came into the store wanting to buy something but there was no one to help them. This only makes the worry twist tighter in my stomach. I look around the store for any indication of a struggle. It only takes a second for me to notice the blood on the floor.

A footprint has smeared some, but I see several more drops leading further into the store. It's hard to imagine anyone not noticing the blood on the floor, but I immediately think of Xavier and his rage against mannequins. Not really mannequins themselves—just how often people say they thought they saw a mannequin when it was actually a body.

In Xavier's words—it is never a mannequin.

People don't just find mannequins lying around. Yet that's the first thought that comes into people's minds. Because they don't want to think they are looking at a dead person. Just like they wouldn't want to think they are looking at blood.

Whoever came in was comfortable enough to pick something out and pay for it. They wouldn't have done that if they thought they were walking across blood on the floor. Regardless of how strange they must have thought it was that no one was there to help them, their minds told them there was something else on the floor.

But I know what it is. And I am afraid I know where it's coming from.

"Nadia!" I call out again, following the blood to the back of the store.

It stops in front of a door marked as the office, but there are more streaks across the knob and the door itself. I don't touch the knob but knock on the door.

"Nadia? Are you in there? Can you hear me? It's Emma. If you're in there, let me know."

Out of the corner of my eye, I see the lights from the squad cars coming into the parking lot. As I hear the officers run inside, a soft voice comes through the office door.

"Emma?"

"Nadia! Are you all right?"

"I think so. Is it really you?"

"Yes, it's me. I am here with police officers. Can you open the door?" I ask.

"Agent Griffin?" an officer calls out.

"I'm back here. Near the office."

I hear a scraping sound from inside the office, and then the lock clicks. Two officers show up in the short hallway leading to the office just as the door opens a few inches and Nadia peers out. She looks at me for a beat, like she isn't completely convinced that it is me. Her eyes slide over to the officers.

"Is she okay?" Nadia asks.

The question sends a shiver along my spine.

"Who?" I ask.

"There was a woman. I heard her. Is she okay?" Nadia asks.

I fill my lungs, feeling a slight bit of relief.

"There is money on the counter. No one else is here or anywhere near the motel. There aren't any other cars. I think she came in and bought something, then left. We will put out a public plea to ask her to come forward just so we can make sure that she is okay. But I believe she's fine. What I'm worried about right now is you. Can you come out?"

The door opens slowly, and Nadia reluctantly steps out of the office. I immediately notice the blood on her hands and up her arm. There's something clutched in her hand. I realize it is a large shard of glass. I look over at one of the officers.

"Get an ambulance started."

I make the decision not to pry any further into what happened until I know Nadia is stable. While she is standing on her own accord and looks to be in relatively good condition with the exception of the cuts and some swelling to her face, the full extent of trauma isn't always immediately visible. I want to make sure she is safe and in a controlled environment before I try to get more information from her. Right now, she needs support and reassurance.

It doesn't take long for the ambulance to arrive, and the paramedics to quickly look over Nadia. She doesn't want to put down the glass, but I gradually convince her to hand it to me.

"Do you want me to ride with you?" I ask.

She nods, and I follow her and the paramedics outside. I wait as they load her onto a gurney and get her settled, then climb up into the ambulance with her. Detective Hawke arrives just before they close the doors.

"What can I do?" he asks.

"I want every inch of this place searched. Get everything you can. Find her phone."

The ambulance door closes, and we head for the hospital. I go to the waiting room as they bring her into the back to check her over. While I wait, I call Lisa to let her know what's going on.

"I'm on my way," she says.

"No. You don't need to do that. Right now, there isn't anything you can do. She's back with the doctors, and once she is ready, I'm going to be questioning her. It's very late, and I'm sure Amelia is worried. The best thing you can do is stay there with her. I will let you know as soon as I know anything else," I tell her.

"This was Brent. Her ex-husband. I know it was," she says. I can hear the tears in her voice.

"We will look into Brent. Right now, we can't come to any conclusions."

I'm off the phone for a few minutes when it rings again.

"It's Hawke," the detective says when I answer. "I got her phone."

"Is it intact?"

"Yeah. It looks like it just fell out of her pocket. I have the CSU coming out to process her car for fingerprints and blood. It looks like whatever went down, at least partially, it happened in the motel office. There's a broken mirror and some blood."

"From the looks of Nadia, I would venture to say quite a bit of it is hers. But maybe we'll get lucky and get some from the perp as well. I need you to contact Mel and let him know what's going on. Have him come out there and give you access to the motel rooms. Nadia mentioned hearing a woman while she was in the office. There was money left on the counter, so I'm hoping she just came through and left without knowing anything was going on, but we need to make sure she isn't in one of those rooms."

Just as I'm finishing my call with the detective, a doctor comes out of the back of the emergency room.

"Are you here with Nadia Holmes?" she asks.

"Yes. Agent Emma Griffin, FBI," I say.

"Dr. Lamont. I just completed my initial exam. She has some cuts and scrapes. The one in the palm of her hand is quite deep and is being stitched up right now. There was some glass in a couple of the wounds, and she told me it was from a broken mirror. She's also being treated for a stab wound to her side."

"Is it serious?" I ask.

"It could be a lot worse. But yes. Right now, she's still running on adrenaline, so I don't think she has fully processed the severity of it. The rest of her injuries are bumps and bruises. She got battered pretty badly. But I'm confident she's going to pull through."

"Good. When can I talk to her?" I ask.

"We need to finish up her stitches and get more medication going. We're going to transfer her to another floor and admit her. She'll need to be here for at least a couple of days. Once she's settled, I'll let you know," Dr. Lamont says.

"Thank you."

She goes back to the large door and scans the ID around her neck to release the magnetic locks. I know it could take quite a bit of time for them to get her fully admitted onto another floor. The time is starting to wear on me, but I'm not going anywhere. Without knowing exactly which floor they're going to put her on, I don't have much of a choice but to stay here in the emergency room and wait. Even the hospital cafeteria will most likely not be open for another couple of hours. I settle for a cup of coffee from the station in another corner of the waiting room and pace as I drink it.

Almost an hour later, a nurse comes out to get me. She escorts me up to the fourth floor and into a room. Nadia is in a gown, tucked into the bed. Her head rests back against a stack of pillows, and an IV pumps fluids into her arm. She's been cleaned up, but her skin is still tinted with blood. Thick bandages protect the wound on her hand.

"Nadia?"

She lifts her head and opens her eyes. "Emma."

I smile and take another step forward. "How are you doing?" I give a short laugh. "Don't you hate when people ask you that when the answer is so obvious? It's what my friend Xavier would call a conversational social expectation."

"He sounds like a barrel of laughs," Nadia says weakly.

"You'd be surprised. Do you mind if I sit?"

"No."

Her head drops back against the pillows again, and she turns it so she can look at me as I sit in the chair I pull up to the side of the bed. The smell of gauze and antiseptic is strong. It brings back waves of memories I push down.

"First, I want you to know, Lisa is taking care of Amelia. I told her I would get in touch with her later and let her know what was going on," I say.

"Thank you," she says.

"As soon as I told her what happened, the first thing she said was that it was your ex-husband."

"No, it wasn't Brent," Nadia says. She sounds adamant. There isn't a shred of hesitation or uncertainty in her voice.

"Do you know who it was? Did you see his face?"

Her eyes narrow slightly, then widen.

"Ron."

"Ron? Maren's boyfriend?" I ask.

"Yes." Her head pops up, and the expression on her face becomes frantic. "You have to find her. He did this. He has her. You have to find her."

I draw in a breath and reach out to rest my hand on hers in a comforting gesture. This isn't the way I wanted to do this, but I don't have a choice now.

"Nadia, Maren was found," I say.

"Where is she? Is she here? Is she all right?" she asks.

"I'm so sorry. She's dead."

Nadia's mouth falls open. Tears create a sparkling veil over her eyes, then overflow and stream down her cheeks. For a second, she doesn't move or make any noise. Then her head gives a couple of fast, small shakes like she's refusing to accept what I said.

"She can't be."

"I'm sorry."

"What happened to her?" she asks.

"I'm not going to get into that right now. What matters at this moment is understanding exactly what happened to you and trying to find who did it," I say.

"It was Ron. I'm telling you, it was him."

"I thought you said you never met him," I say.

"I didn't. But I saw him across the parking lot the first night I was in town. And she showed me a picture of him. Dark hair and a thick mustache."

"What about his eyes?" I ask.

"I don't know for sure. I was too far away the first time I saw him, and he was wearing ski goggles in the picture. But tonight they were dark."

"Probably brown?"

"Yeah." She starts crying harder. "I can't believe this is happening. I can't believe she's gone."

"I know this is extremely difficult for you. And I'm sorry I'm having to ask you these questions and make you go through everything right now. But the sooner I can get all of the information you have to offer me, the faster I'm going to be able to chase this guy down. I need you to tell me exactly what happened. Every detail you can remember. Start with how you ended up at that store."

She recounts what happened step by step. When she describes seeing a car parked behind the motel, I ask if she can describe it. She can only tell me it was a dark, midsized car. She didn't take note of the license plate or anything else about it. Her words slow down, becoming uneven and hesitant as she describes the attack. I listen patiently, allowing her as much space as she needs to work through the traumatic experience. Rushing her or trying to dig out more details could make her shut down, and I could miss critical information.

By the time she's done describing what happened, her eyes look like they are getting heavy.

"Nadia, the detective found your phone. Do I have your consent to look through it?"

"Yes."

"Is there a passcode?"

"1001."

She is already asleep as I leave the room. I go to the nurses station and ask for the doctor. We go into a small sitting room where we can talk without being overheard.

"I'm sure I don't need to explain this, but I need to reiterate the gravity of her situation. I can't reveal any further details right at this second, but I do need the cooperation of the hospital and every member of the staff. No one is to be allowed access to Nadia except for people she specifically requests, Detective Hawke, and me. Officers may be posted outside of her room, and if there will be, I will provide names and badge numbers that will need to be verified before they are allowed on the floor."

"I understand," the doctor says.

"Did you by chance collect samples of the blood found on her?"

"Yes," the doctor tells me. "I took samples of blood from different areas of her body as well as swabs from under her nails. She did specifically say she was not sexually assaulted, and I have no reason not to believe her."

"Thank you. I will check in about her later."

CHAPTER TWENTY-THREE

LEAVE THE HOSPITAL AND MAKE MY WAY TO LISA'S HOUSE. I CALL her from the driveway to let her know I'm here. The sun is just barely starting to come up, and I don't want to scare everyone in the house by ringing the doorbell at this hour. I'm not surprised that Lisa doesn't sound like she's been asleep.

"Come in. I'll unlock the door," she says.

I walk into the house and head for the kitchen where I hear her making coffee. There's a box of doughnuts sitting on the table, and she gestures at them.

"Eat."

I don't argue. I choose a powdered, sugar-coated, jelly-filled doughnut and sit down at the table with Lisa. She's wearing pajamas and a housecoat, but there isn't a trace of relaxation on her face. Her hands wrap tightly around a cup of coffee I'm positive isn't the first she's had.

"How is she?"

"She's going to be fine. She's been admitted, and the doctor wants to keep her for a few days for treatment and observation."

Lisa looks down, a puff of breath escaping her lungs.

"Have you found Brent?" she asks, lifting flashing eyes to me.

"It wasn't Brent," I say.

Lisa looks confused. "What do you mean? Of course it was."

"No. She said it wasn't Brent. She is absolutely sure of it," I say.

"Then who?"

"She thinks it was the man Maren Honeycutt had been dating."

"What?"

It's an active investigation so I can't give her all the details, but I break the news of Maren's death and give her a brief overview of what happened last night. The news of the woman's death clearly has an impact, but since she didn't know her personally, it hits differently. While she's obviously affected by the thought of a woman being brutally murdered, I can tell the harshest effect comes from her making the mental link between that murder and Nadia.

"What's going to happen now?" she asks when she has processed the news.

"I need to find out who this Ron person is and track him down. I also need to get to the bottom of the harassing phone calls and texts to Nadia. We still don't know if they're related. Whether they are or not, I need to know who made them and why."

"Right now, I think what you need is some sleep," Lisa says.

"I'm fine," I tell her.

"You haven't slept at all. You were awake when I called you last night to tell you Nadia didn't come home. You have to rest. It's not safe for you to keep pushing like this."

I know she's right. As much as the thought of sleeping feels like wasted hours that could be spent investigating, I know I can't think as clearly when I'm this sleep-deprived.

"I'll go back to the hotel and get a couple of hours," I tell her.

"No. You'll stay right here. The other guest room is already all made up. There's no point in you driving all the way to the hotel just to sleep."

"I'll need to change clothes too," I point out.

"And you can do that after you get some rest."

She isn't going to take no for an answer. This is the Lisa I remember from college. Forceful, high-achieving, ever-restless, but always nurturing. She was the one who made sure our study groups ate vegetables while we were cramming for exams and got up every so often to walk around and keep our blood flowing. I let her bring me to the guest room, and I thank her before she shuts the door.

Taking off my shoes feels amazing, and within seconds of crawling into the bed, I'm asleep.

I don't know how long I've slept when I wake up, and I worry I've slept most of the day away. A quick glance at my phone reassures me it's only been a couple of hours. I want to burrow back under the covers and enjoy the warmth and darkness for a little while longer, but the sharp rush of thoughts gets me up. Jeff is in the kitchen when I walk out.

"Hey," he says. "How are you?"

"Fine. I needed that. Where's Lisa?"

"She finally fell asleep after taking Amelia to school," he tells me.

"Good."

"Can I make you coffee? Breakfast?"

"Thanks, but I need to get going. When Lisa wakes up, will you tell her that I went back to the hotel and then I'm heading to the police station?" I ask.

"Will do."

"Thank you."

A shower, fresh clothes, and a thin coat of makeup do wonders for making me feel awake and ready to face the rest of the day. The doughnut wore off while I was sleeping, so I grab breakfast from the hotel lobby before making my way to the police station. I call Sam during the drive to update him on what's going on. He tells me he loves me, giving me an extra boost to face the day as I pull into the police station.

Detective Hawke is wearing the same clothes as yesterday, and his hair has the telltale look of a man who spent a few hours curled up on a couch rather than going home.

"Tell me what you've got," I say.

He puts a cup of coffee in my hand, and we go to the conference room where new evidence and records have been added to the table. As he goes over what the team found while processing the crime scene, I try to link each piece to the details Nadia gave me. Everything lines up exactly, from the smashed mirror to the footprints in her blood that must belong to her attacker.

Ron. The man with no last name.

If Nadia is right and he did attack her, the connection between what happened to the women just became far clearer.

"The number that called Nadia when she said the person asked for a room at the motel came back as a prepaid line. No identification," Detective Hawke says.

"Not a surprise. Nadia was smart enough to keep all of the text messages she got, and I compared the number to all of the messages, but it didn't line up. It also wasn't one of the numbers that called her."

"It also didn't show up on Maren's phone records," he points out.

The records just came through, giving us a glimpse into Maren's communications and movements leading up to when she disappeared. It was a temporary moment of optimism when we got the records. We hoped it would mean we could finally track down her boyfriend. That optimism was quickly dashed, however, when we ran the number. It showed up in her records most often, and it was connected to text messages that read like they could've only come from the person she was dating.

The initial results gave us a name. Ronald Parker. But we quickly found out the number was for a carrier famed for its low cost and flexibility. Customers didn't sign service contracts, and those who chose to buy their devices outright didn't have to provide a Social Security number. That meant that while there was a name associated with the number, there couldn't be any real identity verification. No address to follow up with. Nothing to nail him down.

"At least we have a last name now," I say. "It's not much, but it's something."

My phone chirps, and I look at the notification. It's from Sloane.

"She got the footage from the truck stop," I tell Hawke. "It's not great quality, but she got a still of the man the officers talked to that night."

I turn the phone screen toward him so he can see the attached image. With the thick mustache and dark hair peeking out from around a navy beanie, the man fits the description Nadia gave of both Ron when she saw him the night she moved to town and the man who attacked her.

"Did it catch him driving the car with the busted light?" Hawke asks.

"No. Apparently, there's footage of the car driving into the lot, but you can't see the driver. Then this man walks into the frame and goes to the picnic table. From the angle he's walking from and everything, you can make the connection that he was driving that car, but there's no actual confirmation," I say. "I'm going to show it to Nadia when I go check on her." I glance at the time. "Which I should actually go do."

"I'll keep trying to zero in on Ron Parker," he says.

"Okay," I say, gathering my notes and putting them in my bag. "We need to find the other woman he was dating. The married one Maren found out about that made her break up with him."

"I'll keep digging."

"Thanks."

Nadia still looks tired when I get to her room. The swelling in her face has gotten worse, but she is sitting up watching TV.

"Hey," I say. "Can I come in?"

"Of course. I don't even remember you leaving last night."

"The medication got you pretty good by the time I left," I say.

She cringes. "I didn't say anything stupid, did I? One time when my mom was in the hospital for surgery, she kept calling the nurses in to command them to clean the fruit snacks up off the floor. She was convinced there were gummies just all over the place."

I chuckle. "No, you didn't do anything like that. You did give me consent to go through your phone. I hope that's still okay."

"Yeah, of course."

"Thanks. I wanted to let you know that almost immediately after the local news put out the request for information about anyone who might have gone into the store last night, a woman called in. Her name is Beth Hall. She confirmed she stopped at the store because she needed gas and was going to try to get a room at the motel. She said she didn't notice the office. I'm guessing because the lights were off. But she went inside and called out, then put money on the counter for a cup of coffee and left. It fits all the details we saw there," I say.

Nadia sighs. "She's safe."

"Yep. I questioned her about what was going on in the area at the time, and she said she didn't notice anything. She didn't see a man there. She saw the blood on the floor but didn't know it was blood. She thought something spilled. She didn't even know there was a problem," I say.

"I'm so glad to hear she's okay."

"Me too. But again, I'm thinking about you. I want to show you a picture. I'm not going to tell you what it is. I want you to look at it and tell me what you see," I say.

Nadia looks skeptical but agrees.

I show her the picture of the man sitting on the picnic table at the truck stop and see her body react. She visibly tenses up and pulls back.

"That's him."

"Ron? Or the man who attacked you?" I ask.

"Both."

"You are absolutely sure?"

"Yes, that's him."

She sounds adamant. It doesn't seem like she is just saying it because she wants it to be true. Seeing the picture obviously affected her, and I am confident she knows what she's saying.

"When Maren told you that she found out Ron was seeing a married woman, did she tell you anything about that woman?" I ask.

"No. Just that she found out he was seeing somebody else and that he had been as long as he was seeing her and that the woman was married. She didn't mention a name or anything. I don't know if she knew any of that."

"Did she tell you how she found out about this woman? Or that she is married?" I ask.

"All she told us was that she thought Ron was on a business trip and found out he was actually on vacation with this other woman. I didn't ask exactly what happened or how she knew. She was really upset about the whole thing, so I figured it didn't really matter that much. Now I wish I had asked more questions."

"We're going to figure this out," I reassure her. "We just have to go one step at a time."

"What can I do? I want to help any way I can."

"You have already been extremely helpful. I want to focus on exactly how everything unfolded. I want to put together a timeline of everything that happened from the time you arrived in town until now. Tell me about the calls and texts, Christy and Maren, other people you encountered. Anything that stands out to you. There's nothing to show that either of them were dealing with the harassment you have been," I say.

"Which means the situations might not have anything to do with each other," she says.

"We don't know. It's important to look at it from as many different angles as possible. We don't want to risk missing anything." I take a notepad and pen out of my bag. "Are you ready to get started?"

The doctor comes in to check Nadia's vitals just as we are finishing up the timeline.

"Thank you for this," I say. "If you think of anything else or you need anything, don't hesitate to call me."

I leave my card on the table next to the bed and make my way back to the police station.

"Agent Griffin, I was just about to call you," Detective Hawke says when I walk in.

"What's up?"

"DNA came back from Maren's body. They were able to get a profile," he tells me.

"That's fantastic."

"I just started running it through the database. Maybe we'll get a hit," he says.

I know well enough not to get my hopes up too much when it comes to checking the offender database for DNA. While it is an extensive compendium that can prove invaluable when it comes to identifying perpetrators, it isn't infallible. Getting an identification from the database is entirely reliant on that person's DNA already being recorded. Which means they will have had to have been arrested and likely convicted of a serious offense. If they have never offended before or simply never been caught, their DNA won't be on record, and it won't come back with anything.

That's exactly what happens with the DNA on the body. But I am not deterred.

"Run it through the cold case database too," I say. "We need to know if that profile has been identified in any other cases."

This time we aren't disappointed.

Soon I am sitting at the conference table with a list of cases beside me and a computer open in front of me. The DNA collected from Maren came back linked to ten other cases. Five victims were found dead, and three others were severely beaten. The other two cases were young women who went missing and were never found, but DNA was located in their homes or vehicles. It's obvious this man has a very high opinion of himself and his skill as a criminal, not realizing just how much evidence he has actually left behind. But even with this many cases linked by a conclusively identifying genetic profile, there's still a question of who this person actually is.

The name Ron Parker doesn't come up anywhere in any of the cases. I know I have to dig deeper. I can't just rely on the surface information that's available in a quick search. But it does seem strange that Nadia would firmly and insistently identify the man who attacked her as the same man Maren was dating, and yet there is no mention of his name in connection with any of the other victims. Not as a family member. Not as a romantic partner. Not even as a witness.

CHAPTER TWENTY-FOUR

THERE ISN'T A WALL IN LISA'S HOUSE THAT DOESN'T HAVE ANY-
thing hanging on it, so I can't post my usual piece of butcher paper to
take notes. And understandably, Nadia doesn't want something like
that so large and visible to her daughter. At only nine years old, Amelia
understands that something serious and frightening is going on, but she
is still far too young to be faced with the brutal details.

To keep from scaring her and to make sure I can keep everything
organized in a place where I can easily see it, I have set up in the guest
room. I always hesitate to leave any of my case notes in a hotel because
of how many people would have ready access to it, and I didn't want to
have to haul everything around with me. When Lisa offered for me to
establish my own war room of sorts at her house, I took her up on it. I
never want to impose, always preferring to stay in a hotel when possible,
but doing it this way gives me the space and security I need while also
providing continued access to Nadia.

After three days in the hospital, she was discharged with strict instructions to take it easy for another couple of weeks. Mel has stepped up to make sure she has everything she needs. Even though she's new to the community, a quickly put together fundraiser brought in enough support that she doesn't have to worry about missing work for the time she is recovering.

I check on her where she is sitting in the living room, then go back to the guest room to continue working on the cold cases. Several poster boards spread out across the carpet contain lists and clusters of bullet points compiling all the information I have listed from my research. Looking over the notes, what immediately stands out to me is the combination of striking similarities and stark differences between the cases.

The victims are all women within a ten-year age range. They were all either in a relationship or had just ended one at the time of the crime. They'd each gone through either a breakup, the loss of a job, or a death in their family soon before the attacks. None of this is that unusual. Statistically, the majority of victims of violent crime fit those demographics. Women going through vulnerable times are always at higher risk.

Despite these similarities, the cases then diverge dramatically.

The romantic partners linked to each of the victims vary in appearance, age, and even nationality. Circumstances surrounding each of the cases meant these men were never considered suspects.

None of the other material descriptions in the crimes lined up. There were no similar vehicles. No shared locations. Statements from friends and family interviewed at the time of the crimes detailed very different lives and events leading up to what happened to each of them. I feel like I'm looking at a list of completely unrelated crimes, only they are all linked with the iron band of DNA.

I have to step back from the surface facts, the reports provided by investigators. I have to go further and look beyond the crime to the victims and their lives. My first step is contacting the surviving victims. They're the ones who can give me first-person insight, the unique perspective of having actually experienced what happened.

The reports contain current contact information for only one of the victims, Sadie Rosen, and I call her. She doesn't answer, so I leave a voicemail introducing myself and asking her to call me back. I don't tell her why. This isn't something she should hear through a voicemail.

The other two survivors have outdated phone numbers listed, so I start climbing through the grapevine of connections to locate them. Calling other numbers in the file eventually gets me to Prue Bailey, the mother of Noa Bailey. She tells me her daughter has moved out of the country and doesn't keep in touch often.

"What she went through changed her," Prue tells me. "She never really got over it. She said moving was something she'd been planning for years, but I think what happened is what pushed her to do it. She wanted to get away."

"What can you tell me about the man she was dating at the time?"

"I didn't like him from the start. I didn't trust him. He was rude and cocky. One of those men who was completely full of himself and thought Noa should feel honored just to have his attention. She was always talking about him standing her up or being late when they had plans, but somehow he always managed to keep her interested. It hurts me to say it, but I think she stayed with him to prove something to me," Prue says.

"Why do you think that?" I ask.

"Jason was nothing like what Noa usually went for or, admittedly, what I wanted for her. She had always been attracted to really clean-cut, well-educated, ambitious men. I guess the kind of man people would say every mother wants for their daughter. Jason was the opposite. He had blond hair that went almost to his waist, tattoos, and earrings. He had dropped out of high school to start working and didn't think he needed any goals beyond taking over his father's locksmith business."

"That sounds like ambition to me," I point out.

"He didn't have any intention of achieving anything for himself. He just wanted to inherit what was already built and then have people work for him. He thought that made him sound like a leader. Anyway, when I met him, I was really surprised. Noa told me she thought he was interesting and it was fun to be with someone totally new and different. She felt like she had dated the same man over and over, and this was something exciting.

"I should have handled it differently. I should have just accepted that she was an adult going through some learning and growing and that she was going to work her way through it. I really believe if I had just bitten my tongue, she would have seen him for what he really was and broken it off long before he was able to get her tangled up with that crowd. But I didn't. I told her she was being ridiculous and it was never going to work. I said she needed to grow up. That's what made her dig in her heels. And then it happened."

"What do you remember about the attack?" I ask.

"Noa and Jason had finally broken up. I don't know all those specifics because she didn't want to talk to me about their relationship any-

more. I just know that he loaded everything up in his truck and moved. She was really upset about it. Even though things had never been really good between them, she was a mess after he left. She started going out more. She was going to the places he introduced her to. Places she never would have gone before.

"I remember thinking to myself that she had always been such a responsible teenager that I was never really worried about her at that age. And yet now that she was an adult, I was suddenly having to sit up all night waiting for her to call me and let me know she got home safe. She got a speeding ticket for the first time in her life. She was spiraling out of control, and I was terrified something was going to happen to her. Then it did.

"My phone rang in the middle of the night, and I remember being frustrated because I just knew it was her and she had gotten herself into another mess. She was drunk and couldn't drive home or had gone off with somebody she didn't know and ended up stranded. I muttered some things to myself I will never repeat and that I am more ashamed of than anything else in my life. When I picked up the phone, it was a police officer telling me she'd been found under the slide on the playground of an abandoned elementary school just outside of town. They didn't know if she was going to survive."

"I'm sorry you had to go through that," I say. "I know it isn't easy to talk about."

"I'm willing to do anything if there's a chance we'll finally find out who attacked my daughter."

"There's no interview with Jason in the record of the investigation," I say.

"That's because they were never able to find him. It turned out he had lied about everything he told her. The business he said his father owned didn't exist. When she gave them his license plate number, it came back to a completely different make and model. He had essentially vanished."

My next conversation is with Sheila Martinelli. I get her contact information from her mother, and my conversation with her is so different from the one I just had with Prue that it gives me whiplash. She describes how she was going through a difficult time after a sudden divorce left her unsure of what she wanted to do with her life. She met Andy Copperfield in a bookstore when he was so engrossed in the book he was reading that he tripped over her where she was sitting. She laughs softly when she describes him as a little bit of a nerd with shaggy brown hair, which reminded her of her childhood puppy, and thick glasses. He had an affinity for jeans that were just a bit too big and plaid button-up shirts.

He was sweet and gentle, never being too forward or pushing too fast. She found herself falling for his silly intellectual jokes and stories about his college years wishing he was one of the jocks. He even invited her home to meet his parents. She almost went, but she got called into work at the last minute and had to cancel. The next day she got a call from his brother telling her Andy was stung by a bee and died of anaphylactic shock. According to his wishes, he didn't have a funeral and was cremated. I can hear lingering affection and deep emotion in her voice as she talks about him. It hardens when she tells me that two weeks after his death, she was attacked.

"All I wanted while I was in the hospital was him. When I first woke up, there were a few minutes when I didn't remember what happened and I asked for him. I thought he was there. It was like finding out he died all over again."

I'm still waiting to hear back from Sadie when Nadia calls me frantically from the living room.

I run in and find her getting up, heading for the steps to the basement.

"What's going on? What's wrong?"

"I have to get to Amelia's school," she says. "Someone just tried to pick her up."

CHAPTER TWENTY-FIVE

Nadia

“I THOUGHT THIS WAS SUPPOSED TO BE A SECURE SCHOOL. NOBODY is supposed to be able to get inside without permission. How did this person just walk through the doors and get to the office to try to sign my daughter out of school? The only other person on the list of people authorized to take her out of school is Lisa, the woman we live with, and I know it wasn’t her.”

Nadia was so angry she was barely even processing the pain racing through her. Her hands shook, and the edges of her vision were fuzzy from the intensity of the emotion she was feeling. The secretary sitting in front of her looked pale and wide-eyed. Nadia knew some of that had to do with her bruised and swollen face, but it was also the realization of just how badly she had screwed up.

"I'm sorry. That is the policy of the school. No adults are supposed to enter without prior permission or proof of authorization. Whoever let him inside made a serious error in judgment," the secretary said.

"*Him*? It was a man who came to an elementary school and tried to pick up a nine-year-old girl? Who was this person?" Nadia demanded.

Because Lisa was the only other person who had permission to pick Amelia up from school, Nadia knew it would be just as horrifying to find out that a woman tried to sign her out, but somehow she was more disturbed knowing a man was just allowed to walk into the school without anybody knowing who he was. Maybe it was narrow-minded of her, but at that moment, perceived character flaws were the absolute lowest thing on her priority list.

The secretary shifted uncomfortably in her seat.

"Unfortunately, we don't know."

"You don't know?" Nadia asked incredulously. "What do you mean you don't know?"

"He didn't provide a name. He came in and said he was here to pick Amelia up. I asked for picture identification, but he didn't have any to give me. So I told him he would not be able to pick her up, and he left."

"You just let him leave?" Nadia asked.

"There really wasn't anything I could do," the secretary said.

"You could have told him to stop. You could have forced him to tell you his name. You could have called the police because he was trespassing. There was plenty that you could have done."

"How do we access the footage from the security cameras?" Emma asked.

Nadia was so angry she almost forgot the FBI agent who had driven her to the school. Emma stood stoic beside her, looking at the secretary with expectation. This was not a request. She was not asking if they could see the footage; she was making it known it was going to be shown to them.

"I will have to ask the principal," the secretary said.

She didn't move. It was almost as if she thought invoking the principal was going to make Nadia and Emma back off. But they didn't. Emma's eyebrows lifted just slightly.

"Is the principal not in the office right now?"

"She is."

"We need to know who this person was. As of right now, the way I see it, your school is experiencing a serious security breach. Though it worked out in the best way possible because you took steps to ask for identification, you failed in your responsibility to know who was in the school. And whoever let this person inside could have put the entire student body and everyone working here at risk. Allow us to see that footage so that we can identify these people and make sure it doesn't happen again," Emma said.

That was enough to get the secretary on her feet. She went down a hallway leading out of the main lobby, and Nadia heard her knock on a door. She couldn't hear the muffled words that were spoken, but a few moments later, the principal of the school came out with the secretary right behind. It seemed that the secretary had already told her what was going on and what Emma had said, because she immediately escorted both of them into the office and pulled up the footage of the time the man arrived at the school. As soon as she saw him, Nadia's mouth dropped open.

"That's Steven Web."

"You know him?" Emma asked.

"Yes, I grew up with him. He showed up at the store out of nowhere and said he was meeting some woman he met online. But I think he was lying."

"Why would he come to the store?" Emma asked.

"He has always had feelings for me ever since we were kids. Completely unreciprocated. Why would he come here to pick up Amelia? How would he even know what school she went to?" Nadia asked.

"Did you post it on your social media?"

"No. I deactivated my account, and I never posted anything about her. That was a hard and fast rule for me. No pictures of her, no mentions of her school or activities."

"That's good."

"It's obviously not enough," Nadia said.

"Do you have his phone number?"

"I can get it," she said. She stood up and made eye contact with the principal. "This isn't over. I want to know who let him in the building and what is going to be done about it."

She left the school and took out her phone. It didn't take long for her to find Steven's number. It was posted on the website for the company he worked for. She immediately called it.

"Nadia! What a pleasant surprise," he answered, clearly revealing he knew her phone number.

"What the hell do you think you're doing?" she snapped.

"What? What are you talking about?" Steven asked.

"You know exactly what I'm talking about. Who do you think you are, going to my daughter's school and trying to check her out? What is it that you were trying to accomplish with that?"

"Brent didn't tell you he was having me pick her up?" Steven asked.

Nadia felt physically struck by the words. For a second, she couldn't think or form words.

"Brent told you to pick her up?" she asked.

"Yeah. He knew I was going to be in the area again, and so he told me to pick her up and bring to him. He said he was going to get some sort of visitation with her. I figured you knew about this."

"No, I did not know about this," Nadia said.

"Well, the school wouldn't let me pick her up because I forgot my ID. I tried to call Brent to let him know, but he didn't answer."

Without another word, she hung up and dialed her ex-husband.

"Hello?"

"Did you think I wasn't going to notice my daughter being missing?" Nadia asked.

"Nadia?"

"Who the hell else would it be?"

"Amelia is missing?" Brent asked.

"No. She's at school where she is supposed to be. Fortunately, the secretary asked Steven for ID and your little minion wasn't smart enough to have it with him."

"I have no idea what the fuck you are talking about," he said.

He sounded genuinely confused, which made Nadia's stomach twist a little. She squeezed her temples and tried not to scream.

"I got a call from Amelia's school that somebody was trying to check her out from the front office. When I came up to the school, they told me that somebody let a man inside and that he tried to pick her up. I saw the security footage, and it was Steven. I just got off the phone with him, and he said that you told him to pick her up while he was in the area and bring her back to you. He said you told him that you were going to get visitation," she said.

"Have you lost your ever-loving mind? Why would I do something like that? I want my daughter, and I think it's absolute bullshit you won't let me anywhere near her, but I'm not going to have somebody kidnap her for me. I don't need to do that. I could walk into court and show that I am a far more fit parent than you are. I'm not going to risk going to prison for something that stupid."

"Why would he make that up? Even Steven would be able to understand that we could check up on that."

"I have no idea. But I would really like some answers too," Brent said. "I'll call you back."

"Let's get in the car," Emma said. "We shouldn't be doing this standing here."

They walked across the parking lot and got into the car. Nadia called Steven back.

"Brent says he didn't have anything to do with this. He said he didn't message you, and he didn't ask you to pick up Amelia," she said.

"I have the message from him right here on my phone. I can forward it to you."

"Do it."

The message came through, and Nadia saw her ex-husband's phone number and a message giving Steven the address of the school and instructions to pick Amelia up. Fury made her skin burn and her head throb. Why was Brent lying to her about this? How stupid did he think she was?

She called him back, demanding an explanation.

"I didn't send that message," Brent insisted.

"Is there somebody else there with you?" Emma asked.

"Yeah, I'm at work. There are plenty of other people here with me. So this is a fantastic conversation for me to be having."

"Have somebody video call us from their phone and show us your text messages," Emma said.

"Gladly."

He hung up, and less than a minute later, Nadia got a video call. She opened it and saw Brent holding his phone up to the screen so that she could see the messages.

"You could have deleted it," Nadia said.

"I don't think so," Emma said. "Look at the timestamps on the conversations. He would have had to send that message to Steven at the exact same time he was sending another message. While I guess it is conceivably possible, I don't think it happened."

"Thank you," Brent said.

"Then how does Steven have a message on his phone from Brent's number?"

"Is something going on that you're not telling me? I deserve to know if my daughter is in danger," Brent said.

"I can take care of Amelia. Remember, I'm the one who has custody of her."

Nadia hung up and covered her face with her hands for a few seconds, trying to draw deep breaths to calm herself down. She looked up at Emma.

"I don't understand. We both saw that message from Steven. I know he has tried to get my attention in a lot of ways over the years, but I can't fathom him doing something like this."

"I don't think he did. There are spoofing apps easily available to anyone who knows where to look. All somebody has to do is tell the app what name and number to pretend a message is from, and it will show up that way. A lot of scam artists and even unscrupulous telemarketers use the same technique to pretend they are from certain areas," Emma said.

"Somebody else did this? Who would know Brent and Steven?" Nadia asked.

"I don't know. But I think you need to strongly consider finding somewhere else to live and making sure Amelia is driven to and from school until we get this figured out."

Nadia was still reeling from the entire situation later that evening when Lennon came to the house. He had flowers and takeout of the appetizer she loved when they went to dinner. With Amelia downstairs playing, she told him about what happened.

"You can come to my place," he said without hesitation.

Nadia shook her head. "I can't do that."

"Why not? I want you there. I can't stand the thought of either one of you being in danger. No one would have any idea where you were. It isn't all that far from the school, so it would be easy to bring Amelia back and forth."

"I don't know."

"I have an office at my place with a futon. I will take that, and you and Amelia can take my room."

Nadia took a breath. "All right."

CHAPTER TWENTY-SIX

Emma

I T's obvious whoever faked the message to Steven didn't actually intend on him being able to pick up Amelia. Anybody knows there are safety measures in place to protect school children and that it's highly unlikely he would get anywhere near the little girl. They likely didn't even realize he would get so far as to get inside the school. Far more likely is that he would go to the door and say he wanted to pick her up, and they would immediately call Nadia.

This wasn't an actual effort to endanger Amelia. Instead, it was an overt threat. Whoever did this wants Nadia to understand that they are in control. They have infiltrated her life and can manipulate it and her as they please. This changes the urgency of the case. I need to know who is behind these messages and why they are targeting her.

I shift my focus back to the timeline Nadia created for me. She was extremely thorough, putting on full display the precise attention Mel lauded as one of the reasons he gave her a store to run. She didn't just give me bullet points or general ideas. The timeline is full of detailed descriptions of what she was doing and what happened each step of the way.

The timeline starts with the rainstorm and car troubles that brought her to the convenience store that first night. I read about her connection to Maren and the first time she saw Ron. It carries me through Smith fixing her car and Maren arranging for her to get a job at that store. My own discomfort increases as I again read through her laying out the bizarre happenings at the motel as well as the uncomfortable encounters with some customers.

She put particular emphasis on the first text she got the night she was celebrating at the bar with Maren and Christy. She details the text coming in while the other women were in the bathroom and she was talking to Lennon. It was enough to run her out of the bar, but it was only the beginning. From there the calls started, and more texts. Each one was saved on her phone, and she could give precise time stamps and dates to chronicle them.

The timeline tells of a man named Emmett threatening her at the store and Lennon, having gotten a tip from the date of a friend at the bar, being there to help her. It's obvious as I read each of the confrontations Nadia had that there were several men in her life who made her deeply uneasy. From aggressive customers at the store to the short-tempered parent of her daughter's best friend, it seemed she was constantly bombarded.

This sense gets stronger the further I go down the list, and I know some of that is perception. The more anxious she got, the more heightened her awareness and sensitivity became. It doesn't mean these things weren't actually happening, but she likely felt them with much greater intensity than she would have in other situations.

I find myself particularly interested in the night she was asked to cover the shift at the original store and found the faked crime scene inside the motel room. It feels like an unfortunate reality that I'm not surprised by something like that. The types of things that exist out in the Wild West of the internet should be enough to make everybody question the world we live in. What I'm interested in, though, is something my husband would say doesn't exist.

A coincidence.

According to the investigation that was done, the prank of the faked crime scene had nothing to do with the power and phone lines in the store being cut. The phone was already not working when she went into the store, but then the power was cut when she was inside, after discovering what she thought was a gruesome murder scene. But supposedly, these two things, along with the threatening call she received at the same time, had nothing to do with each other. Sam and I might not see eye to eye on the whole coincidence thing all the time, but in this situation, I think he's right.

Curious to see the video for myself, I go onto the app and look it up. I'm actually surprised that it is still available. I would think that because it has been linked to actual crimes, it would have been removed. Instead, it has generated a massive wave of views and comments. The description claims two "adrenaline junkies" and lifelong best friends were embarking on a "quest for excitement" and that included participating in this challenge.

The video is hard to watch. It makes me angry to see the slightly shaky footage, obviously taken on a cheap handheld camera, showing Nadia walking cautiously up to the open motel room door. The voice narrating the video is muffled, and it's almost difficult to understand what he's saying through his giggles. It almost sounds like he's drunk, which I wouldn't be surprised by. In the background, there's another voice adding his own commentary. It's almost impossible to understand what the second person is saying, and it seems like they are standing at a distance from the one with the camera, possibly recording on their own device to make sure they get the best angles.

I watch Nadia step into the room and then run for the store. The voice behind the camera cackles with laughter, and the screen shakes almost violently as he seems to run to get out of sight. The video then cuts to the parking lot full of flashing lights as police swarm and go to investigate.

"They think it's real!" the voice whispers, now almost high-pitched. "They really think somebody got butchered in there."

The second voice mumbles a response, and there are a few more moments of watching the investigation unfold before the video stops. Nadia explained that the police didn't believe the creators behind the video were the ones who cut the lines because they would have included it in the final cut. I understand the logic behind that. But I still can't bring myself to believe there were two forces at work that night in the convenience store parking lot—one team out to create a viral sensation based on cruelly scaring someone with a vandalized motel room, and another person with much darker intentions cutting off communication and electricity to the building. It is too convenient.

I watch the video again, hoping for some mention of the power or phone that I didn't notice before. It's possible they did film that happening but decided to leave it out of what they posted because they knew it could get them in much more serious trouble. But they might have slipped and said something about it. I don't hear them say anything about it, but the second voice is bothering me. It never seems to get any closer or louder. There's no actual conversation between the two of them, only isolated commentary from both.

I don't claim to be particularly well-versed in this type of internet content, but there is something about the uneven cadence and lack of interaction that doesn't sit right. I go down to the comments and read through them, wondering if anybody else noticed. It doesn't take long to see people bringing up the fact that the pair that supposedly traveled around doing stunts and challenges had never posted a video until this one. Several more questioned the creators themselves, but one particular comment caught my attention:

Why does your buddy sound like he's in a tunnel?

I go back to the video and scan through until I find the section with the most pronounced inconsistency in the voices. It isn't glaring. If I was just casually watching the video, I probably wouldn't notice or put any thought into it. But I'm paying close attention to this video, and that makes the odd audio stand out. I listen to it several more times.

I wonder if it's possible that the louder voice is actually a voice-over rather than live audio attached to the footage. But almost as soon as that thought comes to mind, I realize that the sounds coming through are layered with the voice in such a way that it could only be the camera picking up what he's saying at that moment.

I listen again to the voice in the background. It really does sound like the other person is in a tunnel or a hole. And then it clicks. It isn't another person. It's a recording.

The video was not created by multiple people. It is only one. He recorded himself making generic commentary and then probably placed the recorder a few feet away so that it would sound like another person. But the quality of the camera and the recorder are not enough to make it legitimately sound like another person if you pay attention.

I explain this to the detective later when he comes by the house to compare notes on the investigation. It takes me playing it through a couple of times and pointing out the odd audio for him to realize I'm right.

"So this person decided to fake a friend to make videos with. That's strange and kind of sad, but I don't understand what it has to do with the investigation," he says.

"The faked crime scene and the very publicly posted video weren't for some competition. They were to scare and humiliate Nadia. It's just another way this person was manipulating her. That entire situation was orchestrated to scare her and send her back into the store, where they could then cut off the electricity after making another threatening phone call. Those two situations are not happening in separate bubbles in the same location. This is one person doing this to her."

"It's a long shot, but I can get a warrant to see if the app can give us any identifying information about the user. They would have had to register, but that doesn't necessarily mean that they would give their actual name. But we might be able to get a location or an email address. Sometimes people slip up. Criminals are dumb."

"A generalization that is not always applicable, but for the most part, yes. Let me know what you find out."

The detective leaves, and I am still thinking about the video. My mind goes back to using the image search and scouring social media in my efforts to find Denise Stein. I look at Nadia's timeline again. There are several points when she got messages that indicated the person was nearby. We've already confirmed there isn't anything to capture who was moving around outside Lisa and Jeff's house and looking into the window, but there are other options.

I look over Christy's page, but it's sparse. There aren't any recent pictures available. Nadia's page has been deactivated, so I can't search that, and as far as I can tell, Maren didn't have any. This brings me to the official page of the bar where they went out to celebrate. This is where she got the first text message complimenting her on how she looked. That suggested someone was there looking at her.

It doesn't look like the bar itself posts many pictures other than of the bartenders for the night and occasional vanity snaps of cocktails. But when I search for posts that tagged the bar, I get a cascade of results. I scroll through them until I find ones from that night. I look further to include the next day, knowing many people will make posts about a night out the day after when they can think more clearly.

I carefully look over every post. It takes a while, but finally, I start to notice Nadia, Maren, and Christy at their table against the wall. It helps me orient myself when looking at other pictures. Since I've never been inside that bar, knowing where things are positioned helps me to know where to look for people who might be paying too much attention to Nadia's table.

A few pictures in, I catch sight of Lennon sitting at the bar. He's on the far side, facing the door. It puts him at the perfect vantage point to look at Nadia, so it's easy to see why he noticed her. I start taking screenshots of the pictures and arranging them in a document so I can look at them. Using markers like the amount of beer in mugs people are holding, the way items are arranged on tables, and the way the crowd is dispersed throughout the room, I put them in chronological order the best I can.

I include a picture that seems to have been taken before the women arrived and then one after to bookend the timeframe. As I look over the pictures one by one, taking in every detail, something starts to stand out to me. I read through Nadia's account of the night again, then go back to the pictures. Something is off.

CHAPTER TWENTY-SEVEN

Nadia

"ARE YOU SURE THIS IS OKAY?" NADIA ASKED, LOOKING AT THE pile of bags she and Amelia stacked in the corner of the bedroom.

"Yes. And yes," Lennon said.

"What is the second yes for?" she asked.

"You to hold in reserve for the next time you want to ask me if it's okay."

She made a playful face at him, and he wrapped his arms around her. He pressed a kiss to the top of her head.

"I'm glad you're here."

"I just hope it works. I'm still getting messages. The only reason I haven't seen any in the last couple of days is because I've kept my phone off. I'm not at the store, so they can't insist that I am accessible all the time. I gave Mel Lisa's number, so if there is a massive emergency, he can still get in touch with me."

"I think that was even going above and beyond," Lennon says. "Have you ever tried responding to the messages? Maybe this person just wants to see if they can get you to talk."

"I have responded. I have tried calling the number. It doesn't work. It's driving me crazy. But the worst part is not knowing if my daughter is safe. I can't stand the thought of her being away from me. The idea of sending her back to Brent is..."

"Then don't even say it."

"What if it comes to that? What if they can't figure out who is doing this to me and it just keeps escalating?" she asked. "I have to make sure Amelia is going to be okay. I can't keep her in harm's way."

"You won't. You are not going to have to face sending her back to her father. This is going to end. It's inevitable," Lennon says.

"I just can't believe Maren is gone. It hasn't really sunk in yet. I'm still so worried about Christy, and thinking about this person stalking me, it's like my brain hasn't totally absorbed it. And then it will hit me, and I have to realize all over again that I'm never going to have her in my life again," Nadia says.

"And you really think Ron killed her?"

"I don't think it. I know. There isn't a single shred of doubt in my mind," she says.

"But why? You said he was so good to her."

"And then she found out he was in a relationship with somebody else and that woman was married. She broke up with him, and maybe she told him that she was going to tell his mistress's husband," Nadia says. "All I know is that picture Agent Griffin showed me was him. And it was the same man I saw in the parking lot with Maren and who attacked me. And that means he probably went after Christy too. He wanted to punish all of us for being friends or he wanted to keep our mouth shut. I don't know. But it was him. We just have to find him."

CHAPTER TWENTY-EIGHT

Emma

SEARCHING THROUGH COLD CASES CAN BE A TEDIOUS AND DIFFI-
cult task. Using the DNA database is fast and effective, but it only
provides limited information. Sometimes there are other details
about cases that can connect them but aren't as easily located. That's
what I'm looking for now.

DNA connected the ten cases to Maren's murder, but that doesn't
mean those are the only cases that are linked. With my notes in front of
me, I pull out individual characteristics of the cases and search for others that share those elements. I take a new poster board and start group-
ing cases, then print out a map and make marks that end up looking like
a connect-the-dots picture.

A pattern is forming.

Jason.

Andy.
Martin.
Kyle.
Roger.
Oliver.
Mason.
Ron.

Nadia

"If you hadn't moved to Dogwood Valley, where do you think you would be right now?" Lennon asked.

Nadia reached for another dirty dish from the sink and ran it under the water.

"Honestly? I have no idea. So much of coming here was just chance. It wasn't like I made a big plan about it or thought about it for a long time. At that point in my life, it didn't feel like much of anything that I planned was working out. A lot of the time, it felt like I was falling down a mountain and just grabbing on to anything I could," she said.

"I know how that feels," he said.

He took the clean dish from her and dried it.

"Mama?" Amelia came into the room.

Nadia turned to her. "Yeah, baby? What do you need?"

"Do we have any cookies?" She said it with a serious expression, like she was trying to figure out the mysteries of the universe.

Nadia laughed. "I think we do," she said.

"Do we have any milk?"

"I believe so."

"Can I have some of each please?"

"I'll bring it to you in just a minute."

Amelia skipped away to return to playing in the living room. Nadia went to the refrigerator and took out the milk. She filled a cup then put three cookies from the jar onto a small plate. She brought them into the living room and accepted a kiss from Amelia.

Lennon shook his head when she walked back into the kitchen.

"That is the most polite way I've ever heard a nine-year-old ask for cookies and milk."

"She's growing up fast," Nadia said.

"I'm sure that's an interesting experience," he said.

Nadia chuckled softly "You have no idea. I don't think there's really anything that can prepare a person for everything that comes with being a parent. You can read the books, go to the meetings, talk to other parents. It doesn't matter. You're still going to be surprised at the things that come along."

"It's one thing I haven't given a try."

"Given a try?" Nadia asked, furrowing her forehead at the strange statement.

"Yeah, I like experiencing new things. How about you?"

Nadia thought about the question for a second. "You know what? I actually don't know. Does that sound crazy?"

"A little," Lennon said with a laugh. "How do you not know?"

"It's been so long since I've thought about what I want in life beyond just getting from day to day. I haven't had a lot of time or chances to try many new things."

"Because you were too busy sliding down the mountain?" he asked.

"Something like that."

He gestured around himself. "This is a new experience. A new place. New people."

"That's true."

"But you know what I've found?" Lennon asked.

"What?"

"You can try all the new things in the world, it always ends the same way. You always come right back to where you always do."

"So what about you?" Nadia asked.

"What about me?" Lennon asked.

"You said you knew what it was like to feel like you were trying to hold on to anything. What's that story?"

She picked up a stack of plates he had dried and set in the rack. She carried them over to the cabinet and started putting them away.

"It's happened a few times in my life. But I guess the first time I really remember feeling like that was when I was in college and my girl-friend left me."

Nadia scoffed and nodded in commiseration. "Breakups can be really rough."

"I think it probably would have been easier if it had been a real breakup. She just ghosted me," Lennon said.

Nadia paused, her hand on the cabinet handle.

"I don't think we had that word for it then, but that's what it was. I spent so much time watching her run track I ended up failing a class because I never got the coursework done. I was at every one of her competitions and even helped her train. Then Spring Break came, she left, and I never heard from her again."

Heat stung on Nadia's cheeks. She turned to look at him.

"What did you say?

Emma

My heart feels like it's jumping in my chest. Cold rushes through my veins. The familiar tingle goes up the back of my neck.

My hand rests on Nadia's timeline, my fingertips just under the way Maren described Ron and how wonderful their relationship was. I can hear her voice in my head.

"He even told her about his own breakup."

The first line of the article on the screen in front of me stands out bold black against the white background, but the rest fades out of focus like the ink is running down the page.

Police are asking for any information about the death of Brigette Kincaid, a local college track star, who was found in a shallow grave over the weekend after disappearing during Spring Break...

CHAPTER TWENTY-NINE

Nadia

"Y OU KNOW WHAT I LIKE TO THINK ABOUT?" LENNON ASKED. "How many times do you think you walked past me before we met and didn't know?"

"What?" Nadia asked.

Her fingertips slipped away from the handle on the cabinet, and she pressed her back to the counter, starting to ease down it toward the living room.

"Think about it. People walk by each other all the time and never even notice who's around them. They could pass by the same person a dozen times and never realize it. Even if they look right at them, they might not know they've seen them so many times before."

Nadia darted toward the living room. Amelia looked up from the game she was playing.

"Mama?"

"Come on, baby," Nadia said, trying to sound as calm as she could. "We need to go to the bedroom."

That's where her phone was. She'd plugged it into the charger before dinner, not thinking she would need it.

"Why?" Amelia asked.

"Grab your stuff."

Nadia took Amelia's hand and headed for the hallway, but Lennon lunged in front of her, blocking the way. She gasped and took a step back, knocking over the cup of milk.

"Where are you going, Nadia?" he asked.

"To the bedroom," she said. "Get out of my way."

He tilted his head to the side. "That's not a very nice way to talk to the person who brought you into his home. You know, I've always been so nice to you."

Nadia's eyes cut to the side, and she made a move toward the front door. Lennon was too fast.

"A little harder to move so fast now, isn't it?" he asked. "You know, I have to hand it to you. I wasn't expecting you to get out of that office. You surprised me. You're a lot feistier than I gave you credit for. I knew Maren was going to put up a fight, and I made sure Christy never even saw what was coming. But you... I thought you were going to be so much easier. You gave me a fun challenge."

Nadia scooped Amelia into her arms, ignoring the pain that ripped through the wound in her side. She headed for the hallway again and dropped her daughter down to the floor when she felt Lennon's hand clench around her hair again, just like it had at the motel.

"Run! Go to the bedroom. Lock the door. Get my phone and call 911."

Amelia looked at her with terrified eyes.

"Go!"

Nadia hit the ground, her face scraping across the carpet. Lennon stood over her. He lifted his foot, but the sound of the door splintering kept him from stomping down.

"Put your hands up and don't move, or I will take out every single version of you."

CHAPTER THIRTY

Emma

NADIA SCUTTLES ACROSS THE CARPET TO GET AWAY FROM LENNON. My gun is pointed at his face, in between eyes remembered in different colors by the wide swath of people unfortunate enough to cross his path.

"Did he hurt you?" I ask Nadia without moving my stare.

"Not badly this time. I'm going to be fine."

"Yes, you are," I say.

The scream of sirens starts in the distance and gets louder almost instantly as squad cars approach. Lennon looks at the door, then rushes me. In one swift move, I lower my gun and squeeze the trigger. He grunts and collapses to the floor as the bullet embeds in his knee.

I walk over to him, my gun still held in both hands, now pointing down at the center of his chest where he's writhing.

"You don't honestly think I was going to kill you and deprive the justice system of the fun of processing you like ground meat, did you?"

Officers run into the house, and Nadia's hands fly into the air. I release my gun with one hand and hold it up, keeping the gun steady on Lennon.

"Agent Emma Griffin, FBI," I say.

"She's legit," one of the officers says.

"You can relax."

The bedroom door opens, and Amelia runs into the living room. Nadia drops to her knees and pulls the little girl close to her chest.

"You did such a good job, baby."

I step away from Lennon and put my gun in the holster.

"He's going to need an ambulance. But make sure you cuff him first."

Nadia stands up and looks at me, still holding Amelia's head against her.

"Thank you."

"All of them?" Nadia asks three days later as she stares at the pictures lined up in front of her on the conference room table.

"All of them," I say.

"And there's probably more," Detective Hawke says.

I tap my finger onto one of the fifteen photocopied ID cards spread out across the table.

"This is Jared Helmer. He's the original. He stayed under that name until he left college," I say.

"After he murdered his girlfriend for leaving him," Nadia says.

"'Girlfriend' seems like a pretty generous term for what their relationship really was," I say. "I had a chance to talk to Brigette Kincaid's sister and best friend yesterday. They told me Jared was obsessed with Brigette. She agreed to go on a date with him after a mutual friend introduced them, but he wasn't her type. He didn't let go. He sat through all of her practices and competitions. He ran after her when she was working out. Went to the gym at the same time. He started calling her and sending her notes constantly.

"She tried to let him down easy, not wanting to hurt his feelings. But he couldn't take a hint. So when she left for vacation that Spring

Break, she didn't respond to any of his calls or messages. She never came back from vacation. Her body wasn't found for several years. No one ever thought quiet, nerdy Jared would be capable of something like that. And by the time they found her, he'd already learned he could be whoever he wanted to be and live whatever life he wanted to live just by changing his appearance and convincing people what he said was true. When he found the right people, they were easy to manipulate. And when it stopped working out the way he wanted it, he moved on. Leaving bodies and broken survivors in his wake."

"But why me?" Nadia asks.

"The same reason as the others. Amusement. He'd already set his sights on Maren, but then you came along. He wanted to see just how good he had gotten. If he could pull off two different appearances and two different constructed personalities with people who knew each other. Getting your information from Maren was easy. He was also able to take and copy the keys to the stores and the motel. He scheduled texts to show up on your phone when you were with him.

"Then Maren found out about another woman he was seeing. She could have destroyed everything for him. So in his mind, she'd run her course."

My choice of words hangs heavily in the air.

I'm able to meet Christy before I leave Dogwood Valley. It's bitter-sweet watching her mourn Maren but also reunite happily with Nadia. After the hospital, I go back to Lisa and Jeff's house to pack up and say goodbye. Nadia and Amelia are back in their cozy spot in the basement. They won't always be there. But for now, it's good for them.

Lisa walks me outside and hugs me by the car.

"Thank you so much," she says.

"Next time, why don't we get together under better circumstances," I suggest. "Come to Sherwood. I'll introduce you to my cousin Dean and Xavier. We'll sit in the sun and do absolutely nothing else."

Lisa laughs. "Deal. And we'll invite Julia."

"Absolutely."

The drive feels long, and I'm so happy to walk back through my front door. The house smells like spaghetti sauce, and I hear Xavier in the kitchen conjecturing over the mystery of endcap goods that are never put in the cart despite being plentiful and within easy reach. That can only mean one thing.

I walk into the kitchen.

"Dad?"

My father turns in his seat at the table. His face lights up when he sees me, and he gets to his feet.

"Hey, honey. It's me, Dad."

He hugs me, and I laugh at the reminder of the way he has always left me voicemails. Not that I've gotten many from him recently.

"What are you doing here?" I ask. "It's been almost a year."

"Isn't that just the answer to your question, Emma?" Xavier asks. "Wouldn't it make more sense to say, 'It's been almost a year. There you are!'?"

Dad holds out a hand toward Xavier to show his approval of his point.

"It has been way too long, and I've missed you. I've been wanting to come see you. But I'm actually here for another reason too."

"What is that?" I ask.

"I've been keeping tabs on your cases, and I think I might be able to help you with one."

"Thanks, Dad. I really appreciate it, but I know you have enough going on," I say.

Anytime my father sinks off the radar for months at a time, I know there's something serious happening. I've stopped asking. He never tells.

"Emma, trust me."

As he says it, I hear the front door open and Dean's voice. Someone responds to him, and I walk out of the kitchen toward the living room. I stop short when I see my cousin carrying an armful of soda. The man next to him meets my eyes.

"Sebastian McDonnell."

AUTHOR'S NOTE

Dear Reader,

Thank you so much for reading *The Girl on the Run!* Every time I sit down to write another Emma Griffin book, I think, How much trouble can I possibly put her through this time? And somehow, the answer is always a lot. You'd think, after everything she's been through, she might get a break—but where's the fun in that? A quiet town, a fresh start, a simple case… it never stays that way for long. And honestly? I think Emma would be bored if it did. There's a kind of magnetism to the chaos she steps into, a pull toward the mysteries that refuse to stay buried. Maybe that's why, even when things seem impossibly dark, she refuses to walk away. Or maybe she's just as hooked on these cases as I am.

And, of course, Emma's next case is only going to pull her deeper into the chaos. Just wait until you see what she's walking into next. In *The Girl and the Last Scene,* Emma is thrown into the chaos of a film set where actors are vanishing, the director is unraveling at the seams, and the drama behind the scenes is just as dangerous as what's happening in front of the camera. Hidden deaths, blackmail, and a production that was doomed from inception—this case is shaping up to be one you won't want to miss!

While you eagerly await this adventure, I invite you to catch up with Detective Riley Quinn in *Shadows in the Pines.* Emma Griffin isn't the only one who finds herself drawn to the darkest mysteries—Riley has a habit of chasing them down, too. When the daughter of someone she cares about is abducted, Riley is thrown into a race against time. But just as she fights to bring the little girl home, a string of gruesome murders shakes Pine Brooke to its core. Campers, fishermen, and others are being found dead in the woods, each murder more disturbing than the last. With the truth slipping further from her grasp and time running out, Riley must face the shadows of Pine Brooke before they consume everything—and everyone—she's fighting to protect.

Thank you for being part of this journey. I'm eager to hear what you thought of The Girl on the Run, so if you have a quick moment, please consider leaving a review. Your feedback and enthusiasm have been instrumental in shaping the direction of this series, and I'm incredibly grateful for your continued support. Thank you for helping to bring these stories to life!

Yours,
A.J. Rivers

P.S. If for some reason you didn't like this book or found typos or other errors, please let me know personally. I do my best to read and respond to every email at mailto:aj@riversthrillers.com

P.P.S. If you would like to stay up-to-date with me and my latest releases I invite you to visit my Linktree page at *www.linktr.ee/a.j.rivers* to subscribe to my newsletter and receive a free copy of my book, Edge of the Woods. You can also follow me on my social media accounts for behind-the-scenes glimpses and sneak peeks of my upcoming projects, or even sign up for text notifications. I can't wait to connect with you!

ALSO BY
A.J. RIVERS

Emma Griffin FBI Mysteries

Season One

Book One—The Girl in Cabin 13*
Book Two—The Girl Who Vanished*
Book Three—The Girl in the Manor*
Book Four—The Girl Next Door*
Book Five—The Girl and the Deadly Express*
Book Six—The Girl and the Hunt*
Book Seven—The Girl and the Deadly End*

Season Two

Book Eight—The Girl in Dangerous Waters*
Book Nine—The Girl and Secret Society*
Book Ten—The Girl and the Field of Bones*
Book Eleven—The Girl and the Black Christmas*
Book Twelve—The Girl and the Cursed Lake*
Book Thirteen—The Girl and The Unlucky 13*
Book Fourteen—The Girl and the Dragon's Island*

Season Three

Book Fifteen—The Girl in the Woods*
Book Sixteen —The Girl and the Midnight Murder*
Book Seventeen— The Girl and the Silent Night*
Book Eighteen — The Girl and the Last Sleepover*
Book Nineteen — The Girl and the 7 Deadly Sins*
Book Twenty — The Girl in Apartment 9*
Book Twenty-One — The Girl and the Twisted End*

Emma Griffin FBI Mysteries Retro - Limited Series
(Read as standalone or before Emma Griffin book 22)

Book One— *The Girl in the Mist**
Book Two— *The Girl on Hallow's Eve**
Book Three— *The Girl and the Christmas Past**
Book Four— *The Girl and the Winter Bones**
Book Five— *The Girl on the Retreat**

Season Four

Book Twenty-Two — *The Girl and the Deadly Secrets**
Book Twenty-Three — *The Girl on the Road**
Book Twenty-Four — *The Girl and the Unexpected Gifts**
Book Twenty-Five — *The Girl and the Secret Passage**
Book Twenty-Six — *The Girl and the Bride**
Book Twenty-Seven — *The Girl in Her Cabin**
Book Twenty-Eight — *The Girl Who Remembers**

Season Five

Book Twenty-Nine — *The Girl in the Dark**
Book Thirty — *The Girl and the Lies**
Book Thirty-One — *The Girl and the Inmate**
Book Thirty-Two — *The Girl and the Garden of Bones**
Book Thirty-Three — *The Girl on the Run*

Ava James FBI Mysteries

Book One—*The Woman at the Masked Gala**
Book Two—*Ava James and the Forgotten Bones**
Book Three —*The Couple Next Door**
Book Four — *The Cabin on Willow Lake**
Book Five — *The Lake House**
Book Six — *The Ghost of Christmas**
Book Seven — *The Rescue**
Book Eight — *Murder in the Moonlight**
Book Nine — *Behind the Mask**
Book Ten — *The Invitation**
Book Eleven — *The Girl in Hawaii**
Book Twelve — *The Woman in the Window**
Book Thirteen — *The Good Doctor**
Book Fourteen — *The Housewife Killer**
Book Fifteen— *The Librarian**
Book Sixteen — *The Art of Murder**
Book Seventeen — *Secrets in the Acadia*

Dean Steele FBI Mysteries

Book One—*The Woman in the Woods**
Book Two — *The Last Survivors*
Book Three — *No Escape*
Book Four — *The Garden of Secrets*
Book Five — *The Killer Among Us*
Book Six — *The Convict*
Book Seven — *The Last Promise*
Book Eight — *Death by Midnight*
Book Nine — *The Woman in the Attic*
Book Ten — *Playing with Fire*
Book Eleven — *Murder in Twilight Cove*
Book Twelve — *Under the Mask*

ALSO BY
A.J. RIVERS & THOMAS YORK

Made in United States
Cleveland, OH
07 March 2025

14974073R00132